Mollie Hardwick, born in Manchester, is one of the most versatile and successful British writers today. Her range extends from best-selling novels to literary and biographical studies, numerous plays for television, radio and stage, and feature series in leading women's magazines. Her novels include a number of the *Upstairs, Downstairs* novels. She is also the author of many other works in collaboration with her husband Michael Hardwick. Her own novel *Beauty's Daughter* won the Elizabeth Goudge Award of the Romantic Novelists Association as the best historical novel of 1976, and she recently published a new work of historical fiction, *Charlie Is My Darling*. The Hardwicks, whose 'hobby' is running their own professional theatre company, The Hardwick Players, live in an eighteenth century house in Highgate Village, London.

D1342496

Also by Mollie Hardwick:

DUCHESS OF DUKE STREET 1 : THE WAY UP
DUCHESS OF DUKE STREET 2 : THE GOLDEN YEARS

Also by Michael and Mollie Hardwick:

THE CHARLES DICKENS ENCYCLOPEDIA
CHARLES DICKENS: THE GAS-LIGHT BOY
THE PASSISERS

Mollie Hardwick

# The Duchess of Duke Street: The World Keeps Turning

Futura Publications Limited

A Futura Book

A Futura Book

First published in Great Britain in 1977
simultaneously by Futura Publications Limited
and Hamish Hamilton Limited

ISBN 0 8600 7513 3

The author wishes to take this opportunity of
thanking the BBC, John Hawkesworth and others
associated with the production of the original series for
their kind co-operation and assistance.

Printed in Great Britain by
The Anchor Press Ltd
Tiptree, Essex

Futura Publications Limited
110 Warner Road, Camberwell,
London SE5 9HQ

# CHAPTER ONE

Louisa Trotter surveyed her sitting-room on the ground floor of the Bentinck Hotel. *Her* Bentinck, created by her, her own strong personality stamped on every inch of its furnishings, decor and character.

Its exterior, modest enough for smart Duke Street, midway between Piccadilly Circus in the heart of London's West End, and the ancient Palace of St James', gave little indication of the comforts within: the suites of rooms which managed to be both elegant and homely, grand and comfortable, home-from-home to its many regular guests, who might be families or single gentlemen needing a London base for business, pleasure, or both. If Louisa liked one, she asked no awkward questions about what went on in the privacy of those rooms, and would fight like a tigress, any outsider who tried to snoop. But if her delicate antennae recorded disapproval, one would not be allowed there at all, to be snooped upon or not.

From this large, handsome parlour close to the main entrance, she ruled her establishment like a queen spider. It was within earshot of the green-leather hooded chair where Starr, the middle-aged porter, sat. His little brown, white and black Fox Terrier, Fred, his inseparable companion, lay in his basket near his master's military-booted feet. Fred's sensitivities towards new acquaintances were as keen as Louisa's. The wagging of his tail was the equivalent of her welcoming smile and invitation to a glass of champagne in her sanctum; his growl equated with her blunt language of dismissal.

From her room, where the ticking of a mantelpiece

clock, made by her father, was the only sound other than the rustle of burning coals in the grate, Louisa could hear Starr's greetings to new arrivals, and, depending upon the nature of his tone, could be quickly on the spot to deal with them herself. She could hear the passing tread and sniffs of her ancient waiter Merriman as he went about his slow errands, ancient and indestructible. She had inherited him with the fabric of the Bentinck, and he seemed likely to endure as long as it would.

In this room, businesslike and feminine only to the extent of a vase of casually-arranged flowers and some lace drapes here and there, she dealt with her staff, handing out gruff but heart-warming thanks for jobs well done, and colourful Cockney invective towards any-one, staff or guests, who had displeased or disappointed her. On the wide desk, with its imposing brass inkstand and bell, on which her hand struck many an imperious summons, she made up the accounts, and conducted correspondence in response to requests on sheets of the finest notepaper, many of them imprinted with coronets, coats-of-arms and other emblems of nobility and privilege.

As she worked, she was watched by the photographed eyes of favourite guests and friends past and present: the lately dead King Edward VII, who had been her first lover; handsome, smiling Lord Haslemere, Charlie, who had been her second, and would remain the love of her life, though the affaire had ended as quickly as it had begun, and his permanent suite of rooms upstairs had seen many other ladies entertained in it by him, including, recently, his young, county wife.

Pink champagne, and wonderful food cooked by her own hands for a supper with a girl who had disappointed him: those were what Charlie and Louisa had had on that memorable night when they had got ineffably tipsy and had become lovers almost by accident. But the photo-graphs included none of the child who had resulted, little Lottie. Maternity was not for Louisa. Lottie had been despatched to Charlie's ancestral home in Yorkshire, to be brought up humbly, healthily and anonymously, by a respectable childless couple on the estate. Louisa had not seen her daughter since infancy. It didn't trouble her conscience; she was not the type.

There was no photograph, either, of Augustus Trotter, the nominal husband who had been thrust upon her, early in her career, in order to make it 'respectable' for the King to entertain her. The drunken, sister-dominated butler, who had genuinely adored her, but had been defeated by circumstance and Louisa's implacable coldness, had faded out of her life, and was living somewhere in East Anglia. Good riddance, she thought. The late Queen Victoria might have made a fool of herself through melodramatic grief over her departed consort, Albert; but Louisa was the kind of queen who preferred to reign alone.

She had been Louisa Leyton originally, in the long-ago days at Wanstead, Essex, when she was a tough, ambitious girl who wanted no less than to be the best cook in London. It had been a relief to break away from her bossy, snobbish mother, and go into service in Mayfair. But she loved her father—not that Louisa would willingly admit to loving anybody. Something resembling affection and pity stirred in her, whenever she chanced to think of that gentle, downtrodden little man, whose only interest in life was the making and repair of clocks, at which he was so skilful. A disastrous business transaction had ruined him, and forced the Leyton family to move from a comfortable house in Epping to a cramped one in Wanstead, almost on the fringe of the East End of London. Ernest Leyton practised his craft very little now. His heart had gone out of it.

This winter day in 1911 was his sixtieth birthday. Louisa's parents seldom visited her at her hotel, and she scarcely ever visited them at what she had long since ceased to regard as home. But she had asked her father to come to tea today. There had been no getting out of inviting Mum as well, worse luck.

Louisa did not bother to go to the mirror over the mantelpiece to inspect her appearance. She looked good enough, she knew. More than all right for any sort of company, in fact. Now in her early thirties, she still had the delicate porcelain complexion of her girlhood, setting off the great blue eyes that were her most striking claim to beauty. Her fondness for champagne was not reflected in the almost nun-like purity of her features, or in the pretty figure, graced by one of the elaborately lace-trimmed blouses she fancied, and a fashionable narrow, floor-length skirt.

She patted her hair as she got up from the desk. There was no grey in it yet, she knew; only worriers got that, and she was above worrying. Worry had nearly killed her before Charlie had rescued her. No, it got you nowhere, and Louisa had resolved on getting somewhere. She patted the firm coils of rich auburn hair, dressed high on her head. She could afford to pay others to do any worrying for her, now.

The clock showed three: about time they arrived. The hotel was very quiet this afternoon. Starr was out there on duty, with Fred no doubt sleeping heavily in his basket. Major Smith-Barton, Louisa's former guest, and now employee and unofficial adviser, was away at a race meeting—silly old sod, won't ever learn, she thought. Conditions were just right for doing her duty by poor old Dad.

She checked the tea-table, precisely set by old Merriman with her best plates. Three gleaming-white napkins were folded crisply into elegant shapes. The essential features of a tea-table were missing, however. Where cups and saucers would normally have stood there gleamed three champagne glasses. A bottle was in an ice bucket on a stand beside the table. Tea was not Louisa's style at all.

Her sharp ears caught a shuffling approach towards the outside of her door and a laboured breathing which she knew was old Merriman's. There was a fumbled attempt to turn the knob, which failed. Louisa moved towards it, but the brisk squeak-squeak of Starr's boots told her that he was coming to his colleague's help.

'All right, all right,' she heard him say, and the door opened. Merriman lurched in, staggering under the weight of a vast, round cake, iced and decorated to represent the face of a clock. He conveyed it safely to the large area of tea-table left vacant to receive it, and rid himself of the burden thankfully.

Louisa nodded approval of his having got it there intact. She had worked hard on that cake. She was still the best cook in London, even if she only cooked for special occasions such as this.

Starr, in the doorway with his little dog looking up from his feet, looked at the cake admiringly.

'That the right time?' he asked. Actually, it was. Louisa had had the forethought to set the angelica hands on the iced clock-face at three.

'Astonishingly heavy, for a cake,' Merriman gasped, holding his side.

'You'd be heavy, if you was as full of fruit as that cake,' Louisa told him. 'Now, don't go wheezing all over it!'

'Indigestion mixture, fruit cake,' Merriman pronounced balefully.

'Thank you, Merrylegs,' Louisa said, and he shambled to the door, only to pause with it open as other voices sounded in the hall. Louisa recognised her mother's loud, put-on gentility; but there was a deep male voice that certainly wasn't her Dad's. She frowned as she heard it say, 'Trotter! Fancy marryin' a bloke with a monniker like that!'

Louisa sailed past Merriman into the hall. Yes, as she had expected: Mum was overdressed, in a copy of one of those fashionable tailored suits with long jackets, for which her figure was too stout, and an enormous cartwheel feathered Nell Gwynne hat, as worn by Miss Julia Neilson in *The Scarlet Pimpernel*. Mr Trotter had

obviously been ordered into his Sunday suit, but it hung
on him in loose, ugly folds, like an elephant's skin. He
seemed to have shrunk over the years. He looked yellow
and ill. Louisa went directly to him and gave him a
hearty kiss and a hug, bestowing a mere peck on her
mother's much-powdered cheek.

'Many happy returns, Dad,' she said; and only then
did she turn her glance to the other man with them, who
must have made the disparaging remark she had over-
heard. He was big, and would have been hulking, but
for his erect carriage. He was in his thirties. Something
about him seemed familiar to her, but she couldn't
instantly grasp at it.

Surprisingly, he winked at her. She glared back and
drew a deep breath, ready to tell him off; but before she
could utter a word, her mother had cried, 'Surprise,
Louisa! Surprise!'

The man laughed raucously, showing good white
teeth. Light dawned on Louisa.

'It's not . . . *is* it?'

'It is,' replied her mother. 'Our Arthur.'

'Who else?' laughed the brother Louisa had not seen
since his boyhood and her girlhood.

'Good Gordon Highlanders!' she exclaimed, and
stared round for a chair. Starr saw her need and deftly
slipped one under her.

'Just what I did when I saw him first,' Mrs Leyton
said. '*Just* what I did. Wasn't it, Ern? Only no-one put
a chair for me.'

Mr Leyton made no reply. Louisa examined Arthur
with mixed feelings. She was glad to see him again, in a
way; but somehow he was different from what she had
envisaged on the rare occasions she had thought of him.
He was well set up: carried himself like a soldier, though
that was only natural, considering that he had left his
insurance job after four years, at the age of nineteen, to
enlist in the army as a trooper, and shortly to go off to the
Boer War.

'Well, give us a kiss, gel,' he said, coming over and leaning down to her. Instead, she held up a cheek. He gave it a smacking wet kiss, which made her frown with distaste; since Charlie, she had not liked anyone to touch her. Arthur stood up again. 'Cheek like a peachy rose,' he said. 'You ain't half come on, Louie. Quite a woman.' His eyes travelled up and down her figure. 'All that your own?'

'Of course it's me own. Anyway, you can talk. You was a skinny lad when you went away. How long you been back?'

'Docked two days ago. Straight home to Mum and Dad, like the good boy I am.'

'That's right,' Mrs Leyton said proudly. Arthur had always been her favourite, as a child. He had been more biddable than the rebelliously independent sister who was three years his junior. All the same, Louisa had resented the favouritism he had been shown. She had resented even more his being allowed to stay at school until he was fifteen, whereas she had been put out into service while still only a child. But she wronged her parents in this: they had never told her how they had intended she should become a teacher, as she had wished, but how they had been forced, due to her father's financial disaster, to abandon the plan. In withholding this knowledge from her they had, for once, acted in accord with one another; and it was a pity, for if they had been frank with Louisa, who was intelligent enough, even as a child, to have understood their situation, she would have felt sympathy, instead of lifelong bitterness.

Mr Leyton was looking down at the cake. He raised his melancholy eyes and stared questioningly at Louisa. She got up swiftly and went to him.

'That's right, Dad. It's your birthday, isn't it?'

'But . . . I never had a cake on my birthday before.'

He looked fit to cry. This embarrassment was saved, unintentionally, by Arthur asking, 'Does it chime, Lou?' She had always hated diminutives of her name. She

11

looked at him scornfully. Mrs Leyton saw her expression and stepped in quickly.

'I hope you didn't mind us bringing Arthur, Louisa? He is your brother.'

Arthur added, 'I was all for coming straight over, when I heard you were here . . .'

'But I said, "No, Arthur. Don't go rushing round there. She's invited us for your Dad's birthday, so we'll all go then. Make it a double celebration".'

Louisa unbent. 'Yeh, of course. Why not?'

Arthur grinned. 'Let's get on with it, then, eh? Shall I open the liquid rations?' Louisa nodded, and he turned his attention to the bottle.

Mr Leyton said quietly, 'You needn't have gone to all this trouble, Louisa.'

'No trouble, Dad. I enjoyed making the cake, and I'll enjoy seeing you eat it. Now, you sit here and have a sandwich.'

Her parents sat and accepted dainty sandwiches. Arthur startled them by getting the cork out with an inexpert pop. He poured sloppily for them all, filling the tulip glasses excessively.

'You could've knocked me down with a feather,' Mrs Leyton was rattling on to Louisa during this. 'We was sitting by the fire, like you know we do every evening, when there was a knock on the back-yard door, and then the kitchen door opens and he pokes his head round.' She jerked the thumb of her sandwich-holding hand at Arthur. 'I gave a scream, I don't mind telling you, and then he winks and says, "No need to kill the fatted calf. A nice soused herring'll do me fine".' She repeated this, laughing, until she choked on crumbs and lapsed into a coughing fit.

'I thought we'd seen the last of you,' Louisa told her brother.

'The bad penny, gel. Always turns up. Here you are. If you've done coughing, Ma, we'll raise our glasses to the old man.'

They drank to Mr Leyton, who nodded silent acknowledgment.

'And now, to the bad penny,' Arthur said. They drank again. Louisa noted that Arthur had drained his glass in the two toasts. She rang for Merriman, and ordered two more bottles to be brought smartly. Arthur's and Mrs Leyton's eyes gleamed appreciatively. They were making equally rapid inroads into the salmon sandwich supplies. Mr Leyton, who had barely sipped from his glass, was still on his first sandwich, taking infrequent tiny nibbles. Louisa watched him, concerned.

'Done very well, our Louisa,' Mrs Leyton said to her son through a mouthful of bread. 'Moved up in the world.'

Suddenly alarmed that her mother was going to add something indiscreet about the circumstances of her leap from obscurity—had she told him already, even?—Louisa changed the subject.

'What brought you home again, Arthur?'

'A yearning for the old faces, as you might say. No—tell you the truth, I'd had enough of foreign parts. After a time they pall. Here—when are we going to cut that cake?'

He had already opened, uninvited, one of the bottles Merriman had brought, not bothering to wait for it to chill. Louisa answered, 'When Dad's ready.'

'Oh, he won't mind,' Mrs Leyton said. 'Hardly eats more than a bird, anyway. I didn't get no cake for my birthday,' she added reproachfully.

'You wasn't sixty, was you? Sixty's a big step in life. Have another sandwich, Dad.'

'No thanks, love. This'll do me.'

'You . . . all right, Dad?'

'Yes. Oh, yes.'

Mrs Leyton snorted. 'Been complaining of aches and pains for days. All over the place. Getting on, that's all. Fair wears me out, his moaning. You can't stay young for ever, I keep telling him.'

Louisa put an arm round her father's shoulders,

13

noticing how narrow and hard they felt under his jacket.

'Old bones, you know,' he said with an apologetic smile. 'Feeling tired all the time. I haven't looked at a clock for weeks.'

'Well, you've got a nice one to look at now, Dad. And you can eat it—a whacking big slice. That'll put life into you. You ready to cut it, eh?'

Her father stood up stiffly. Arthur passed the knife across the table. Mr Leyton stood looking at the beautifully decorated cake.

'Shame to spoil it,' he mumbled. Louisa and Arthur insisted, though. But when their father tried to make the first cut he could only just pierce the icing. With a jest about giving the bride a helping hand, Arthur came round and put his big hand over the bony one holding the knife. The blade slid through. Arthur stood back and joined Louisa in applause. Their mother's hands remained in her lap, and she did not smile.

'Make a wish, Dad,' Louisa reminded him. He looked at her, and she could almost imagine what his wish was.

As they were eating the slices of cake, Arthur gulping his down with draughts of champagne, there was a knock at the door and Gwyneth Davies looked into the room. This was the aunt of Louisa's principal maid and deputy, Mary. Louisa had taken her on part-time after the middle-aged Welshwoman had pleased her during a spell as temporary helper at a hectic period.

'Yes?' Louisa asked.

'Excuse me, ma'am. I finished hemming the curtains for Room 8. Shall I start making up the new pillow cases now, or would you rather I concentrated on the ironing?'

'Ask Mary, Mrs Davies,' Louisa ordered impatiently. 'That's her department.'

'It's her afternoon off, ma'am.'

'Oh . . . Do the ironing, then.'

But Gwyneth persisted, 'Is that a good idea? I mean, the pillow cases will be needed tomorrow, when Number Ten's beds are changed.'

'Then do the bloody pillow cases! Use your head, for Gawd's sake.'

'Yes, ma'am. Only I don't want to do the wrong thing. Oh, and Mr Monkford, Number Seven, is in the hall, wanting his bags brought down, and no one to fetch them but me, and I can't carry weights like that . . .'

The Welsh gabble caused Louisa to throw up her hands. 'Where the 'ell is Starr?'

'Getting a cab for Mrs Brown, Number Ten. And I don't think Merriman is fit for lumping luggage down all those stairs, ma'am, and . . .'

'It isn't your job to decide who's fit and who isn't, Mrs Davies. Just tell Merriman to see to it—and get back to them pillow cases.'

Arthur intervened at her elbow. 'I'm fit—Mrs Trotter.'

Louisa swung round. 'You?'

Arthur walked toward Gwyneth. 'Fit as a fiddle. Show me the luggage, lady, and I'll soon shift it.' He turned to Louisa, grinning and flexing his right arm. 'Look at that. Desperate for exercise.' He winked, and firmly ushered Gwyneth from the room before Louisa could object.

'Quite a card, our Arthur, isn't he?' Mrs Leyton giggled. Her husband looked as affronted as did her daughter. Mrs Leyton didn't notice, though. She took the cake knife and crudely hacked herself off another slice.

'A cab for you, sir?' Starr asked Mr Monkford, when he had finished ushering Mrs Brown out to the one he had obtained for her.

'It is being attended to,' the gentleman answered.

'Beg pardon, sir?'

At that moment Arthur Leyton came back through the main entrance door and smirked ingratiatingly at the guest.

'Your cab awaits, sir. A very lucky capture, as you might say.' Before the bewildered Starr could move towards the baggage which he noticed had materialised near the foot of the stairs through no act of his, the man

15

he had gathered to be Mrs Trotter's brother had picked them up and was taking them out ahead of the departing guest.

When this extempore porter returned a few moments later, he thumbed a coin into the air, caught it cleanly, then flicked it over to Starr, saying, 'Yours by rights. I'm only here for the day, not for the dough.'

The man grinned and swung away into the proprietress's parlour, without troubling to knock on the door.

Inside, he made straight for the cake and chopped off another slice, pausing only for a swig of champagne before sinking his teeth into it.

'You got some terrible old crocks working for you, Louisa,' he said, crumbs spilling out between his lips.

'That's right,' Mrs Leyton put in. 'That old Merry . . . what's his name? He could do with pensioning off, for a start. And that porter—allowing him to keep that snappy little dog of his in the hall . . . You could do with a man like Arthur about the place, my girl. He'd keep things moving for you.'

'Would he? I'm not exactly standing still, meself.'

'Needs a good man, though. Like Arthur. He's looking for a job, aren't you, dear?'

'Now, love . . .!' It was a muted protest, but all the more telling, in that it came from mild Mr Leyton. His wife treated him to a look of scorn.

'Why not let the boy help Louisa?' she demanded. 'He's itching to be useful to his sister. Aren't you, dear?'

Arthur, squirming under the description 'boy', muttered that he was willing to do what he could for to help. Louisa regarded him.

'You've changed,' she said at length. 'Never wanted to do anything for no-one when we was kids.'

''Course I've changed. Ten years, you know.'

'Mum's little darling, you was.'

'Wasn't he, Ern?' Mrs Leyton enthused, addressing her husband directly for once. 'A lovely baby. Like a little angel, I used to think. Should've been the girl, I always said. Now, Louisa, she was nothing like a girl. Always dashing about and . . .'

'Shut up, Mum!' Louisa ordered. Even Arthur was looking embarrassed. 'It's Dad's birthday. We're here to give him a treat, not to go on about me and Arthur. Speaking of which, get that other bloody bottle open, will you?'

Arthur moved willingly to obey. Louisa leaned over the cake and picked off the angelica strips representing the clock hands. She caught her father's eye again as she popped them into her mouth and straightened up. His gaze flicked away to Arthur, then back to her.

Poor old Dad! Anyone less like a man celebrating his birthday and his son's homecoming, Louisa couldn't imagine.

That evening, after her guests had gone, Louisa sat on in her sanctum. She was working determinedly at her books, fighting to stave off the yawns and ennui left by the afternoon champagne. She wished there were some party going on in one of the suites to which she might have been summoned, or could gatecrash; but it was a winter Sunday, and just as dead as that implied. Louisa had no pleasures, other than bright, boozy, chatty company. She had no time for hobbies. Reading held no interest for her. Thank goodness, whenever she was at a bit of a loose end there were always arrears of book-keeping and correspondence to occupy her.

Mary came in to see her, pink faced from the cold, dark of hair and eyes, smiling fondly at the former fellow servant at Lord Henry Norton's house who had become famous and had subsequently taken her in as employee and confidante.

'Hello,' Louisa greeted the little Welsh girl. 'Had a good day off?'

'Oh, yes, ma'am, thank you. I did some shopping for a new dress. Auntie Gwyneth is going to make it up.

17

Auntie was telling me just now your brother's come back from abroad, ma'am. Oh, you must be pleased about that!'

Louisa twitched a little smile, but made no reply. Sitting back in her desk chair, she regarded Mary for some moments, then asked, as casually as she could, 'Mary . . . What do you think of Mr Merriman these days?'

'What I always think.'

'I mean, is he getting past it?'

'Oh, no! He'll go on forever. He's one of those who are always tired, but never stops. Like my grandad. He was driving his pony to market right until . . .'

Mary's late grandad and his pony were not unfamiliar to Louisa by now. She interrupted, 'Yeh, yeh. But we are short-handed, aren't we?'

'Well, we could do with someone in the kitchen to help with the veg. Or a parlourmaid. But most of all we need a strong person to lug coal and stuff about. I mean, I don't mind doing it once, now and then . . . But with Mr Starr refusing to soil his hands, saying he's got to keep clean on the door, and quite rightly, only . . .'

'Thank you, Mary,' Louisa stopped the flow. 'That's all I wanted to know. Good night, now.'

She gave the girl her radiant smile, a welcome gift to anyone, to be valued for its rarity. But when Mary had gone out, Louisa's expression turned deeply thoughtful; almost apprehensive. It was as though Mary had carried away the gift with her.

# CHAPTER TWO

'I got your message,' Arthur told Louisa unnecessarily; he would not have been sitting there in her room again, at 9.30 a.m. a few days later, if he had not. 'You might have said what it was all about, though.'

Louisa held a pencil horizontally between her upraised hands as she regarded him from behind her desk. She had thought hard before reaching her decision. There was still time to change her mind; but she didn't draw back.

'I'll be frank, Arthur. I don't like the idea of employing family . . .'

'Employing . . .!'

'Don't let's beat about the bush. That's what it would amount to. I'm short-handed. There are plenty of people out of work, but not the sort I want.'

'Particular, eh?'

'This isn't any sort of hotel. I run it as a home-from-home. But it's a business. Now, you want a job. I could do with a strong man to do carrying and so on. But one with some intelligence, and clean. One who might move up as he learns all the ropes. So, what about it?'

Arthur grinned uncertainly. 'Mum said you was a tough customer.'

'I am. If you don't like the idea, say so and go. Understand, you couldn't come in here making yourself comfortable. You'd have a job to do and I'd expect you to do it.'

He speculated for a moment. 'All found, of course?'

'Of course.'

'I like a girl with spirit, Louisa.'

'I'm no girl. I'm a woman.'

'That's what I mean by spirit. All right. I'll do it—ma'am.'

He sprang up and stood to attention before her. Louisa had to smile.

''Ere,' she exclaimed, 'Come to think of it, who's doin' who a favour?'

They laughed together briefly.

'Mind,' he said, 'I'm no-one's skivvy. Not even yours.'

'There's no skivvies here. We all do a job of work as well and as cheerfully as we can. I don't ask nobody to do anything I couldn't do myself. And the customer comes first, of course.'

'Can't say fairer than that. What about my wages?'

'Fifteen bob a week. And all found, like I said. Start tomorrow morning, six o'clock sharp. And no preferential treatment.'

'What a sergeant-major you'd make!' he declared admiringly. 'All right.'

Louisa threw down the pencil she had been twiddling, and relaxed at last. 'Coffee to clinch it?' she invited.

'Why not?'

She reached across and pulled the bell near her chair. Arthur sat again, smiling at her, admiring the stretch of his sister's bosom against her blouse as she leaned over her chair arm. Luckily for him she didn't notice the glance. She would have resented it.

Instead, she said, 'Remember when you and me pinched Mum's bottle of port and you went singing down the street? Said you was off to join the opera.'

'Those were the days!' he laughed.

'For you, maybe. Being a boy, you could do things.'

'What things?'

'Anything you wanted. I mean, you got away, didn't you? Into the army.'

'I had to get away. After that row with the boss I couldn't ever have done that sort of work again. It was stiflin' me.'

'Yeh. But I had to be stifled from the start. Sent out to skivvy in some old doll's kitchen . . .'

Merriman interrupted them, and was sent for coffee and to bring back Starr. He looked suspiciously at Arthur, who winked at him, unseen by Louisa. Merriman drew himself up as far as his stoop would allow and went out. Starr came in a moment later, with Fred, as usual, at his heels.

'Starr,' said Louisa, 'you know Mr Leyton by now. I'm taking him on to help with carrying and general duties. He'll help with coal and fires, and then change and help with portering.'

'And the boots?' Starr asked pointedly. 'If you remember, madam, we have no boot boy at present. Will *Mr* Leyton be cleaning the boots?'

Louisa did not glance at her brother. 'Yes,' she said firmly. 'His duties will include boot boy. That'll be all, thanks, Starr. I'll send Mr Leyton out shortly.'

Starr went. Arthur grinned at his sister.

'Old soldier. Tell 'em a mile off. Got everything worked out.'

'You was a soldier, too,' she reminded him. 'How long was you actually in?'

'Long enough.'

'You hardly ever wrote. What you been doing since?'

'Bit of this, bit of that. Prize-fighting for a time. Coal-heaving. Bit of mining . . .'

Merriman returned soon after with the coffee. When he had gone again and Louisa had handed Arthur his cup she said, 'Right, then—this is the last time I entertain you in this parlour.'

'Unless I call in my private capacity.'

She shook her head. 'Don't do that while you're working as dogsbody.'

'Suppose I rise to maitre d'hotel, or something?'

'No such thing here. Can you cook?'

'I can make a drop of tea over a camp fire in a howling blizzard, if you ever get one.'

21

They both laughed, brother and sister, who had once been children together. There had been a gulf between them then; it had grown immeasurably wide by now. But, just briefly, it was spanned.

No one else in the Bentinck laughed about Arthur's appointment, however. At first, only Merriman and Starr—and therefore, of course, Fred—regarded him with unconcealed dislike. The female staff were merely suspicious, uneasy in this relationship with a man who was in theory no higher than any of them, but was known to be the brother of their formidable employer. They treated him warily; and it was as well to be wary of Arthur Leyton, they soon discovered, for he had an unpleasant habit of brushing against them on stairs and in doorways, leering into their faces and, when their faces were not towards him, pinching their bottoms. If he had been truly one of them they would have used their tongues on him, and perhaps the palms of their hands across his cheek; but because he was who he was, they felt it would somehow be taking a liberty to do either.

Unhappiness prevailed, and in no one more than in Fred, Starr's little dog, the sole intimate of his life since the army, the recipient of his confidences and complaints, the comforter, with his wet nose and reassuring tongue, on occasions when they were alone in Starr's room and Starr fell to ruminating about the tragedy of poor Lizzie, who had loved him once and had died in the Thames so soon after returning into his life.

Fred showed Arthur Leyton his feelings about him more directly than any of the others. His low growl was a sure signal to Starr whenever Arthur drew near. Stroking his dog to quieten him, he would feel the fur rising into angry spikes along the spine.

Arthur knew he was disliked by them all, and took a good deal of pleasure in it, knowing there was nothing they could do to retaliate. They might complain to Louisa, perhaps, but she would send them off with a flea in their

22

ear. He reckoned himself a good worker—the guests were appreciative of his youthful alertness—and he had done nothing that could be counted a major offence.

The dog's case was different. His open hostility annoyed Arthur. It irked him that he could not communicate what he would have liked to say to the animal. He had to be content with grimaces and sharp gestures when Starr was not looking. But they were not enough.

It was Fred's disadvantage to be tethered to a leg of Starr's chair. Louisa had allowed him to bring the dog into service with him—he had, in fact, given her no chance to object—but Fred was only allowed to wander loose at his master's heel. At other times he had to stay where he was. Arthur recognised his chance.

One morning, a few days after his arrival, Arthur saw that Starr's chair was empty. No one was in the hall. The little dog was sitting outside his basket, flicking busily with a hind leg at an itch behind one of his ears. Arthur swiftly went over to him, glanced round again to see that he was unobserved, and, at the risk of a nip in the ankle from the now-growling Fred, brought down his boot on one of the splayed forepaws.

Fred emitted a piercing shriek. It was followed immediately by a crash of metal and crockery, as cups, plates and cutlery came cascading down the stairs. After them came bouncing a large silver tray. Arthur looked up to see Merriman hanging on to the banisters, his face white.

Starr came hurrying in from the street, where he had been seeing some guests into a cab. He scarcely spared a glance for the shattered crockery, but went to his whimpering dog. He slipped his lead from the chair leg and gathered him up in his arms.

Arthur, who had stepped away a few paces, called up to Merriman, 'You all right, Mr Merriman? You know, you oughtn't to be carrying heavy trays of stuff, not at your age.'

Merriman came slowly down, holding the banister rail.

'Never dropped a tray in my life,' he quavered. 'Never,

in all my years of service. It was that dog, barking suddenly, just as I was turning the bend, and made me hit the
tray on the banister post.'

Starr had by now located the place where Fred had
been hurt and was massaging it tenderly.

'You trod on him,' he said to Arthur. 'You trod on his
paw.'

'Me? I never. You should teach him not to bark sudden
like that and upset old men.'

'Fred only barks under provocation. I know you've
been itching to have a go at him, because he can't stick
the sight of you . . .'

'Here, here, what's this?' Louisa demanded, bustling
on to the scene. She had heard from the kitchen the dog's
cry and the crash. 'For Gawd's sake, Starr, put that dog
down and help clear this mess up. Arthur, go and fetch
Violet with a brush and pan.'

'He trod on Fred's paw,' Starr objected, still holding
the animal.

'Did you?'

''Course not. What's he think I am? You never knew
me hurt an animal.'

'*I* know,' Starr insisted.

Louisa went down on her knees, gathering up fragments of crockery. She said impatiently, 'Look, will someone just do as they're told around here? I want this mess
cleared up before any guests see it. Now get a move on,
the lot of you.'

Merriman went shakily to the kitchen, followed by a
defiant Starr, taking Fred with him to have his paw
bathed in warm water. Arthur got down beside his sister.

'Bit of a risk—an old codger like that up and down
stairs with loaded trays,' he murmured as they worked.

'He's never been no trouble before.'

'He's getting older every day, though. I could do his
job for you, if you like.'

Louisa paused to stare at him. 'What? You serve meals?'

'Why not?'

'You haven't got no finesse.'

'Thanks! I could learn, though.'

Violet, the 'tween-maid, arrived with brush and dust-pan, and the conversation ended unsatisfactorily for Arthur. He had no chance to re-open it; but, as it turned out, there was no need. The mishap had affected Merriman more than he would admit. Mary and her Aunt Gwyneth made him sit down in the kitchen and drink some hot sweet tea. He remained pale, and trembled visibly. Starr, who knew shock when he saw it, told him firmly to go off to bed, and helped the reluctant old man to do so.

With Mary and Violet busy enough with their own work, there was no question but that Arthur should take over from Merriman, at least for the time being. He did so triumphantly, and what the room service lost in expertise it gained in speed.

Louisa had other things on her mind than her brother's pressing ambition. She had had another visit from her parents.

'. . . If only he'd see a doctor,' Mrs Leyton said, referring to her husband as if he were not there beside her in Louisa's parlour. 'If I've asked him once, I've asked him a thousand times.'

'I don't need a doctor,' he said wearily. 'There's nothing wrong with me.'

'Of course something's wrong with him. He's lost interest in things.'

'I just want a bit of peace and quiet. To do nothing for a bit.'

'There, you see, Louisa! I mean, he's never been a man of great energy, your father, but at least he still used to mend a few clocks. Now he does nothing.'

Louisa thought she saw what was expected of her. 'Perhaps you could do with a bit of a holiday, Dad?'

'Just what I was thinking,' her mother agreed quickly. 'Only there isn't the money for one.'

Louisa's suspicion had been confirmed. She said, 'I'll

pay. I want to see Dad looking better. Now, what about Southend? Or Brighton. You haven't been to Brighton, have you, Dad?'

He shook his head, embarrassed to be pushed yet again into spongeing on his daughter. But he knew what Mrs Leyton had come intending to say, and now heard her saying it.

'No, Louisa. It's very kind of you, but we don't want to put you to expense, especially when you're having a slack time here.'

'Who says I'm having a slack time?'

'Arthur did. When he came to see us yesterday.'

'Bloody cheek! What's it got to do with Arthur?'

'Language, dear! It's only that he said there was a few rooms vacant just now, and a nice little suite at the back that would just do for your father and me . . .'

'Oh, did he! Well, next time you see him you can tell him I said you can't come here.'

'Louisa!'

'The girl's right,' Mr Leyton roused himself to say. 'She's got a business to run.'

'She means we're not good enough for her, more like. Sitting here all la-di-da with all this wealth round her . . . Playing Lady Bountiful to her own brother and the parents who gave her her start.'

'You gave me no start,' Louisa retorted, flushing. 'I made me own.'

'Just because we're not snobs with our noses in the air,' her mother carried on. 'I never thought to see the day she'd be ashamed of us.'

'Listen, I've said I'll pay for you to have a nice little holiday by the sea.'

'No thank *you*. Come on, Ernest. We'll not stay where we're not wanted.'

Mrs Leyton put her cup and saucer down noisily and began to get up. Louisa said, 'But it's for Dad's good. It's him we were talking about.'

'Well, never mind. He'll just have to see a doctor, or

lump it.'

Louisa was a match for most people, but her mother was an exception. There was no love between them. It was just the thought of the reprisals which would be visited upon her poor father that forced Louisa to capitulate.

'Dad?' she asked. 'Would you like to come here for a week?'

'We . . . I don't want to trouble you, love. I just want a bit of peace and quiet—anywhere.'

'Then you'll come. It'll do you good to be waited on, and you'll have your breakfast in bed every day.'

Mrs Leyton sat down again, expressed condescending thanks, and said she thought she would take another cup of tea, after all. Mr Leyton said nothing; but his eyes told Louisa, 'Sorry, love. You know how it is.'

There was further trouble when they arrived, the day after Merriman's fall. Louisa came out of her parlour in time to hear her mother ordering an astonished Starr in her most affected voice, 'Be so good as to take our luggage up to our rooms, Starr.'

'*Room*, Starr,' Louisa corrected. '*Room* seventeen.'

'You said a suite,' her mother snapped.

'Arthur said a suite, not me. Number Seventeen, Starr.'

Louisa swept on her way. That was one skirmish her mother had not been able to win.

Merriman's resilience had been deeply dented by his unhappy experience. Although he wanted badly to get back to work, he had reeled and nearly fallen when he had got out of bed that morning. There was nothing for it but to get back in. Mary and Gwyneth fussed over him and brought him his meals, and Louisa insisted he have a half-bottle of champagne with his lunch and dinner as the world's best pick-me-up.

He was in bed for several days. Gwyneth, whose principal work was the laundry and sewing, was delighted to be able to join Mary in the dispense, polishing glasses, getting out wines and making coffee. Arthur's bid to take over Merriman's duties entirely had not succeeded. Louisa saw best to keep him on a fairly tight rein.

'Number Seventeen!' Gwyneth said to her niece as a bell jangled amongst the rows on the board. 'Mr and Mrs Leyton again. She's been ringing that blessed bell every five minutes since she got here.'

'She'll be wanting tea now, I expect,' Mary said. 'Tea and muffins. She eats like an elephant. That poor Mr Leyton, though. Real sorry for him, I am.'

'Shall I go up?' Gwyneth offered.

'No. Let her precious son go when he's free. I'm sick of her, Auntie, and so is the rest of us. Driving them mad in the kitchen. Mrs Trotter shouldn't do such things, bringing her family here. It's not right.'

'It's her hotel.'

'It's not as if they were a nice family. You know Starr's thinking about giving his notice? That poor little Fred's still so upset he won't even eat a bit of chocolate cake.'

The bell rang again, long and insistently, as Arthur came in and looked at it. 'Number Seventeen,' he said. 'Why isn't someone answering it?'

Mary rounded on him, her dark eyes flashing. 'If we run every time Mrs Leyton rings that bell there's nothing else will get done in the place.'

'Oh? Mutiny is it?'

'Don't be silly. They're not even proper guests.'

'They're your employer's parents—and mine. I'll go.'

He went away, leaving the two women crushed.

'Five times I've rung that bell,' his mother fumed at him. 'I thought you was all dead.'

'Sorry, Mum,' Arthur said. 'I can't be everywhere. As to the rest of 'em—well . . .' He spread his hands expressively. 'You know, I worry about our Louisa, watching how hard she works, while them lot just idles their time.'

'So do I,' his mother said. 'I've been thinking about that. And I've had an idea about it . . .'

Her husband, unnoticed by either of them, rubbed his brow and closed his eyes. He wished he could just sleep

28

and sleep and sleep. But he was driven downstairs to Louisa's parlour, where he sat down miserably beside his wife, while Arthur went away to get the tea things.

'You shouldn't, love,' he protested mildly, when his wife, after a good deal of exasperated sighing, got up and moved a chair to a position where she had declared over and over it would be better placed. Mrs Leyton ignored him and resumed her own seat, stiffening her back like a queen.

When Louisa came in she frowned to see the two of them there, then frowned again when she noticed that the chair had been moved. But she said nothing and merely went to her desk to get some papers from a drawer.

'How is Merriman, dear?' Mrs Leyton asked, in honeyed tones.

'Improving. He'll be up, soon as I knock off the champagne treatment.'

'Yes. An old malingerer, if ever I saw one. But what a good job our Arthur turned up when he did.'

'If he hadn't, Merriman wouldn't be in bed now.'

Mrs Leyton ignored this. She had heard only Arthur's account of what had happened, and had never thought to disbelieve it.

'Nice to have the family round you in troubled times,' she went on. 'You know where you are with family.'

'Yeh. I know.'

'I mean, no dipping in the sugar when your back's turned.'

'No one dips in my sugar.'

'Only in a manner of speaking, that is. But, you know, Louisa, you might do well to make it a family affair.'

Louisa's head jerked up from the open drawer. 'Eh?'

'I mean, the service you're getting here—and giving. I'm sorry to say—well, it's very poor.'

'Oh? Since when?'

'Well, all this dilly-dallying. I rang five times for breakfast, and if Arthur hadn't been on the boots we'd have been walking barefoot round the shops all morning.

Lunchtime we'd have starved, if Arthur hadn't brought us a tray. And just now I had to ring seven times—*seven* times—for tea, and if it hadn't been for Arthur . . .'

Arthur came in at that moment with tea things. Mrs Leyton gestured towards the table near her and he obediently laid the tray down, watched amazedly by Louisa.

'I was just saying to Louisa,' her mother addressed Arthur, 'I was just going to say, why not make this place a family concern? I could superintend the meals. Ernest can look after the door . . .'

Louisa looked towards her father. He was positively squirming.

'I see,' she said. 'And I'd be dogsbody, I suppose?'

'Nonsense, dear. Arthur, fetch another cup for Louisa.'

'Don't trouble yourself,' she told him. 'I've got work to do.'

She dragged out the entire contents of the drawer and marched from the room with them. Mrs Leyton sighed. She picked up a sandwich and examined its contents. 'Salmon again?'

'You like salmon, Mum,' Arthur reminded her.

'Yes, but not every time. You'll really have to speak to them in that kitchen, you know.'

But in the kitchen, at that moment, they were speaking of her.

'Getting out of hand, it is,' Starr was saying to Mrs Cochrane, the cook, and Gwyneth and Violet. 'I may say, it comes hard for me to talk like this. Me and Fred's loyal characters, ain't we, Fred? But there is such a thing as self-respect.'

'That's right,' Gwyneth agreed, and Fred all but said so, too.

'I mean,' his master went on, 'this bloke comes pushing in, no respect for nothing, and what happens? Mr Merriman laid up in bed. Poor Fred here half lamed. And the place isn't our own any more. Now, I'm as fond of Mrs Trotter as any of us, but I came here on the clear understanding that . . .'

'Oh! Somebody loves me, then,' Louisa declared, hurrying in with her stiff gait. 'What's this, then? A blooming meeting? Well, come on—what's biting you?'

Starr pulled in his stomach, inflated his chest, and replied manfully, 'Your family, ma'am. I am forced to speak frankly, ma'am. We are no longer servants in our own home . . . as you might say.'

'The thing is, mum,' Mrs Cochrane intervened, 'I'm not having any more of it. That Mr Leyton is never out of my kitchen. Forever getting himself snacks and things for them parents of his.'

'My parents, too, Mrs Cochrane.'

'Well . . . It's all very well, mum, but I'm being thrown all over the place. Why, I never know what I've got. I go to my currant cake, and half of it's gone. Yesterday there wasn't a spot of salmon to be found, and Lady Talbot was asking for it specially. It's not right, mum, him pinching my food *and* Violet's bum.'

Louisa would have smiled at this if she hadn't recognised the dangerous build-up of the situation. Still, she tried to lighten it by saying, 'I'm sorry about your food and Violet's bum. As for Lady Talbot, I'll have a word with her meself. The other thing, I'll have to think about. If you'll all be kind enough to carry on normal for the time being, I'll sort it out somehow. I promise.'

That evening she sat in the lamplight beside her parlour fireplace and thought about it. It was herself she blamed mostly, for being such a soft touch. All her life, it seemed, people had been pushing her the way they wanted her to go; yet there she'd been, thinking how tough and independent she was. She'd been turfed out of school and into service by her parents. She'd been manipulated into marriage with Augustus Trotter, to satsify the whim of a king. It had been her own idea to take on the Bentinck, not for her benefit, but to keep Trotter's self-esteem up for him and stop him pestering her with his unwanted attentions. When she'd wanted nothing better than to die peacefully in the hospital bed to which overwork had brought her, Charlie Haslemere had as good as forced her to start up the Bentinck again in its new form.

She'd been married, though she had never wanted marriage. She'd had a child, yet didn't like children and had never dreamed of having one of her own. She had achieved her ambition of becoming the best cook in London, but it hadn't ended there, and seemed to have brought endless responsibilities for other people in its train. Her father's words sounded in her mind: 'Just a bit of peace and quiet . . .'

And then she looked up, and he was there, hovering apologetically in the doorway, with the door half open.

'I knocked, love,' he said, 'but I wasn't sure whether you'd answered.'

'Come in, Dad,' Louisa said, and pulled a chair to the other side of the fire for him. 'How about a glass of wine?'

'Not for me, love, thanks. I didn't want to disturb you.'

'You make yourself comfy. Where's Mum?'

'Doing the town with Arthur. It's his evening off, isn't it?'

'Oh, yes. I forgot.' Giving me own brother the evening off, she thought. What topsy-turvy state had things come to?

'Still keeping good time?' her father asked. She followed his gaze to the mantelpiece where the clock ticked.

'Nicest wedding present we had,' she said.

'All in the past,' he said. 'All in the past—but the old clock ticks on, like me.'

She took a breath and said, 'You'll have to go, Dad.' Topsy-turvy again, giving her parents the order of the boot. But he answered, 'Of course we will. I never wanted to come. I mean, putting on you like . . .'

'You feel a bit better for the change, though?'

'I wasn't ill. She gets these bees in her bonnet.' He jerked his head significantly. 'Tell you the truth, love, she gives me the pip.'

'Worse than me, is she?'

'You're a different kettle of fish.'

'I'm like her. I want me own way. I want to manage everything. But everything seems to manage me.'

'You don't moan about it, though.'

'S'pose not. Dad, I don't want to hurt her. I know she'd enjoy herself here, lording it about. She'd do the running of it quite well, I expect. But I can't have her under the same roof as me.'

'I have to, love.'

'Oh, Dad!'

'It's different for you, girl. You're the boss and she's your mother. That combination would never mix. No, we'll go. And Arthur ought to, too.'

'That what you think?'

He nodded. 'He wants to be boss, as well.'

'Runs in the family, eh?'

'Not me. Peace and quiet. That's all I want.'

The door opened abruptly and Mrs Leyton flounced in, wearing a hat and coat over an evening gown. Arthur was behind her.

'Oh—waiting up for us?' she asked, frowning at the sight of her husband. 'What are you doing, Ern?'

'Just talking to our Louisa, dear.'

'Mm! Arthur, d'you think you could fetch a drop of coffee for us? And a few sandwiches?'

'But not salmon,' Louisa interposed.

Her mother failed to detect the sarcasm. She said, 'No, not salmon. A nice bit of ham off the bone, or tongue . . .'

'No!' Louisa said sharply, halting Arthur who was turning to go out.

'Eh?'

'I said, no. You can have a cup of coffee, if whoever's in the kitchen will kindly make it. But you'll stay out of there, Arthur.'

'What for?'

'Because I'm telling you. Mrs Cochrane doesn't want you messing about in her kitchen no longer.'

'I thought it was your kitchen.'

'Mrs Cochrane runs it for me, in her way, which is my way, and we can't neither of us be messed about. So go and ask them for some coffee for us all. Tell them it's my orders.'

Arthur shrugged elaborately, gave a low bow, and went out. Louisa turned to her mother, who had sat down and was unpinning her hat.

'You've been here a week now, Mum . . .'

'And very nice, too—apart from the staff.'

'The staff are threatening to leave.'

'Good riddance.'

'I don't want them to leave. I want you to, Mum.'

'Of all things! Us before that lot!'

'Listen, you've had the week we agreed . . .'

'Your father isn't anything like better yet. And I don't like your tone, my girl.'

She was taken aback by the intensity of Louisa's cry: 'Oh, why can't I deal with me family like I deal with the rest of life? I made this hotel what it is, and I intend to go on running it me own way. It's me livelihood—me *life!* Mum, I'm telling you as nicely as I can—you *are* my mother . . .'

She knew she had blundered as soon as the words were said. Tears had sprung to her mother's eyes and she was groping for her handkerchief. It was the weapon against which Louisa's defences were weakest.

'She's putting us out,' Mrs Leyton sobbed at Arthur who had just returned. 'Me and your poor, sick old dad.'

Feeling at a disadvantage with him looking down on her, Louisa stood up to face her brother. Even so, he was a good deal taller than she; but she could put her hands on her hips and stiffen her back in an attitude any of her staff would have known meant that battle was about to be joined.

'I'm asking them to go home, having had their week,' she told him. 'And I'm sacking you.'

His eyes widened, but he laughed. 'No references?'

'I'm serious.'

'Well, I don't think I want to go. Send Mum and Dad home, if that's all you feel for them. But you need me, Louie.'

'I don't need no one—and that's not me name.'

'Yes you do. This servant trouble, for instance . . .'

'There was no servant trouble till you got a foot in here and started acting Lord Muck.'

Arthur's smile faded and he leaned towards her. 'You're Lady Muck, more like. Too big for your boots by far. Well, you can't just turn me out as and when it suits you. I have my rights.'

'Arthur, I'll put a bleedin' bomb under this place before I'll let you walk roughshod over me.'

'Suit yourself about that. What is it anyway, but a stamping ground for a few bloody nobs with handles to their names?'

'Arthur! You shouldn't talk like that!' Mrs Leyton rebuked him.

He turned and said savagely, 'Shut up, you silly old hag! Time you learnt to keep your stupid mouth shut!'

A silence dropped between them all. Mrs Leyton sat aghast, her handkerchief half raised. Louisa stared. Even mild Mr Leyton flushed and seemed likely to get up and attack his son.

'Don't you speak to Mum like that in my place!' Louisa stormed. 'Get out of it. Go on—before I smash a bottle over your bleedin' head!'

'I'm going,' Arthur sneered. 'I was a fool to set foot in the place. Sack me? You couldn't keep me here chained down. I tell you something though, Louisa. You said "No skivvies here". Well what d'you call yourself? You're a bloody monumental skivvy—with gold edges. You live in a world of dreams . . .'

She was reaching for a vase.

'Don't worry about references,' he smirked, edging round the door. 'I wouldn't want them from this high-class whorehouse.'

The vase shattered against the closed door. It was a

repeat of her ejection of Augustus Trotter and his sister, except that she had thrown bottles then. She turned back to the fireplace. Her parents were staring, looking half-terrified.

As on that previous occasion, her violent act had drained her instantaneously. Her shoulders slumped. She said dully, 'It's all right, Mum. You can stay another week.'

But her mother scented another victory. She jumped up and gesticulated to her husband to follow suit.

'I'll never enter this place again,' she declared. 'You've spoiled everything . . . driven Arthur from me. He called me a hag! I had a lovely night out, and you've spoiled it. I never get nothing nice happening to me. You've got all this—and I've got nothing. Nothing!'

She burst into sobs and fumbled her way out of the room. Her husband followed, giving Louisa's arm a little pat as he went by. When they had gone Louisa, too, began to cry, and collapsed on to a chair.

Mary, bringing the coffee Arthur had ordered, came in and found her.

'Put that down!' Louisa moaned. 'Pour me a cup and get some brandy.'

'Yes'm.'

'They're going—thank God!—and I don't think they'll come again.'

Mary poured, not comprehending the logic of the tears. Louisa seized the brandy glass from her and drank some straight down. Between sobs, she stammered, 'Oh, poor Mum! Poor Mum! She's got nothin', and I've got everythin' . . . And he called me a skivvy and her a hag. Oh, Mary, poor Mum! Poor, poor Mum!'

Mary knelt beside the chair and put her arm round her. She still did not understand; but then, neither did Louisa. She just wept and wept.

# CHAPTER THREE

Louisa had never been one for holidays. A visit to the French estates of a noble guest from that country had turned out disastrously when he had taken to pursuing her through his vineyards with obvious intentions. Her sojourn in a rented house at Cowes, on the Isle of Wight, had been an act of revenge for a snub, with an impact upon the neighbouring Royal Sailing Club from which its lady members would never recover. Other than on these occasions, she had scarcely ever left the Bentinck, preferring to sit there like a spider at the centre of its web and let the world come to her.

So it was a surprise to Mary to be told by Louisa, who had a letter in front of her on her desk, that she was leaving for Yorkshire at once and might be away for some time.

Mary knew from whom the letter had come; she had brought it in and had recognised both the postmark and Lord Haslemere's crest on the envelope. Charles, Viscount Haslemere, had once been a familiar figure on the premises. It had been he who had rescued Louisa from financial ruin and despair by setting her up in the hotel in the first place, on the excuse that he wanted a set of rooms in London and the best cook in the capital to cater for him. He had been the Honourable Charles Tyrrel in those days, tall, handsome, young, with no other career than man-about-town, and one of his many conquests—unpremeditated for once—had been Louisa herself. She had borne his child, and Mary had been her confidante at that time. She knew that the baby, christened Lottie, had been fostered out to servants on the Haslemere estate in Yorkshire, shortly after Charles had inherited his late father's title.

Mary, who had never been invited to marry anyone, let alone have a baby, had sorrowed a good deal at first at the thought of her mistress being deprived of her child like this. But years of close acquaintance with Louisa Trotter had taught her that she and Lord Haslemere had taken the right decision. Any attempt by Louisa to bring up a child would have failed notably, and the Bentinck would have been an utterly unsuitable place for attempting it. Having rejected Lord Haslemere's gentlemanly offer to marry her, Louisa had put their daughter out of her life completely, and out of her mind so far as she could.

And then, some years later, Lord Haslemere had decided the time had come to give up bachelorhood, marry a suitable girl, and beget an heir to perpetuate the family line. Mary remembered the unmistakable tension Louisa Trotter had displayed when he had introduced her to his chosen mate, a twenty-year-old, rather characterless type, Margaret Wormald, who had been brought up in country seclusion by a guardian, both her parents being dead. They were married, from the Bentinck, in 1910, and had then gone to live on the Haslemere estate, Bishopsleigh in Yorkshire. The Bentinck had seen little of them since. Mary had noticed few envelopes bearing the crest she knew so well.

It was now the beginning of February, 1914, almost three years after the disruptive invasion by Mrs Trotter's brother, of whom, thank goodness, no further sight had been seen. He was as much forgotten as Lord Haslemere appeared to be. The suite of rooms kept vacant at all times for his lordship's brief visits to London had been relinquished by him two years or so ago and was used now for the hotel's most honoured guests. So the arrival of the letter with the crest and Yorkshire postmark, and Louisa's prompt decision to go there, aroused curiosity in the Welsh girl's mind. No explanation was given her, and she had more tact than to ask questions. She noticed, though, that a considerable amount of luggage was loaded into the hotel 'bus in which Major Smith-Barton drove their employer to King's Cross. It seemed to presage a long stay, during which Mary would be in charge of the hotel, with his assistance.

Louisa was no connoisseur of Nature, but the grandeur of the Yorkshire dales impressed her, as she was driven through them in a closed horse-carriage bearing the Haslemere coat of arms, which had been there to meet her at Harrogate Station in response to her telegram. The contrast between these majestic slopes, carved into jigsaw-like patterns by endless walls of loosely piled stones, and the artificiality of London, where everything seemed man-made, gave her the feeling that she had transported herself to some foreign land, an illusion which had been heightened by the flat accents she had encountered at Harrogate, with some words quite incomprehensible to her Cockney ears.

Bishopsleigh was impressive, too, though in a different way. It was huge—much larger than Louisa had expected, although Charlie had shown her photographs of it years ago. It was stone-built, and the mist enshrouding it on this bleak February afternoon gave the impression that it would prove to be as cold inside as it was without. Louisa would suddenly have been glad to be back in her parlour, with a nice fire glowing in the grate and an open bottle of bubbly at her side. That one room and her bedroom were the centre of her world; in them she felt contented and secure. She would not have swapped them for all the Bishopsleighs in England.

But her welcome from Charlie was warm. He almost ran out of the front door, preceded by barking, yelping dogs, which pranced around as he helped her out of the carriage, and hugged her to him, crying out that she couldn't know how glad he was to see her again. Her spirits rose.

They fell again, though, when she took in the atmosphere of the vast hall-cum-sitting-room into which he led her.

'Blimey!' she said, craning her head back to stare up to the distant darkness of the ceiling. The walls seemed like acreages. She shivered. A broad staircase led up towards shadowy nothingness.

'Pickering,' Charlies ordered a short, silver-haired servant, 'see to the fire, will you? The wretched thing's practically dead.'

'Soon get you warm,' he told Louisa, who was glad to keep her coat on for the time being. 'You know, you're sweetness itself to come all this way.'

'Sweet I may be, but salt's generally what you need, Charlie. What you been up to now? I couldn't make head nor tail of your letter.'

He laughed. 'Margaret and I both need a tonic—who more obvious than you?'

'I've got an 'otel to run, remember?'

'It runs you, more likely. A change will do you good. Come on. To keep your circulation going until the fire's burnt up I'll show you over the family ruin.'

He tucked her arm through his, and, with the dogs padding excitedly ahead of them, led her along passages, up and down staircases, and into an almost bewildering number of rooms. There was an air of vastness and gloom everywhere. For the most part the furnishings were oaken and heavy, the people in the dark pictures forbidding. It was a dynastic house, with nothing of the still-boyish Charlie imprinted on it, and even less of his wife— wherever she might be.

They encountered her on the stairs leading back to the hall. Louisa was startled. She had not thought of Margaret as lovely; she was not one for appreciating women's looks. But there was undeniable beauty in this girl whose height almost exactly matched Louisa's own five feet five inches, whose eyes were almost as large as Louisa's own, though brown and wistful, not bright and blue like hers, and whose youthful slenderness made even the trim Louisa conscious for once that she herself was almost into her forties.

Yet Margaret's hair, scraped into a knot on top of her head, looked somehow untidy, and even uncared for. She wore an unbecoming white dress, which seemed remarkably flimsy for these chill surroundings. And when they shook hands, Louisa could feel an almost electric force tensing up the younger woman's muscles.

When they had greeted one another Louisa turned to smile at Charlie. He smiled back, and led them down into the hall; but she had caught the anxiety with which he had evidently been watching them. She knew suddenly that it was not only the house that was making her wish again she was snugly back in the Bentinck.

They all sat together in the hall before dinner, with drinks in their hands. Louisa was in an armchair, yet, as usual, poised as stiffly upright as if the corset she wore every day now, was holding her like that, and not her own gesture of independence towards the rest of the world. Charles and Margaret were together on the sofa, his legs stretched far out towards the brass fender, she with hers so tightly tucked together that they might have been in a knot. She played incessantly with a curl which had dropped loose beside her left ear. Louisa's initial impression of her tense state was confirmed by the way she spoke.

'The point is, Louisa, you understand Charles so well. Now that the shooting season's over, he's been getting so frightfully bored. After all, to go without slaughtering pheasants and woodcock four times a week must be a great hardship for a man.'

Louisa noted the brittle tone in which it was said, and the grim twitch of Charlie's lips as he heard it. And she saw the effort he made. He took his wife's hand, saying, 'You're probably right. Getting to be just like Father. Good God, if you'd told me a few years ago that I would, I wouldn't have believed either of you!'

'Poor love!' Louisa mocked him. 'What a shame!' Margaret was not within her range of vision as she spoke, but she could feel that her gaze had turned sharply towards her. Then she heard her change the subject in a way that was all too obviously unsuccessful.

'Was it the summer of '08 when I first came here, Charlie? I think it must have been. I remember the house was simply swarming with people. I was quite dazzled. Then, in the afternoon, we went out on the lake. You rowed right out into the middle . . .' she turned to Louisa, 'though, of course, we couldn't agree where the middle was, exactly. Then he put up the oars and we drifted. It was sunny. Very warm. Every so often a moorhen called. But otherwise, not a sound. Nothing. No one. Just us—drifting.'

Louisa gave Charles a quick glance. His glass had been nearly full a few moments earlier. Now it was empty.

She jerked her attention back to Margaret, as she heard her almost cry out, 'Oh Louisa, where are all the happy, innocent times gone?'

Louisa, who had seen little of their happy, innocent times, had no pat answer to give, for once. But she brooded on the question a good deal during the following hours. The next morning—Sunday—she leaned towards Charlie during the singing of a lusty hymn in the ancient little church whose walls bore memorials to so many of his family, and asked, 'Is one of them our Lottie?'

Her question startled him. He could see that her gaze was on the girls in the small choir. He shook his head hurriedly. He hadn't imagined she would allude to that matter. But she had; and again, she felt Margaret's look turned swiftly towards them.

Whenever she could during the rest of the service she watched Margaret, and during luncheon she came to a decision. The soup and fish courses were concluded. During them, Louisa had been unaccustomedly quiet, letting Charlie prattle on about the content of the sermon by his friend the vicar, a sporting, outspoken man of late middle-age whose subject that day had been the crime of bigamy. Now the meat was on their plates and the vegetables had been served. Louisa's watchful eyes had noted how small a portion of each Margaret accepted. As soon as Pickering had left the room she got up from her place and went swiftly round to where Margaret sat. She siezed the napkin from her hostess's lap and held it up by one end. Pieces of fish cascaded to the floor.

Charles cried, 'Louisa! What the devil are you doing?'

She ignored him, and addressed Margaret. 'When did you last eat a proper meal, my girl?'

Charlie watched with astonishment as his wife, instead of reacting with resentment, slumped suddenly against the back of her chair and covered her face with her hands, muttering, 'I can't! I can't eat!'

'Why the 'ell not?' was the unsympathetic response she got from the woman standing over her.

'It . . . makes me ill. When I eat, I'm sick.'

Louisa looked at her for some moments, then gave her stiff shrug and went back to her place. She prodded her own portion of meat. 'Small wonder, to judge from the muck your cook serves up!'

She went on to eat it silently and fastidiously; but her dramatic action had had its effect. Margaret stayed as she was, making no further pretence of eating her luncheon. Charles picked at his unhappily. Louisa knew now why she had been summoned to Yorkshire.

When she and Charles had some time alone after the meal she said without preamble, 'This kind of nonsense has been goin' on for months, hasn't it?'

He had to nod agreement. Then he lifted his head and snapped out, 'What the hell am I supposed to do with a woman like that? What is it she wants? She's a spoilt, demented child.'

'All right, then—treat her like a child. What they won't do, make 'em do.'

He looked at her in a strange, questioning way. 'What . . . do you mean by that?'

'Make her eat. I will, if you can't. You sent for me. All right, then I shall prepare her food meself, and that old cat of yours in the kitchen can like it or lump it, if this is all she can dish up. What your Margaret needs is good food, a bit of fun, and . . .'

She stopped herself. Then, watching him closely, she added with an effort, ' . . . and some more lovin' attention from his bloomin' lordship.' It surprised her considerably when, at this, he shook his head angrily and walked out of the room.

Louisa pondered for some minutes, then went in search of Margaret. After losing herself in the upstairs corridors she eventually located a room which, she recognised, Charlie had pointed out during his conducted tour as Margaret's. She hesitated outside the closed door for a few moments, wondering whether Charlie might be in there. She doubted it very much. She knocked. Margaret's muffled voice called out.

Louisa went in. Margaret was in bed, in her under-clothes. Her dress was lying rumpled on the carpet; Louisa picked it up and folded it over her arm before placing it carefully across a chair back. She went to the bed and sat on it, regarding its occupant. Margaret was deathly pale and noticeably haggard. The beauty Louisa had fancied she had seen, had been an illusion of powder and rouge in grim surroundings.

'Is it all right if I speak my mind?' Louisa said. It wasn't often that she asked anyone's permission to say or do anything.

The reply was a dull, 'Of course.'

'Then, I don't think you're ill. You're just letting your-self go.'

'I feel so tired . . .'

'What's gone wrong between you two?'

'Nothing.'

'Garn! Given half a chance you'd just turn your face to the wall and give up, wouldn't you? I know, 'cos I felt like that once meself. And, come to think of it, it was *he* who snapped me out of it.'

Margaret's dulled eyes glowed with a sudden spark at this. Louisa went on hastily, 'In a business sort of way,

44

that is. He made me work at my life. And you're goin' to have to work at yours, my girl.' And so is he, she added to herself silently, though Gawd knows why I should have to be the one to make him!

She addressed him in the hall some minutes later, having elicited nothing from Margaret but a refusal to discuss her personal affairs with her. He was lying on the sofa, pensively smoking a cigar. Louisa went straight to the brandy decanter and, without asking permission, poured generous measures for them both. Then she took a chair opposite him. He swung his feet to the floor, to sit up facing her.

'You don't think Margaret knows about Lottie, do you?' Louisa asked. Her directness startled him.

'No! Why?'

Louisa shrugged. 'There's always gossip.'

'Not about that. Nobody knows. Not even her . . . . parents, the Richards. They just think she was a by-blow of some relative of mine.'

'Poor little b . . . . bleeder. I've been thinking, Charlie, since I've been here, and she might be within ten yards of me, for all I know . . . I've been wondrin' what her future's goin' to be. I mean, what sort of a choice has she got, compared to what she might have had?'

'What choice have any of us got?'

'I knew what I wanted—and I got it. Maybe I was just the lucky one. What about her, though?'

Charlie said seriously, 'Louisa, dear, I know what you're feeling. But neither of us can step in now. We both gave up that right when Lottie was only a few weeks old. The Richards are decent people. She's an intelligent, tough little thing, believe me. She'll be all right.'

Louisa nodded mutely, sipped some brandy, and blew her nose. Then she pulled herself up and said, 'I wonder what sort of choice your Margaret's had?'

'You mean, marriage or no marriage?' he joked, but she shook her head.

'I mean motherhood. I never wanted it, but it happened.

45

How about her?'

Charles dropped his gaze. He took a large mouthful of brandy, swilled it between his cheeks, then swallowed it. At last he said, 'I'd resigned myself to giving up our daughter—yours and mine. I settled all my hopes on Margaret. The estate . . . children. I thought she was just the type . . .'

'Not like me, eh?' Louisa said softly, trying to ease his obvious pain.

'Not a bit like you, Louisa. The idea disgusts her.'

'I thought as much. Well, look at the way she was brought up. There was I, worrying about our Lottie! Thank God she hasn't got just a crusty old godfather for a guardian. Why, I expect he taught her she'd crumble into dust if any man so much as breathed on her.'

'I know! I've borne all that in mind. I've tried to be gentle, considerate, but . . . Honestly, I sometimes think she believes the whole business is some sort of perversion of my own.'

Louisa shocked him with a harsh laugh. 'I reckon it's a miracle the upper classes 'aven't died out altogether. You're not the only one, Charlie, believe me. I've heard tales of some honeymooners in my hotel.'

'That's all very well. But most upper-class young ladies have a highly developed sense of duty, too. They grit their teeth and bear it. Margaret, poor girl, just vomits.'

Louisa stared. 'But . . . you've been married over three years. That can't be all it is.'

'She's wasting away, Louisa. I don't know why, and I can't do anything. Our doctor can't help. She's got no mother or sisters or women friends I could talk to. That's why I asked you to come, don't you see?'

'Me—of all people?'

Charles nodded guiltily. Louisa regarded him for some minutes, during which neither of them spoke. Then she said, 'When your uncle, Lord Henry Norton, came to me to break the news that he wanted to marry you off to her,

I said it wasn't none of my concern. And then you came, too, asking me if you ought to pop the question to her. And after you had, you came again and said how you must break away from the Bentinck, from me, because I was tryin' to hold on to you, and it wouldn't do. I wasn't, Charlie, you know I wasn't . . .'

'I know now, Louisa.'

'Then why come to me about this? Why's it got to be me in the middle all the time?'

'I also said I'd been relying on you for too long—that I'd got to learn to be responsible for myself. Well, I have to admit I've tried, and I've failed. That's all, I'm afraid.'

Another silence fell, until Louisa said, 'Well, apart from talking to her—and I still think I'm about the last one she's likely to listen to—all I can do is feed her proper and hope she'll get back her taste for that, at least. As to the other, well, that's your department.' She hesitated, then added, bashful for once, 'Unless you've changed a lot, I can't see it bein' anything lacking on your side.'

She left him abruptly. She went straight down to the kitchen and, ignoring the protests of the cook, proceeded to prepare a chicken soup to a recipe of her own, a standard favourite at the Bentinck. When she had tasted it for the last time, and approved it, she poured it into a warmed bowl, sprinkled in small, crisp croutons, and took it quickly on a tray to Margaret's room. Margaret tried to refuse it. Louisa stood firm and watched as the delicious soup was slowly and reluctantly sipped.

When about half it it had been swallowed Margaret put the spoon down and pushed the tray away. Louisa made no effort to force her further. She smiled and lifted the tray off the bed.

'There you are, dear,' she said triumphantly. 'That was nice, wasn't it?'

'Yes, thank you.'

'It'll do for a beginning. I'm going to cook everything for you meself till there's colour back in them pretty cheeks.'

She swept out, feeling highly pleased with herself. What she did not know was that within seconds of her departure Margaret was noisily sick into the basin she kept ready for these frequent occurrences, and lay gasping and exhausted, overwhelmed by nausea.

When Louisa got back to the kitchen the cook was not there, but someone else was. This was a girl of eleven or twelve years old. She was plainly dressed in a short, dark frock with a pinafore and thick black stockings. Her hair was tied back in a knot. She was standing beside the table in the middle of the room where the cook had left a tray of newly-baked biscuits to cool. At a glance, Louisa saw that there was a gap in one of the uniform rows in which they had been laid out. She put down her tray and went to the child, whose pretty, oval-shaped face had reddened.

'Where are they?' Louisa demanded. 'You eaten 'em?'

The girl shook her head. Louisa pointed at the pinafore pocket.

'Let's have them, then. Quick—before cook comes back.'

The child produced the biscuits. Louisa snatched them from her and put them back in place.

'Don't they feed you at 'ome? Who are you, anyway?'

All the answer she got was, 'Don't tell, will yer?' It was said in the local accent.

They both heard the cook approaching, scolding her kitchenmaid. Before Louisa could ask any more questions the child had dashed out of the back door and gone. But she had jerked the door shut behind her and the cook heard it bang. She glared suspiciously at Louisa, at her biscuits, then snapped, 'Who was that, coming in my kitchen? That Richards brat, I expect. Not but what everyone comes swarming here lately, as if they thought it was their own.'

A brief argument followed, in which Louisa conveyed her firm intention of preparing Lady Haslemere's meals personally and told her rival to go and ask Lord Haslemere, if she didn't believe her.

It wasn't until afterwards that Louisa remembered the girl, and the name the cook had mentioned—and realised with a wave of shock that she had been face to face with her own daughter.

Two more light meals Louisa cooked for Margaret and saw them satisfactorily accepted; and twice more Margaret was sick after them, without Louisa's knowledge.

It was February the fourteenth, Valentine's Day. Louisa had duly received a card, and knew very well from whom it had come: he gave her a little kiss on the cheek, for old time's sake. Then he told her that the vicar, with whom he had been doing some mild archaeological digging in recent weeks, was coming for tea, and that Margaret had said she would join them. Louisa, of course, was invited as well, if she would promise not to make any disparaging references to her rival's cake.

The February dark settled early, but the hall wore a more cheerful appearance for once, due to a big, bright fire, which dispelled most of the shadows and made the best china twinkle colourfully on the table. The vicar was a tall, lean man with nice, silvering hair, a hearty handshake and a lively personality. Louisa, who no longer swore as much as had once been her habit, but was very apt to let slip an oath or two, decided that she would not need to guard her tongue too carefully in his presence. She relaxed and prepared to enjoy herself.

The appearance of Margaret cheered them all. She was beautifully dressed in an elaborately embroidered teagown. Her hair was carefully arranged and there was a welcome touch of pink under the powder on her cheeks. If Louisa had looked closely enough she would have detected that it was rouge, applied with deceptive care. But she had no reason to do any such thing; and it certainly never occurred to her that Margaret had gone to great lengths over her appearance in a deliberate effort to outshine her.

They enjoyed a long tea, throughout which they all talked nineteen to the dozen on a range of topics, with occasional breaks into hilarity, generally sparked off by the jolly clergyman and the stories of goings-on at the Bentinck Hotel which he and Charlie persuaded Louisa to relate in her inimitable way. Louisa kept no eye on Margaret to see how she reacted, or how much she ate. She was off duty just now. In fact, Margaret ate nothing at all. She accepted a few things and concealed them under the table, as a child would its unwanted crusts.

They got on so well, that afternoon gave way to evening with them still rattling away. Charlie proposed they have some wine and the vicar accepted eagerly. After a glass or two he declared that he would sing them his party piece, if Charlie would play. The offer was applauded and Charlie opened the grand piano and sat down to the keyboard. He knew the piece well enough. He had heard the vicar perform it often, and had accompanied it before.

> *They saw me dance the Polka,*
> *They saw me cover the ground,*
> *They saw my coat-tails flying*
> *As I jumped my partner round.*
> *When the band commences playing,*
> *My feet begin to go,*
> *For a rollicking romping Polka*
> *Is the jolliest fun I know . . .*

The vicar's coat-tails were literally flying, as he jigged about to his own zestful singing. The infectious quick rhythm had Louisa clapping hands in time to it, and she noticed Margaret's foot tapping more and more vigorously. Suddenly Margaret sprang up and began whirling round, her loose skirt swirling. Louisa saw Charlie throw her a look of alarm, and she herself feared that Margaret, in her debilitated state, might make herself dizzy and perhaps faint. But the song was soon over. To general applause the vicar bowed elaborately. Margaret collapsed into a chair, but she was still smiling, as well as panting heavily.

The vicar took a long draught of wine and told Louisa, 'There's no doubt about it—I missed my true calling in life.'

She agreed. 'If ever you was to get kicked out of your present job, come to me and I'll take you on at the drop of an 'at.'

Charles got up from the piano stool. 'Speaking of hats,' he said, 'that reminds me, I've got a secret admirer.'

He went over to a side table where some papers lay. He picked one up and brought it back to show them. It was a hand-crayoned Valentine card, on rough paper. Its picture was a fair likeness of him, wearing his coronet.

Louisa and the vicar exclaimed in admiration of it, but Margaret asked in a cold voice, 'Who sent that?'

'The Richards child, of course. She always draws our greetings cards. I found this here this morning.'

The rest of them froze as Margaret jumped to her feet, swayed unsteadily, and cried with a rising note of hysteria, 'That brat! I've said before I won't have it in the house. Its mother can't control it. If they can't keep it out of here, they can pack up and go, the lot of them. Do you hear? I wish I could never see the beastly little thing again!'

Charlie went quickly to his wife and gently forced her back into her chair. She was trembling and wide-eyed. What had alarmed Louisa even more, though, was that the outburst had been directed partly to Charlie, but partly also towards her. Her fear that Margaret somehow had discovered the secret about the child returned, and chilled her.

'I, er, I think I ought to be going,' the vicar said diplomatically. 'Good heavens, if that's the time I've long outstayed my welcome.'

But Margaret's contorted features straightened and she smiled weakly.

'Don't go on my account, please,' she said, getting up slowly. 'I'm so sorry, everyone. The dancing made me giddy, and I don't think I knew what I was saying.'

Charlie went to assist her again, but she evaded him and came over to Louisa, surprising her by kissing her on the cheek.

'Goodnight, Louisa,' she said. 'Thank you for looking after me.' She turned to the others. 'I'm so terribly tired suddenly. If you'll excuse me, I'll go to bed.'

Before Charles could move again she had gone quickly and quite steadily to the wide staircase. She went up, assisting herself by the banister rail, and disappeared from their sight.

'I'm sorry,' Charlie told the vicar. 'Over-excited, I'm afraid.'

'I know, old chap. So sorry. Anyway, I really must be going. I enjoyed myself so much—especially meeting you, Mrs Trotter.'

'Louisa to my friends, Vicar.'

'Alec to mine, Louisa. When I pay my next five-yearly visit to London, I shall certainly call at the Bentinck. Goodnight and God bless, meanwhile.'

When Charlie returned from showing him out he found Louisa kneeling by the fire, warming her hands. A strange chill had come over her which the flames seemed unable to dispel.

'I liked him,' she said. 'He's a delight.'

'He'd shock some of the old types rigid.'

'That's why I liked him. You known him all your life?'

'Since I was a young man. He came here, oh, about the time I first met you, I'd say.' Charlie paused, then added, 'I wish I were that young man again, Louisa.'

'Never look back, Charlie. Never. I've just found out what a bad thing that is.'

She got up and stood in front of him, searching his eyes seriously.

'You shouldn't have fetched me here. She knows. I know she does.'

'She can't, I tell you. Anyway, it was years ago—long before her time. And such things are common enough, God knows.'

'God may know, but not her. Brought up by stuffy old Sir Jimmy Rosslyn. Wonder she even knows the facts of life, if you'll pardon me saying so.'

'I don't think she does—even now. Or if she does, she hates them.'

Louisa shivered suddenly. The gloom had descended on the hall again. The brief festivity had been like some manic interlude in that usually sombre place.

'Charlie,' she said, 'I'm afraid!'

He moved to put his arm round her, but realised he must not and checked himself.

'Don't worry, Louisa. I'm truly sorry I dragged you into it. You go back to the Bentinck and leave it to me.'

There was a sudden flurry of movement at the head of the stairs and Margaret's old nanny, who had looked after her from infancy, came part of the way down.

'My lord!' she cried to Charlie. 'Something's the matter . . .'

He hurried to the foot of the stairs. 'What is it?'

'Miss Margaret—her ladyship . . . She's nowhere to be found. I'd undressed her and put her night things on, and I went out to fill her water decanter. When I came back she'd gone, and I can't find her anywhere.'

Charlie was hurrying up the stairs. 'She's upset, Nanny. In rather a state. She might have had a dizzy turn and had to sit down somewhere.'

'I've looked everywhere, sir.'

'I'll look. Get Pickering to come as well.'

Louisa called up, 'I'll come, too.'

She hurried up after him and began her own search. The four of them went separately from room to room, passage to passage, in the big house, until every possible place had been explored. They converged finally on the hall and agreed that Nanny had been right.

Charles ordered Pickering to fetch every man and search the entire estate. He told Louisa and Nanny to stay indoors, because of the bitter cold, then dashed off into the darkness, not even pausing to get a coat.

It was more than an hour before he found her. Growing fear and certainty had taken him to the edge of the lake. It would be impossible to search the dark, icy-cold water that night, but he knew that it would have to be done next day, and thought he was certain what they would find.

But he was wrong. He noticed that the little blue boat, in which he and Margaret had once drifted in the sunshine, laughingly essaying the hopeless and pointless task of defining the exact centre of the lake, was absent from its mooring. Peering hard, he thought he could see its dark shape out on the water. Another little boat was tied up close to where he stood. He got into it and rowed out.

Margaret was in the other boat, lying across its stern, one hand trailing in the water. She wore only her nightdress. Her head was arched back and her hair hung loose. Whether the intense cold had killed her, or something before that, didn't concern him just then. She was dead.

Louisa stayed on for the funeral, which was conducted by that same vicar who, less than an hour before the tragedy, had capered abandonedly in front of them all. Margaret's guardian, Sir James Rosslyn, now looking very old and infirm, attended. So did Lord Henry Norton, who had arranged the marriage, and in whose household Louisa had set her first confident foot on the ladder to success and fame. Apart from Nanny, the other servants and one or two parishioners, it was a small party in the snow at the graveside.

Louisa saw the couple she knew to be Mr and Mrs Richards, her child's foster-parents. They were older than she had always pictured them. Lottie herself was not there. Louisa was glad of that: it would have made the occasion doubly painful for her.

She saw Lottie once more, though. The carriage was taking Louisa away from Bishopsleigh to her train next morning. Charlie had wanted to accompany her, but she had refused to let him. She wanted no company but her own until she could be back at the Bentinck, as soon as possible, to submerge her thoughts and memories in the bustle of work.

She turned from waving back to him, and saw through the carriage window the girl, standing beside the drive, looking at her. She was scowling. Louisa returned her stare expressionlessly. Her hand did not rise to wave, even instinctively.

The child turned her back in what looked like a deliberate gesture. The carriage passed on. Louisa did not trouble to turn round again. 'Never look back.'

# CHAPTER FOUR

The conclusion of the inquest was that the death of Margaret, Viscountess Haslemere, had been caused by misadventure. After that there was scarcely any fuss. The Press merely noticed the tragedy in passing. Margaret had been little known in society, and since his marriage to her Charlie's name had seldom appeared in print. As there were no children, and no close relatives on her side, no major consequences were precipitated. After less than four years of a marriage that had been fruitless in every sense, Charlie simply lapsed into bachelorhood again, under the new title of widower.

It would have been truer to say that Margaret lay on his conscience, rather than that he grieved for her. They had been quite unsuited to one another and should never have married. Of all the women and girls Charlie had known, in varying degrees of intimacy, she had been the least known to him, and the least intimate beforehand. Perhaps that was why he had chosen her, to most people's astonishment and the dismay of a few hopefuls: she had been untarnished, and he had seen that as a principal qualification for helping him further the Haslemere line.

Louisa had said little at the time. Secretly, though without realising it, she had resented his marrying at all. Although they had agreed within days of the start of their own relationship that it must end, she had always regarded him as to some extent her property. When he had told her, immediately after the wedding, that he must free himself of her, he had been telling her in effect that he must go away and do his duty; but she knew as well as he did that a dull marriage and a squire's life in the heart of remote Yorkshire, was not for him.

Now Fate had released him from it. Throughout that Spring he remained at Bishopsleigh, sorting out what loose ends Margaret's death had left, brooding about mortality, examining his past and future. Then one day in early July, when the trees were in the pride of their green again, and the sun shone warmly in an impeccably blue sky, with promise of a marvellous summer, he shook himself, telegraphed to the Bentinck, and set his man to packing his things for a return to London.

Louisa was pleased by the news. Charlie's return to his home-from-home was always a tonic to her, though she expected to find him less his old cheerful self this time. Well, a few weeks of her cooking and bossing would soon have him back to normal. She fancied she could read him like a book, and that she, more than anyone, knew what was best for him.

She could not offer him his former suite. Although it still contained all the furnishings he had bought especially for it in the first place, and he could have slipped back into it as easily and comfortably as putting on a favourite pair of his Lobb's boots, it was let to an elderly member of a Balkan royal family and his new young Austrian bride. He had often stayed at the Bentinck before, and had promised the princess-to-be that her honeymoon should be spent in the hotel he regarded as the best in the world, in the heart of the capital city he preferred above all others. Louisa had agreed to cook for them herself, throughout the month they would be staying. They had duly arrived. Louisa had been charmed by the naive little princess, and had made a great personal effort to get the marriage off to a perfect start. It never occurred to her how contrasted her attitude towards it was to what she had felt towards Charlie's.

She was able to provide Charlie with a much smaller but pleasant set of apartments. His telegram had stated that he did not know how long he would wish to stay, and she didn't question him when he arrived.

He was paler than she was used to seeing him, and had lost some weight, which somehow seemed to have added to his height. His dark hair had acquired the first grains of silver at the sides. He still had his neat military moustache, and the semi-mourning suit he wore accentuated the impression of romantic melancholy.

Of course, Louisa took him straight into her parlour and poured champagne for them both.

'Isn't it your cricketing week, or whatever it is, up in Yorkshire?' she asked, determined to strike a cheerful note from the start.

He nodded, unsmiling. 'I chucked it this year.'

'Oh? Pity. You've always looked forward to it so much. Enjoyed it.'

'That's the point. She . . . Margaret . . . it was one of the few things she really joined in. Used to keep the score for us and make everyone laugh with the muddle she'd get into. She'd be everywhere if I went this year.'

'Nice to have some happy memories,' Louisa said, trying to keep the tone up.

'Yes. As a matter of fact, one of the first things I want to do is see a fellow about an idea I've had for a memorial to her. I'd rather like to talk to you about it first, if you don't mind.'

'I think I do mind,' she startled him by replying. 'I'm sorry, Charlie. It's been bad for you, but it was bad before it happened, remember? It's over and done with, and I don't want you coming turning my hotel into a morgue with your moping.'

'Very well! I'll find somewhere else.'

She changed her tone quickly, realising that she had been too blunt, even for Charlie.

'It wasn't your fault, love,' she said quietly. 'She did herself in.'

'That wasn't the coroner's finding.'

'Letting you down easy, so it wouldn't be all over the papers. It wasn't her fault, either, poor thing. She . . .

couldn't face up to life. It was something . . . in here that
was wrong.'

She touched her temple significantly with a forefinger.

'That's what I tell myself. But I married her . . .'

'For better or for worse. Don't you remember what
was said in this very room before it?—you pays yer
money . . . Marriage is a lottery, Charlie. Crikey, I
reckon the Major's got a better chance of winning, putting
his pennies on the ponies! Sorry, love, there I go again. I
won't say you should forget it. You won't, anyway. It
might have . . .'

'What? Might have what?'

'Well, made you a better person. You was pretty spoilt,
you know.'

At last, to Louisa's relief, Charlie smiled, and responded, 'Tempered me in the fierce furnace of life, sort
of thing?'

'Yeh. That's it. Memorials is all right and proper, but
not when you put 'em up to your own misery. That way
you'll get like poor Margaret.'

Charlie stirred and drained his glass. Louisa was pleased
that he held it out willingly when she raised the bottle
towards him.

'What shall I do?' he asked. 'Go back to Yorkshire? I
don't want to. That life doesn't suit me.'

'I could have told you that. Don't go, if you don't have
to. Chuck them clothes, for a start, and get yourself
something more cheerful. You know what women do
when they're a bit down? They buy a new hat, and cheer
'emselves up fancyin' themselves. Get out and do something.'

That reminded her and she glanced at the clock.

'Here, I can't sit all day gossiping with you. I got more
on this month than since the Coronation, what with
cooking for my love-birds in your old rooms.' She
drained her glass and stood up. ''Fraid there won't be no
time to cook special for you . . .'

She paused and looked into his face as he rose. Then

she said more kindly, 'But if you've any special dinners you want me to do, I'll see what I can manage. Welcome back, Charlie, love. I'm glad you know where your friends are.'

She stepped forward, gave him a kiss on the cheek, then bustled out, smoothing her skirt as her stiff backed gait carried her down to the kitchen.

Charlie was back in the parlour again a few mornings later. He was wearing a pearl grey suit now, and a discreetly coloured tie under his high collar. Gloom had been replaced now by a look of anxiety.

'Oh, lor', what now?' Louisa demanded, and sent for Merriman and coffee. Ten o'clock was early for champagne, even by her timetable.

Charlie held up a letter on stiff paper. 'They've asked me to become a Gentleman Usher at Court.'

'What's that? A sort of glorified Merriman?'

'A part-time courtier. On duty at royal functions—garden parties, court balls, diplomatic occasions. Old Johnnie Farjeon's behind it, obviously. Trying to be kind.'

'He's a kind bloke.'

It had been the former Major Farjeon, now Sir John, who had acted as go-between in the relationship between Louisa and King Edward the Seventh. He had been unfailingly courteous and helpful to her, then and since.

'Well, congratulations, Charlie! It's a step in the right direction, eh? P'raps we *will* have some bubbly, after all.'

But Charlie's expression was still perplexed. He said, 'I think I'm going to ask them to excuse me. I . . . don't feel up to it.'

Louisa jumped up and came pugnaciously round from behind her desk.

'I see it! Johnnie's getting sick and tired of you wanderin' round spreadin' gloom and despondency wherever you go. I know a lot of your friends are, me for one. That's what he's tryin' to buck you out of.'

She shook a finger in Charlie's face.

'And if King George does you the honour to ask you to help out at his do's, I reckon it's an insult to refuse. After all, you're a bloody viscount. Doesn't that mean you have *some* responsibilities?'

'I . . . hadn't looked at it like that.'

'I can see you hadn't, and it's about time you did. I'm proud of our aristocracy, Charlie Haslemere. Most of 'em I've had dealings with has been gentry in the best way— though I wouldn't always say the same for some of their jumped-up wives. But if I heard any one of 'em say he couldn't be bothered to do a bit for 'is king, I'd show 'im my door—and I reckon I oughtn't to make an exception of you.'

Charlie raised his hands in the traditional gesture of surrender, and actually grinned.

'Louisa, your sharp tongue is more subtly persuasive than all the honeyed words in the language. I'll accept at once.'

She glowered at him for a little longer, daring him to have second thoughts afterwards.

'Yeh,' she said at length. 'You do—or never darken my doors again . . . as once I said to Trotter and his bloody sister.'

Merriman found them laughing together when he arrived with the tray. They sat beside the fireless grate, filled for the summer with an arrangement of dried flowers and leaves, and sipped their coffee.

'Will you have to wear a special uniform?' asked Louisa.

'Lord, yes! Very special and very expensive. More like a glorified footman than a glorified Merriman.'

'I could use a glorified footman some evenings, if the King can let you off.'

'My poor tailor is going to have to work night and day. I'll have to dash round to him as soon as I've written my acceptance.'

'They go short-staffed at the Palace, then?'

'The invitation says that if I do accept, I'd have to

make my debut at the court ball on the 23rd.'

'Crickey! What you lounging here for, then? No, take your time, love. A couple of cups of coffee won't set back your tailor or my book-keeping that much. Oh, Charlie, I wish I could be at that ball to see you. You'll look so . . . Tell you what! So's I can see you in your full fig, and because you're being such a good, obedient boy, I'll give you a lovely dinner first. Ask Johnnie and any of your other friends who'll be mixed up in this, and their wives, and I'll cook every scrap of it with me own hands.'

'No, Louisa. I'd rather you sat down with us.'

'I can't sit down in me pinny, and I can't cook proper unless I'm downstairs to concentrate. No, it's full dress and orders for all of you lot, and full cap and pinny for me—and them's my orders. Besides, it's the way I want to do it for you, love.'

Charlie finished his coffee and put the cup and saucer back on the tray. Before he left the room he kissed Louisa, holding her lightly by one cheek so that she was forced to accept his lips on hers. It was a soft, brief kiss—nothing more—but it spoke his gratitude for forcing him to take up his part in life again.

When the door had closed behind him Louisa finished her own coffee. She sat for some moments afterwards, letting her mind wander freely. Then she snapped back into action, hurrying to her desk chair to get on with the accounts. But the blank menu cards in their rack caught her eye. She drew one out, took up her pen, and wrote at the head of it, in her fine, copperplate hand:

Ld. Haslemere. Diner du 23 Juillet, 1914.

She paused, thought hard for some time, then slowly began to compile the menu, partly from inspiration, but also from her memory of notably successful blendings of the past.

Several times during the next few days she changed her mind, in some instances subsequently changing it back again. When at last she was ready, and all the crossed-

63

out and scribbled-on versions had been thrown away, she summoned Major Smith-Barton for a consultation about the wines.

The ageing Major had been a fixture at the hotel for several years, ever since his arrival as a guest out of the blue with a monocle in his eye, the initials of the Distinguished Service Order after his name, and a small amount of well-worn luggage. He had taken a small room, rapidly engaged the interest of Starr as a fellow-fancier of the horses, and proceeded to gallop along that downhill course which leaves the bookmakers richer, their client poorer, and his creditors unpaid.

Louisa had characteristically put up with his unsettled bills until financial trouble of her own had forced her to deliver an ultimatum. He had been unable to pay, but he had readily accepted the alternative—that he stay on as an unofficial employee, helping with all sorts of tasks from driving the hotel 'bus to carrying luggage. His professed expert knowledge of race form (he had been an honorary steward to the Calcutta Racecourse in his time) had proved of no benefit to Starr, who, fortunately, placed only occasional small bets; but his acquaintance with many society families had helped Louisa greatly. It had pleased, though mystified, many guests of the aristocratic sort to be welcomed to the Bentinck and shown to their rooms by an old army or school colleague, who greeted them by their Christian names, enquired after the health of the members of their families, and asked, as any fellow clubman might, whether the partridges were rising well this year? If asked what on earth he was doing in the hotel, the Major lapsed into vagueness, returned some airily uninformative answer, and wandered off, remarking that they must foregather for a glass of something or other soon.

His opinion about wines was as excellent as his knowledge of horseflesh was deficient. Louisa always discussed her menu with him before a special function.

He screwed in his eyeglass and looked at the card,

reading it aloud:

> *Melon Glacée*
> *Potage Bisque*
> *Truite Saumonée Norvegienne*
> *Blanchailles*
> *Soufflé de Cailles au Riz* . . .

. . . I say, Mrs Trotter, that makes my mouth water just to read it out.'

She nodded. 'The dear old King used to love his quails, God bless him. Read the rest, though.'

> *Jambon de Prague*
> *Dindonneau aux Froids*
> *Salade*
> *Glace d'Ananas*
> *Pêches Bonnes Femmes* . . .

. . . My word! Now, let's have a look in the old book.'

Major Smith-Barton handed back the menu card and took up the Bentinck's cellar book. The worn leather volume had been begun well before Louisa's time, by two proprietors preceding her. Some fantastically venerable vintages were listed in its earlier pages, and not all had yet been crossed out as drunk. But by far the bulk of the entries, all in ink, had been made during her tenure. More wine had been consumed on those premises in her thirteen years there than in the preceding thirty, and not a little of it by herself and favoured guests in the parlour where she and the Major now stood.

'Let us consider the pièce de resistance,' he said judicially. 'The quail soufflé, of course. We can build round that, so to speak. Now, my first thought was a burgundy. But a quail is a small bird, *en soufflé*. It's warm weather. You'll be drinking champagne during a good deal of the rest of the meal, I imagine? Yes. Then, in that case, I think, perhaps, a bordeaux.'

He leafed back and forth amongst the pages, until he found what he sought.

'Yes. Pichon-Longueville '02. A tricky year, '02. Bad thunderstorms over France in October. Affected St

Emilion and Pomeral. But the Medoc, being nearer the sea, escaped them.'

'I must say, Major, I never did!' Louisa exclaimed admiringly.

He wagged his head. 'Ah, dear lady! Now, a question—how is the salmon trout to be cooked?'

'In aspic. Served cold, you know.'

'Quite, quite. In that case, we might do worse than turn our minds to Chablis Grenouilles . . .'

The dinner party was one of the most colourful gatherings the Bentinck Hotel had seen in its history. A small crowd collected and lingered near the front door to see if any further resplendently dressed people would be arriving, hoping, even, for a glimpse of royalty. Starr persuaded them to disperse. Definitely no royalty, and definitely no-one still to come, he told them lightly, and they drifted away.

The meal was to be served in Charlie's old dining-room. The Bentinck had no public dining-room—all meals were served to guests in their apartments—and the limited quarters he had been occupying since his return did not include separate dining accommodation. By a lucky chance, three days before the occasion, the Balkan prince had come to Louisa with a sorrowful expression to say that, due to the growing consequences of the assassination at Sarajevo of the Heir-Apparent to the throne of Austria–Hungary, he had been summoned back to his country. His councillors had left him as long as possible to enjoy his honeymoon, but now that accusations and counter-accusations were flying between Austria and Serbia his state's stability depended to some extent on his presence to support his ancient father.

'Charlie,' Louisa had called to Lord Haslemere a few minutes later, as he was crossing the hall to go to the final fitting of his uniform trousers, 'your old rooms—they'll be free from tonight. Do you want 'em for your party?'

His face lit up. 'I say! Wouldn't it be too much trouble?'

"'Course it will. But, for you, I daresay we'll struggle through.'

'Thanks, Louisa. That'll put the perfect touch to it. I must dash, though. Tailor's a tyrant.'

'Ta-ra!'

They were short-handed at the moment. Violet, the Tyneside maid who had been with Louisa for years, had suddenly been swept off her feet by an actor and whisked off to the provinces with him in a state of happy sin. Mary, Ethel and Louisa herself briefly left their other duties and worked on the newly-vacated suite to restore it to an exact semblance of how Louisa and Mary remembered it. When Charlie asked to see it, Louisa refused to let him. He'd know his way about it when the time came, she assured him. She wanted his evening to be as special as possible for him, as well as his guests.

So it was Merriman who stood at the door to welcome the party. Charlie was trim and handsome in his new court dress, with its distinctive usher's coat, as he entered his former abode and looked round appreciatively at the familiar surroundings and all the well-remembered things.

But his uniform was positively sober compared with those of his fellow-diners. Captain Evelyn Marjoribanks blazed in the scarlet full dress of the Grenadier Guards. Major Billy Fitzsimmons contrasted with him in the peacock full dress of the Queen's Own Irish Hussars. Sir James Farjeon had found himself unable to attend. There was a good deal of urgent activity in military circles just now.

The youngest of the ladies, a Lady Victoria, a marquis's remarkably beautiful, deplorably feather-brained daughter, in a white silk sheath dress, was like a moving candle, lit atop by the dazzle from one of the most valuable parures of diamond tiara, earrings and necklace in the British Isles. Major Fitzsimmons' pretty blonde wife, known for reasons no one could remember as Puffin, sparked less in dress than in personality and endless, inconsequential chatter. The third lady, Antonia, a dowager countess, lately widowed in her forties, was known as Toni to her face but 'the Marmalade Tart' behind her back. Her voice was ginny and gravelly, her brain sharp, and her hair a new, interesting shade of henna, as she carefully prepared herself for a new and, she was determined, more interesting role in life than the dull county existence which had been her lot for the past twenty years.

'Stunning rooms,' Mrs Fitzsimmons remarked, with barely a glance round. 'As I was saying, Billy mutinied.'

'Did they throw you in the Tower?' Charlie asked the Hussar Major.

'We didn't actually mutiny. You know how Puffin exaggerates. We were all called together in a tent on the Curragh, and the General said that if it came to civil war between Ireland and Ulster we'd have to stop it. Well, I mean to say, there was I, in an Irish regiment, and my own estates only thirty miles away. We'd have been fighting our own people. It would have been ridiculous.'

'Complete farce,' the Captain of Grenadiers agreed. 'Generals seem to have cotton-wool for brains. God help us if there's a real war.'

'I'm sure He will, Evelyn, dear,' the dowager said. 'It's taken for granted that He's on our side, isn't it?'

'Oh!' the Lady Victoria exclaimed. 'I thought the Germans were so religious.'

'Wasting their time, in this case. God's ours. We've always counted on God. That's why the generals don't bother to do their stuff properly!'

'Bravo, Countess!' Major Fitzsimmons cried. 'Charlie, old boy, great quarters you've got here. Snug as a bug.'

'Thanks,' Charles said, a little ruefully. 'But they're not mine any more.'

'Too bad, too bad.'

'Yes,' the Countess agreed. 'You could have invited me tête-à-tête, Charles.'

'The Dragon would get you before you were up the

stairs,' Captain Marjoribanks warned her. 'Where is she, Charlie?'

'Cooking. Specially for us.'

There were enthusiastic cries at this, and Charles was glad to have the subject changed by Merriman dispensing pre-dinner drinks. Charles had never known how widely his past connection with Louisa had become known, and he always felt uneasy when she and he were mentioned in the same breath by such gossips as he knew these women to be.

He thought she might just have come up and shown herself after the meal, which, inevitably, was superb. But she did not. He knew how hard she would have worked during these past two hours, rushing between ovens, tables, saucepans, serving dishes . . . Shouting orders to everyone, yet doing most things with her own hands. Her face would be red, her hair flying, her impatience nearer to boiling over than any of her pans. When the last course had gone up, and it was only left to Merriman, in attendance on the party, to make and serve the coffee, Louisa would fling herself down in a kitchen chair and call for champagne for herself and the harassed helpers whom she had driven with scorn and abuse.

All the same, when the party descended to the hall, ready to leave for the ball, cloaks over their shoulders despite the hot night, and the men's swords clinking, he left the others briefly to cross to her parlour and look in. She was at her desk, tidy and calm, and writing composedly.

'Louisa, darling,' he called softly as she looked up. 'Thank you for a wonderful dinner. You certainly earned your sovereign tonight.'

She grinned at the reference to the first reward Edward the Seventh had given her for cooking for him.

'Thanks, Charlie . . . Give my kind regards to the royals.'

He blew her a kiss and returned to his party, being ushered out to their carriages by Starr.

Louisa looked at the inside of her closed door, listening to the hearty departure. Then she shoved aside a wistful thought that had come to her in the aftermath of all the kitchen bustle, and went on with what she was doing.

She thought she heard them return after midnight. She was still at her desk. The recent hectic times had thrown her far behind with her accounts, and night gave her the best opportunity of catching up undisturbed.

She heard the scuffling of feet, and male and female gigglings. It could have been any of two or three parties at present staying in the hotel, but she fancied she heard some metallic sounds, as of spurs and swords. She did not trouble to go out and see.

'I'm quite famished,' Puffin whispered, as they made their less than steady way towards the stairs. 'Hope you've got plenty to eat in your room, Charlie.'

'Damn!' he exclaimed. 'I was only using the dining-room for the evening. I didn't give any orders, and there won't be anything in my bedroom.'

'Thoroughly unsatisfactory arrangements!' the Countess condemned him, putting on a voice like Lady Bracknell's, which made them all giggle again.

'Sssh!' Charlie said. 'Look, all of you go down to the kitchen.' He pointed the way. 'There won't be any staff on duty now. We'll have to manage for ourselves. I'll get some booze.'

They shuffled off and he tiptoed across the hall to the dispense. He saw the slit of light under Louisa's door, hesitated, then decided not to disturb her. He knew she sometimes fell asleep in her easy chair and spent the night in it as happily as if she had been in bed. Its parlour was where this spider belonged.

He got a bottle of champagne under each arm, and one in each hand, and pulled the dispense door to with his foot, before creeping back across the hall and down to the kitchen. His guests were foraging about, peering into cupboards, chattering and generally looking helpless.

Cloaks and swords were strewn about.

The two officers thankfully seized champagne bottles and opened one each, pouring their contents into the mugs the kitchen staff used for their tea.

'Yummy!' Puffin exclaimed, savouring a familiar drink from an unaccustomed vessel.

Lady Victoria took off her tiara with both hands and laid it on a scrubbed chopping board.

'The beastly thing weighs a ton,' she pouted.

'Quite apart from looking like a fender,' remarked the Marmalade Tart.

'What're we going to eat?' the Grenadier asked plaintively.

'Eggs and bacon,' said the Hussar. 'Always the thing, late at night.'

'Yum-yum!' contributed Puffin. 'What do we cook them in?'

'A saucepan,' her husband told his wife, who had never cooked an egg in her life. Neither had he.

'I think it's a sort of flat thing,' Lady Victoria hesitated. 'Isn't it?'.

'A frying-pan,' Charlie said, lifting a copper one down from a row gleaming in the electric light. 'I think the eggs are over there somewhere, Billy. As to the bacon . . .'

'I've found some!' Lady Victoria cried. She had actually recognised it. 'Oops!' she cried again, though less triumphantly this time. In reaching up to take the bacon from its wire-grilled safe she had caught her gown on a saucepan handle. As she straightened up the pan was jerked to the floor, where it bowled about with the maximum possible din.

They all looked at one another.

'Not to worry,' Charlie told them. 'I'll light a gas ring while someone breaks some eggs.'

'Oh, please let me do one!' Puffin pleaded. 'I'd love to break an egg.'

Her husband handed her one. She tapped it carefully against the basin he had the initiative to provide her with.

71

When nothing happened she brought the egg down hard on the basin rim. The shell broke, but its contents slithered down the outside of the bowl and from there to the floor.

'Oh dear! I don't think I'd make a very good cook . . .'

'Nor do I, Mrs Fitzsimmons, if you'll excuse me saying so.'

Louisa's voice from the head of the kitchen stairs caused them to jerk round like guilty children. She had heard the pan fall, just as she was crossing the hall to go to bed at last.

In silence she descended the stairs and stalked across the kitchen, as upright as if she had been starting her day, not ending it well after midnight. She took an egg and broke it briskly and accurately into the bowl.

'Got it?' she demanded. 'Only, you don't break no more into the same bowl until you've used each one. If you get one bad 'un it'd ruin all the rest, see?'

A chorus of admiration and apology arose around her. She ignored it and began bustling about setting eggs and bacon to fry in separate pans.

'Here—doesn't the poor chef get any of that?' She jerked her head at the champagne bottles. Captain Marjoribanks hurried to pour some for her. She looked disgustedly at the mug, but drank from it.

'How was the bloomin' ball, then?'

In their various ways, and to a large extent simultaneously, they told her how stiff and formal the King and Queen had been, just sitting watching everyone dance and looking frightfully bored by the whole thing.

'It was rather like an animated version of Madame Tussaud's,' Charlie said. 'But too hot for any waxworks. Luckily, the King and Queen go early to bed . . .'

'So we melted back here,' quipped the Countess.

Louisa gave her a broad smile. 'Very clever, dear.' She turned to the others. 'What sort of dances did you 'ave?'

'Waltzes, waltzes, waltzes!' they chorused.

'No modern stuff?'

'At the palace?'

Lady Victoria was pouting again. 'And I adore the Bunny Hug and the Turkey Trot.'

'So do I, love,' Louisa said warmly. 'Can't say I've had much practice at 'em, but I'm willin' to have a go, if anyone else is.'

This received a storm of approval. Charlie jumped up up on to the main table and put out his hand to help Louisa up.

'Just follow me,' he instructed. 'Right, everyone?'

They had seized saucepans and began to beat out a rhythm with them, accompanying their singing of 'Florry was a Flapper'. Charlie went into the convolutions of the dance, jerking Louisa with him. The pans of frying food were forgotten. The chorus of voices and the ragged clatter filled the room.

But at length a man's voice somehow overbore it all. They looked towards the stairs. At their foot stood Major Smith-Barton, in his dressing-gown, swelling his lungs for another cry for attention in his long-disused military fashion. His expression was serious.

Louisa remembered the frying pans and scrambled down as the racket ceased. The Major went to Captain Marjoribanks.

'Captain Marjoribanks, sir?'

The officer recognised another gentleman's voice.

'Yes, sir.'

'Sorry to disturb you . . . all,' Major Smith-Barton said. 'Your soldier servant's in the hall, Captain Marjoribanks. He has a taxicab and orders to take you back to barracks immediately.'

'Eh? What for, does he say?'

'Not my place to question him, old boy. I get the impression you're in for a pretty quick move, though. Your battalion, that is.'

Marjoribanks was already hurrying to gather up his things.

'Do you, by God! Ireland? Or this European thing

73

blowing up?'

'There was a special edition of the papers this evening while you were all at the ball. There's an ultimatum of some sort flying round from Austria to Serbia. No more details yet, but if it isn't met there could be hell to pay.'

'And we'll be dragged in for certain,' Major Fitz-simmons put in. 'I'd better report in, too. They might not know where to come looking for me.'

Louisa suggested they eat their eggs and bacon before going; but the two officers, now quickly sobered up and concerned about their duty, declined, and the ladies said they had better go with them because of the carriage arrangements. They gathered up their things, thanked Charlie and Louisa, and left, a subdued, preoccupied quartet.

'Well, come on,' Louisa said, indicating the food, 'we're not wasting all this.'

Major Smith-Barton succeeded in persuading her to let him go back to the bed from which he had been roused. So she and Charlie sat down at the table on which they had been dancing and ate bacon and eggs, washed down with the remains of the champagne.

'What about you, Charlie boy?' she asked after a while.

'Me?'

'If there's a war, would you have to go?'

He shrugged. 'I'm not a professional soldier. They'll deal with it.'

'Just like that?'

'Chaps like Marjoribanks and Billy might seem rather wet when it comes to conversation or anything serious. When it comes to fighting, you'll find there's a different side to them.'

'Oh, I know. I've had plenty of their kind through here. Anyway, you're too ancient.'

'I like that! Louisa . . . Seriously . . .'

'What now?'

'This settles it for me. I can't go back to the wilds of Yorkshire and bury myself away while all this is going on.

74

Anything might happen. I want to stay where all my friends are, right at the centre. Louisa, if I asked nicely, could I have my rooms back—permanently?'

She was looking hard at him, wondering what she ought to say and what she wanted to say.

'Please,' he asked.

She sighed, and smiled. 'Of course, love. You always said this was 'ome. Nip up and fetch another bottle of bubbly, will you? We got these bleedin' eggs to finish if they come out of our ears, so we'd better wash 'em down proper.'

# CHAPTER FIVE

'War!' Louisa exclaimed. 'What the 'ell are we doin' at war?'

It was August the fifth, 1914. She had come down from her bedroom at her usual early hour, to find Major Smith-Barton conversing seriously in the hall with Starr, a newspaper held between them. The Major had gravely given her the news that for several hours already, while she had been sleeping peacefully, the nation had been at war with Germany.

The news shocked and bewildered her. Like almost everyone else in Great Britain she had never believed such a thing would come to pass.

Yet all the portents had been there for them. Throughout that extraordinary July of oven-like heat alternating with sudden cold, dazzling blue skies and violent storms, the situation in Europe had been deteriorating daily. One of the few ways in which Louisa was typical of her sex was that she seldom read a newspaper. It was left to the Major to convey to her anything which he felt might interest her, which was not much. Outside the running of her hotel, and gossip about society people of her acquaintance, she took little heed of events in the world at large.

The anti-climax of Captain Marjoribanks's sudden recall to barracks during the extempore party in the kitchen had left her with no sense of foreboding. She had gone off to bed and slept soundly. Neither had she lost sleep on the night of Sunday, August the second, a day which had seen crowds gathering anxiously in Whitehall, and later singing the National Anthem before Bucking-ham Palace. Extra editions of the newspapers had told, in two-inch headlines, that German troops had crossed the French and Luxemburg borders.

'Very serious indeed,' Major Smith-Barton had said, shaking his head over one of those extras.

'I dunno why,' Louisa told him. 'If the Jerries and the Frogs want to fight each other, let 'em get on with it.'

The Major sighed. He had tried to explain the situation several times before, but she had shrugged it off always.

'It's Belgium that is the danger,' he told her again. 'We warned France not to take our intervention for granted. But we have a treaty with Belgium. If the Germans invade her, we're bound to go to her help.'

'Huh! I'll believe that when I see it. I know them politicians. Find a way to wriggle out of anything, when it comes to it.'

'Well,' the Major had to concede, 'it's certainly said that the Foreign Secretary hasn't the whole Cabinet behind him in favour of honouring our pledge.'

'You see? And that Eddie Grey's as much a ditherer as any of them. If he'd given Kaiser Billy a warning to stop all this nonsense before it started, there wouldn't have been any of it. I dunno, what with suffragettes and Ireland, and all these unions striking! And slap in the middle of Bank Holiday, when people just want to enjoy themselves.'

'Dear lady, the Kaiser's in no mood to listen to warn-ings. The Germans have been working themselves up to war pitch for months—years. "Der Tag", they've been openly calling it—the day when it would all begin; and now it has.'

'I'd have warned him off meself!' she retorted. 'Bloody cheek! He's jealous of our country. Always has been. I wish I'd put strychnine in his soup, the last time I cooked for him.'

The prospect of Louisa warning the Kaiser to his face not to start a war made the Major smile secretly. She would have been quite capable of it. But it was too late now. It was unlikely that Kaiser Wilhelm II would ever again sit down to a meal cooked by Louisa Trotter.

Events moved swiftly. On the following day, the Monday, with the beaches packed, holidaymakers everywhere calculated whether they had enough shillings left to give them another day away from home, for it had just been announced that the Bank Holiday had been extended by a day, while the City institutions wrestled with the implications of the doubling of Bank Rate to ten per cent. The Germans, it was reported, were poised to go into Belgium. A sense of general excitement prevailed, but no apprehension that within a few more hours Britain would be at war. An event of such magnitude was beyond the grasp of most minds. Like Louisa, most people believed that the politicians would fix it. Didn't they always?

The Foreign Secretary, Sir Edward Grey, issued at last the ultimatum which Louisa, reflecting the opinion of many other people, had said ought to have been made weeks earlier. He warned Germany that unless she guaranteed by midnight to leave Belgium unmolested, Britain would go to her ally's aid.

But it was Major Smith-Barton who had been right in the end. Germany was too far gone in aggressive intent to listen to reason any longer. While Louisa slept, midnight, August 4, came and passed. The ultimatum was ignored, and Britain went to war.

Starr tapped the newspaper he and the Major had been reading together.

'Sir Edward Grey reckons it'll change the world, this war, madam. England, too.'

'Oh, will it? Right, Starr. Get all the staff up here.'

'Here, madam?'

'In the hall. Sharp.'

'Yes, madam.'

'And bring a hammer and some nails back with you.'

Mystified, Starr went off. Louisa turned to the Major,

who was looking equally baffled.

'Major, be good enough to pop into my parlour and take down that signed photo of the Kaiser from off my wall.'

'Delighted,' he smiled, sensing something of her intention, though by no means the whole of it.

The staff assembled: Mary, Merriman, Mrs Cochrane, Ethel, Starr, the Major—and Fred. Louisa ordered them to follow her and set off up the stairs, leading a procession whose rear was brought up by Starr's little dog, bounding up the steps on his lead.

She led them along a passage on the first floor to the door of one of the few communal lavatories in the building. She pushed open the door and went in. The rest crowded round amazedly as she went to kneel on the fine mahogany seat, beckoning to the Major to hand her the framed picture of the "All Highest".

'Hammer and nails, Starr,' she ordered.

He passed her the nails. 'Sorry, madam, I couldn't find the hammer straight off. I'll nip down again . . .'

'Never mind.'

Louisa reached back and took off one of her shoes. Taking it by the toe, she proceeded to use the heel to hammer two nails into the wall above the lavatory seat. Then she picked up the picture and hung it on them.

'There!' she said, standing up. 'That's the only throne you're going to have in this hotel, your Imperial Bloody Majesty. Come to think of it, let's have your face to the wall, where it should be.'

She reversed the picture, then turned to the others, addressing them incongruously from within the lavatory, while they stood clustered outside it.

'This hotel's at war with Germany from now on. You men—you've all been military—put up your medals. And Starr—get a union jack on that bloody dog's collar before I see him again.'

'Yes, madam,' Starr replied willingly. 'Fred'll want to do his bit. Won't you, old son?'

The little dog looked up at his master and wagged his tail enthusiastically, sensing that something exciting was in prospect, and that they were going to let him join in.

When first the little Union Jack was affixed to Fred's collar, though, he did his best to get rid of it, as an irritant; but he couldn't get his mouth down sufficiently to reach it, and flailing at it with a hind paw had no effect. And then, suddenly, he began to realise that, whatever it was, it was producing beneficial effects. Even those guests in the hotel who had been in the habit of ignoring him as they passed by, would now pause to speak to him, with smiling faces, and stroke him.

His master looked very fine with his buttons given an extra polish and a row of medals on his chest. Merriman, too, wore his mementoes of ancient campaigns in the dust of Egypt. Major Smith-Barton had gone even further in obedience to Louisa's Order of the Day. He had resurrected his old but still respectable 17th Lancers uniform. Ethel had pressed it for him, and he now wore it proudly, with his D.S.O. and other medals up.

As soon as the initial shock of the outbreak of war had passed, the nation had come to quick terms with its new state. The many known German spies in the country had been smoothly rounded up by the Secret Service. Paper plans to have an army in readiness had been put into effect, and the British Expeditionary Force of 160,000 men was assembling, ready to cross to France. The newly created Earl Kitchener, on leave in England from his duty as British consul-general in Egypt, had been asked to leave the Channel boat which was to have taken him on the first leg of his journey back there and had been appointed Secretary of State for War. Within a week he was appealing for a hundred thousand volunteers. In little more than another fortnight he had them.

'Miserable old blighter!' Louisa remarked to Charlie Haslemere. 'He reckons the war'll last four years.

Everybody else is saying it'll be over by Christmas.'

'If I've anything to do with it, it will,' he responded. She looked at him sharply. He had just come in, immaculately dressed in frock coat, top hat, spats and kid gloves.

''Ere, what're you looking so pleased about, Charlie? Where you been?'

'Off to take the King's shilling.'

'The . . . You've . . . joined up?'

'That's it. I've been to see the lieutenant-colonel of the Coldstream Guards, an old friend of the family, and he's agreed to take me on. You see before you Ensign the Viscount Haslemere.'

'Coldstreams . . .' Louisa said dazedly, her mind reeling.

'Not Coldstreams,' he corrected pedantically. 'Coldstream Guards, Coldstream, or Coldstreamers. They're very particular. In any other regiment I'd be a second-lieutenant, but it's ensign in the Coldstream.'

'But . . . what's all the rush?'

'A prompt response to Kitchener's call. The war will never be over by Christmas if people like me just sit about waiting for someone else to fight it. The more who get in quickly, the sooner it will be finished.'

Unusually for her, Louisa was experiencing the chill of alarm.

'It was only the other day you said leave it to the professionals.'

'Kitchener is *the* professional, so far as I'm concerned. If he says my country needs me, he means it.'

'You only just settled back into your rooms! Oh, Charlie, why didn't you ask me?'

'Because, Louisa, my dear, you reminded me recently, and quite rightly, that I'm always coming to you for my decisions. Well, I decided that this was one I should make for myself. Anyway, it wasn't entirely up to me. I had to get through a medical exam, and that might have ploughed me there and then. But I passed A1.'

'So that's why you're looking like an over-excited schoolboy!' Louisa flared. 'Want to prove yourself to yourself, don't you?'

'There are times when you are the most illogical, stupid, annoying woman. You drink to victory, you curse the Kaiser and hang his picture in the lavatory—and then you're angry because I do my duty and join the army.'

'It doesn't have to be *your* duty. There's millions of young ones before you. Someone like you should use your nut and look round first, to see where you're needed most.'

'Louisa, look at me. If you were a man, wouldn't you be joining up?'

She looked at him, hesitating, before answering evasively, 'How do I know . . . not being a man? Oh . . . push off if you want to, then!'

She stalked away to her room and closed the door violently.


'Quite an excitement, this war starting, isn't it?' Mary Phillips said. 'Everyone's so jolly, all of a sudden.'

'Jolly!' Merriman exclaimed, putting his tea mug down on the kitchen table. 'Contemplating half the human race trying to kill the other half. I don't call that jolly.'

'Oh, you know what I mean, Mr Merriman.'

'No, I don't.'

'Well, go and listen outside Mrs Trotter's door, then. You won't hear jollier than that!'

The war had been in progress some three weeks. British jubilation was at its height. On August 18 the news had come that the entire British Expeditionary Force, with its guns and equipment intact down to the last item, had landed safely in France and was preparing to give the marauding Germans what for. Thousands of men, like Charlie, hastened to enlist, anxious to take a share in this history-making adventure before it was over.

Thousands of others flocked to the colours in response to the appearance in British streets of pathetic evacuees from little Belgium, whose resistance had been so brave, if so brief. Their stories of brutality, pillage and rape stirred up true hatred in the hearts of hitherto easygoing Englishmen, who visualised the same threat to their own land and womenfolk if the beastly Hun was allowed to cross the Channel. War fever, which had not existed at the outset, was suddenly rife and proving to be most contagious.

The news was good. The B.E.F. was marching confidently to join the French offensive. Wherever they went they were greeted with cheers, garlands, Union Jacks, Tricolors, and kisses from both women and men. It promised to be a short, sharp, inevitably triumphant campaign.

So there was no question of pressing the new recruits into uniform and throwing them into battle with all speed. They would be properly trained at home first, to the chagrin of the more impatient of them, but to the relief of Louisa Trotter and thousands of other women who would be gladder to see the whole business finished before their men could become involved.

Charlie was training at Chelsea Barracks, so had plenty of opportunity to spend his time off-duty at the Bentinck. Louisa encouraged him to bring as many friends as he wished, and established a pattern which was to become legendary, of plying them with as much champagne as they wanted and charging it to the bills of rich guests who would never notice it or miss what extra it cost them. Suddenly, Charlie had become everything to her: neither lover, sweetheart, son, husband, yet . . . She did not stop to analyse what she felt about him, but only knew a great new urge, after all these years, to keep him near her and to fling herself into concentrated celebration of his presence.

On this occasion the brother subalterns he had brought round with him were Ensigns Willie Watling and Jack

Hubbard, both his juniors by fifteen years or more. The three men, proud of their brand-new, Savile Row-made service dress and glistening Sam Browne belts, lounged with their glasses in the parlour, watched by a radiant Louisa, like a proud mare admiring her leggy colts' friskings. They talked, they joked, they sang, all inconsequential nonsense in tune with that time.

'Did you know, Mrs Trotter,' Willie Watling asked Louisa . . . He paused to sip champagne. 'Did you know that an elephant drinks twenty-five gallons of water a day, an ox eight gallons, and a sheep or pig only six to eight pints?'

'Can't say I did. Ever worked out how much bubbly a Coldstream ensign gets through?'

They all laughed excessively. Willie produced a slim book from a breast pocket of his khaki tunic.

'Not given in here,' he said, waving it. 'Only go by what's in here.'

'Oh? What's that, then?'

'It's our Bible,' Jack Hubbard told her. 'Field Service Pocket Book. Every officer has to carry one.'

'Well, I hope it proves bloomin' useful to know how much an elephant drinks, I'm sure.'

'Ah, but listen to this,' Willie said, thumbing the pages. '"To calculate the weight of a sheep. Kill eight sheep, weigh them, and take the average."'

'You're havin' me on!'

'Well, only a bit. Honestly, some of the stuff!'

Merriman came in with two bottles.

'More champagne you ordered, madam.'

'Thanks. Bung 'em in the ice and take the empties.'

'Yes, madam. Who shall I put these down to?'

'Lord Kitchener.'

'He's taken the pledge not to touch alcohol until the war is over. Anyway, he isn't a guest at present.'

'Well, I haven't taken no pledge. Put 'em down to me.'

He went away, sniffing. The two young guests expressed renewed thanks.

Louisa said, 'If that's your Bible, who's your God, then? Your C.O.?'

'Lord, no!'

'Drill-Sergeant Robinson.'

'Definitely Drill-Sergeant Robinson.'

'Who's he, when he's at home?'

Charlie told her, 'His uniform *is* his home. Six foot ten, the smartest man in the regiment, without a doubt. He said to me on parade this morning, "We've got two things in common, me lord. We've both got crowns. You wears yours on yer 'ead, and I wears mine on me sleeve. An' if I says 'Jump!', sir, you jump!"'

A gale of laughter greeted this imitation, delivered in stentorian tones, which caused Merriman, in the kitchen, to sniff, and Mary to smile 'I told you so' at him.

After another quarter of an hour Jack Hubbard said to Willie, 'Come on. We're on extra picquet this evening.'

'Lor', yes,' said Willie, lumbering to his feet. 'Thanks for a lovely drink, Mrs Trotter.'

'Louisa.'

'Louisa. Thanks.'

'That's all right, dear. Any time you're passing. Either of you.'

The two young men picked up their caps and swagger-canes and went, with less than military steadiness in their gait. Charlie stayed on. Louisa poured him another glass.

'I hope Drill-Sergeant What's-'is-name won't have 'em tied to wheels when he sees 'em. Nice boys.'

'The best. They make me feel quite old.'

'They make me feel young.' She smiled affectionately across at him. She thought how becoming that uniform was, and how it made him look even more handsome and distinguished than ever, and certainly younger, whatever he felt. He seemed to read her thoughts.

'Do you know,' he said, 'I don't think I've felt so jolly well and pip-pip for years.'

'Taking a bit of exercise for a change. Getting your

liver on the move.'

'Probably. But I think it's having something worth-while to do. A reason for living, after wasting so much of my life. I mean, I know it's all nonsense, this "For King and Country" stuff, but . . . well . . .'

'Nice to be needed, eh?'

'Something to aim at. And everything having to be just right. No sloppiness about anything, which is why Drill-Sergeant Robinson's crown means more than the one he thinks I wear. We're the best, and that's how it's got to remain. D'you see what I mean?'

Louisa nodded, and said, trying not to sound too hope-ful, 'Lots more training to do, I suppose?'

'Field training, yes. But it won't be too long, I hope.'

She felt the prick of alarm again. 'Don't you go jumping no queues, Charlie, just because the colonel's a pal. There's plenty of young 'uns ahead of you.'

He wrinkled his brow seriously. 'Don't you think they're really the valuable ones—the next generation?'

'Crikey! You sound like grandpa. No, let them get on with it, and you get fixed up with a nice interesting job on the Staff, or training, or something.'

He stared. 'Louisa, you still don't seem to have the foggiest idea why I joined the army. It was to beat the Germans, not mess about on the Staff and be the butt of all my friends.'

'Is that all you ever think of—what other people think of you?'

'No, it isn't.'

She got up. 'Well, I got duty to do as well—in the kitchen.' She turned to go to the door, but stopped and looked at him searchingly before saying, in a softer tone, 'I know how you feel, Charlie, love. It's how I feel about my cooking. It's a pig at the time, when you're sweating like hell—but it's something that's got to be just right, and it's worth all the effort. So take no notice of me, love. I suppose I was being a bit selfish.'

She nodded and went, leaving him to digest the remark as he finished his last glass of champagne.

The news turned sour on the last day but one of August. It told of the French army virtually smashed and the British Expeditionary Force in full retreat.

The story of that long, terrible retreat brought the reality of war home to the Bentinck Hotel and everywhere else in Britain at last.

'A hundred and sixty miles!' Mary exclaimed, some days later, after Merriman had read out a bulletin. 'Oh, those poor boys!'

'Ten days' marching,' he sniffed. 'Some with only rags on their feet. Men falling down and not being able to get up again, and those coming after 'em too tired to lift their feet to step over 'em.'

Starr shook his head. 'Yet they could still show Jerry how to shoot, by all accounts. I read that in some of those rearguard actions our lads were firing their rifles so fast that the Hun mistook 'em for machine-guns.'

'Well,' Mary sighed, 'I don't know. I was going to start knitting woollens for them, but you said they'd be home by Christmas. Now it looks as if you're right, though not how you meant. Perhaps I'd better take up first aid instead.'

'Whatever's the use of that?' Merriman asked.

'Looks like there will be fighting over here before long, that's what.'

'Don't you worry,' Starr tried to reassure her. 'They'll stand and hold somewhere. Then, when spring comes and the ground gets hard again, and the second hundred-thousand's out there to help 'em, they'll push old Jerry back again. Won't they, Fred?'

If his dog could have understood, he would probably not have believed him, any more than Mary did.

The B.E.F. turned and stood amongst the orchards of the Marne, on September 5. The exultant Germans, seeing Paris within their grasp, lunged forward, only to be thrown back in a pitched battle, with the loss of some of their finest soldiers. The battle of the Aisne followed. From these and smaller engagements it began to become clear that neither side was going to have its own way. Like cats staring at each other, awaiting the moment to pounce, both sides dug themselves into the earth, in a trench system extending virtually from the North Sea to the Alps. Sir John French ordered his troops to fortify their positions as strongly as wood, sandbags, piled earth and wire made possible. He would send them forward again as soon as possible, he promised. When, in October and November, the Germans launched their greatest effort, trying by sheer weight of numbers to smash through Ypres and secure the Channel ports before the onset of winter, the B.E.F. fought them off for three weeks. There was no going forward in turn; but it was the end of the retreat. The British Army was staying in France for the duration.

Even Louisa felt the impact of the mounting losses reported in every day's newspaper during that first battle of Ypres, in which the B.E.F. lost over 2,000 officers and more than 50,000 men. Inevitably, many of the names she read were familiar to her, conjuring up faces she remembered as laughing, carefree, confident, healthy with youth and zest for living. She started a scrapbook of obituaries from *The Times* and photographs from the *Illustrated London News*.

One morning, as she was pasting up the latest batch in her parlour, Charlie Haslemere came in, looking exceptionally cheerful. He gave Louisa a smacking kiss on the cheek.

'Come on,' he ordered her, 'I'm going to take you out to lunch.'

'Oh, are you? What's that in aid of?'

'We've been told to send our swords to the armourer to be sharpened. It . . . means we'll be off soon. Probably the next draft.'

Louisa strove to hide her sudden feelings. She indicated her book.

'Looks like you're going to be needed. Can't be much of the old army left. Seen Billy Renfold's name today?'

'I hadn't. Poor old Billy! Well, they've had a hell of a biffing. But there are literally hundreds of thousands of us new people now. They won't be calling us bloody civilians any more when we get out there to help them.'

'S'pose not,' she answered, unconvinced; then, with a rush, 'Charlie—take care of yourself. Don't go getting yourself killed, will you?'

Her intensity surprised him.

'Of course I'll take care . . .'

''Cos I'd rather have a live Charlie than a dead hero. Don't . . . you never think of it? 'Cos I do.'

'Yes, Louisa, I think about it. We all do, only we don't talk about it, except when there's someone we know in the casualty lists. But the prospect doesn't seem frightening. Perhaps it's partly because we don't really know what it's like out there. Anyway, it's a decent way to die . . . A good cause.'

'For King and Country, eh? Yeh. Well, I'll go and put me hat on.'

Charlie had unbuttoned one of his side pockets where there was a small bulge. He drew out a little red box.

'Louisa, there's something else I'd very much like you to wear . . . for me.'

She came forward curiously to accept the box and open it. Her mouth opened. She saw a superb little star-shaped brooch, in diamonds and rubies.

'The Coldstream star,' Charlie explained. 'If . . . you wear it, it means you're . . . my girl. Did you know that in the old days knights used to give their wives or their girls something to wear while they were away at the crusades?'

Louisa was glad he had gone on speaking. She was near to tears. As usual, though, she managed to stem rising emotion with a quip.

'I thought they locked 'em up in chastity belts.'

She was pinning the star to her bosom with trembling

fingers. She stepped quickly to the mantelpiece mirror to admire it, then turned and went to Charlie to give him the warmest, most heartfelt kiss on the lips that he had had from her since an evening many years before.

Charlie's kit lay in the hall. It was an almost pathetically small pile, little more than most guests would bring for a single night's stay. There were a valise, a haversack and a small suitcase. His sword lay on top of them.

Starr and Major Smith-Barton stood side by side, looking down at the things, which Fred circled slowly, sniffing thoroughly.

'Travel lighter than in my campaigning days,' the Major said. 'Used to take trunks of stuff.'

'Though I say it myself, Major,' Starr said grimly, 'better him than me. Makes our wars look like backyard scraps, this one.'

The Major nodded. Starr went on, 'They say the Hun's using poison gas at Wipers. Can't really believe that, sir. Probably just another of them rumours . . .'

'True enough, from what I hear, I'm afraid. Absolutely devilish!'

'A year ago, who would have dreamed that one lot of human beings, if you can call 'em that, would try to kill another lot by choking 'em with poison gas? Fred, old son, we're well out of it, I can tell you that.'

Their ruminations were interrupted by Louisa's emergence from her parlour. She was wearing a fur-trimmed coat and a large, flowered hat. The Coldstream star sparkled radiantly on her breast. She was very pale.

'Let's have the others up here, Starr,' she ordered. 'Give his lordship a proper send off.'

Starr hurried down to the kitchen. The Major said to Louisa, 'Why don't you let me take you and Charlie in the hotel 'bus?'

'No need, thanks, Major. Going to drop him at the barracks, then I'll go on to the station to be there when they march up.'

The staff were hurrying up from below, the women smoothing their aprons and dresses and patting their hair. Merriman was the last, stooping and holding himself with a hand above one hip.

'Line up—quick,' Louisa commanded. 'Here 'e comes.'

Some other guests, among them a general and an admiral, stopped to watch this parade of honour for a mere ensign, at that moment coming down the stairs. He was wearing service dress and Sam Browne, but the jodhpurs and the beautiful boots had been replaced by more practical serge plus-fours and puttees.

The reception touched him visibly. He went along the line with a handshake and an individual word for every one. The women curtseyed. At the end of the parade Charlie stooped low to caress Fred's muzzle, grey with age now, and to whisper to him, unheard by the others, to guard Louisa well till he came back.

Then he put on his cap, took Louisa's arm, and hurried her out, with Starr and Merriman carrying his kit.

Mary Phillips sniffed away her tears.

'Come on,' she mumbled to the other women, all of whom were crying. 'Guests mustn't see us standing about here.' They trooped away to the kitchen; but it was several minutes before any of them was capable of carrying on working.

The only light in Louisa's parlour in the dark of that late afternoon was the glow from the fire, and its reflection in the brandy glasses she and Major Smith-Barton held. They sat on opposite sides of the grate. Louisa had taken off her hat, but not her coat; she felt chilled by more than the cold of being out of doors for several hours on a dank, cheerless afternoon.

'He was leading his detachment,' she told the Major. 'He looked marvellous, and so did his men—all about six-foot nine, I thought. You could hear the drums thumping first, and then the music, and the cheering got nearer and nearer, and then, there they was . . .'

She downed her brandy and hastily poured some more, handing the bottle across to the Major, who did the same.

'His colonel friend was there, and Rummy Tummy and some of the others he's brought round here. And there was some mothers and wives, and they was ever so nice to me—not a bit snooty. And then the men was all told to get in the train, and the soldiers' wives and girls were blubbing and holding hands and holding up kids, and that. But we didn't do so much of that, bein' officers' ladies.'

The Major smiled. 'Stiff upper lip. Traditional.'

'Yeh, well, mine wasn't so stiff as all that. On the way back here I made the cabby drop me at St. James's Church, and I went in and prayed he'll be all right. I don't expect God knew my voice—He 'asn't heard it all that much; and anyway, how can He keep an eye on all those millions of blokes? But what else can you do?'

'Bit of comfort,' the Major muttered.

'Yeh. Funny thing, I suddenly don't feel quite so bleedin' patriotic as I did. You know what I mean?'

'I do. Puts a very different complexion on things, now we've got a boy of our own at the Front. All very well watching the others go, but when it comes to sending one of our own . . . Bless me, I'm sounding as though we're all family . . . Though I do feel a bit as if I'm an uncle to old Charlie.'

Louisa was staring into the fire.

'I dunno what I am to him,' she said, almost to herself. 'But I know I won't have a day's peace till he comes back safe.'

Her voice trembled, and she turned her face further aside. The Major reached over and took her hand.

As they sat in silence, thinking similar yet differing thoughts, the sound of male voices singing reached them. It was nothing unusual in the Bentinck. Only the most insistent complaints from guests ever moved

Louisa to remonstrate with roistering young officers anywhere on the premises.

These were evidently out in the hall, the Major thought, as he noticed Louisa's head jerk up sharply. He heard, in wild chorus:

'Oh we don't want to lose you,
But we think you ought to go,
For your King and your Country . . .'

Louisa's eyes were flashing. She hurled herself out of her chair and across the room to the door. She yanked it open. The Major heard the singing end abruptly, as Louisa yelled to the startled singers, 'Stop singin' that bloody song! Sing anything you want, but I won't have that one—never again in my bleedin' hotel!'

# CHAPTER SIX

'Out you go, Fred, and do your duty. I'll leave the
door open a few minutes, but I don't want to see you
back until you've done it.'

His dog hesitated and looked up at him. Starr give it
a gentle push with the shining toecap of his boot and the
animal waddled slowly and reluctantly into the yard.

Fred was an old fellow now. He had come to the
Bentinck when Starr had literally engaged himself as
porter there in 1902. He had been only just out of puppy-
hood then, but it was more than fourteen years ago,
which made his age the equivalent of a human being
quite some way past his century.

His years had been idle and comfortable, spent for
the most part in his basket beside the green leather hooded
porter's chair in the hall. But Starr had never spoilt
him with titbits and had allowed others to give him only
the occasional one. There had been regular exercise in
St James's Park, with many a long Sunday run on
Hampstead Heath. Fred had kept his health and his
figure and was still sprightly.

He had developed a growing aversion to one thing,
though—the cold. The warm interior of the hotel for
him, any day, even on days when a mild sun shone.
And this morning there was not even that; just cold,
smelly mist. It swirled in through the door from the yard
to the kitchen and Mrs Cochrane called from the table
where she was preparing a dish of kidneys, 'Ooh, Mr
Starr, you're letting all that nasty fog in. Shut the door,
for heaven's sake!'

He broke his promise to Fred and obeyed.

'Give him a few minutes' privacy,' he said. 'Mind, you don't want to complain about fog, Mrs C. Better than bombs.'

He was referring to the increase in the air war against Britain. It had begun within a few weeks of the outbreak of war when the first Zeppelins had nosed their way over coastal resorts where only weeks before the beaches had been crowded during that long Bank Holiday. The first bombs had fallen on Great Yarmouth, and the first on London soon afterward. Curiosity amongst those who craned their necks to the sky, from which came the menacing growling of the engines, turned to fear, and people learned to make for cover as soon as they heard the football rattles, wielded by bicycling policemen, which warned of a raid.

At first there were no defences against the monster airships. These evolved gradually: guns capable of extra-high elevation, powerful searchlights, finally fighter aircraft and a new breed of gallant young men able to fly them by night with no more instruments or aids than they normally had by day. Several of the so-called 'Zepps' were shot down near London in 1916, and the staff of the Bentinck had thrilled with the rest of their nation at graphic photographs of the mighty, burnt-out skeletons, felled in cornfields and draped on trees.

But they came still, always by night. It was rumoured that their inventor, Count von Zeppelin, had made a personal vow to destroy Buckingham Palace, or die. The Kaiser's intention of leaving the palace unscathed at all costs, so that he could move into it as soon as Britain was overcome, had drowned in the mud of the Western Front, in which millions of his men and their enemies had lived, suffered and died, during more than two wretched years which had gained neither side any advantage, but had wiped out the flower of their youth.

'Well,' Mrs Cochrane retorted to Starr, 'Zepps or no Zepps, I'll thank you to keep that door shut, please.

You'll have all the breakfasts getting cold, and then there'll be hell to pay from *her*.'

'Yes, there will,' Louisa's deep-chested voice boomed from the stairs. 'And who's "*her*", I'd like to know? The cat's mother?'

'Sorry, madam. We're in a real rush this morning.'

'Why? What're you doing serving breakfasts?' she demanded seeing Mary picking up a laden tray. The little Welsh maid, now in her late thirties and seemingly a spinster for life, was wearing a black crêpe mourning band on one of her sleeves. She was pale, and her old placidity was missing.

She almost snapped back, 'Because Merriman was kept up half the night with that young officer's supper-party, and he isn't down yet. It's all very well them sitting up drinking till all hours, but it puts on those of us who've work to do.'

Louisa stared. Mary indicated her tray with a nod of her head. 'And I don't see why that old general shouldn't wait for his kidneys till Merriman is ready. He's lucky to get them at all, living here at his ease and sending boys off to die in the trenches.'

She clattered away up the stairs from the kitchen. Mrs Cochrane said quickly, as she worked, 'Mary's not herself, madam. Losing one of her brothers at the Front . . .'

'Come off it, Mrs C! She said she hadn't seen him since they was four. There's enough grief and misery in this war without carrying on over someone you hardly know.'

There was a scratching at the back door. Louisa glared in that direction and Starr hurried to admit Fred, opening the door the minimum amount and quickly closing it again. He gathered Fred up.

'That was quick,' he said suspiciously. 'Out and back, in scarcely time to shake your tail. Never mind—it is a bit nippy.'

'For Gawd's sake take that perishin' dog out of my

kitchen!' Louisa said. 'It's hard enough struggling to keep up our standards without dogs running underfoot.'

Starr beat a hasty retreat with Fred. Mrs Cochrane said, 'He looks after that dog better than a lot of folk care for their kids. Ah, there you are, Mr Merriman. Just in time to take Lord Pratt his herrings.'

'Yes,' Louisa told him, fixing him with a menacing eye, 'and I'll want a word with you in my parlour, soon as breakfast's done.'

She went back upstairs, in the wake of Starr, whom she found in the hall taking letters from a postwoman. Louisa quickened her step. He smiled and held out an envelope marked 'Forces Mail' and written in a hand familiar to them all.

'Thanks,' she said. 'I'll have the rest later.'

Louisa bustled into her parlour and closed the door. Reading Charlie's letters was an occasion for privacy from all others.

He was by now a captain. He had been back several times on brief leaves, which he had clearly needed. On the last occasion he had scarcely stirred from his bed. Exhaustion and privation had thinned his cheeks, and dreadful sights had burnt themselves into his eyes. He would not tell Louisa or the Major exactly in which battles he had taken part. The Major had a shrewd idea about them, but he was saying nothing to Louisa, either. The casualty lists from them all had been dreadful.

She had wondered how long he could go on. She wanted to suggest that, in view of his age and two years' almost unbroken service at the Western Front, he should ask for something quieter now. But she knew he wouldn't listen to her if she did. He had spoken more than once of the great value of really seasoned leaders, when so many raw soldiers were constantly being sent to replace the dead, the missing and the wounded. He wore his confidence like a charm, in the way that Louisa constantly wore her Coldstream star. And each two or three days' respite seemed to restore him remarkably. Louisa could only leave him to do as he felt best.

'Is his lordship all right, madam?' Starr asked, when she went out to him at last.

'He was when he wrote this. "We expect to return to the first-line trenches tomorrow".'

'Did he get the hamper safely?'

'Yeh, ta. He says the wine and game pies went down a treat.'

Louisa saw the newspaper in her porter's hand. 'Anyone . . . today?' she asked. He knew what she meant.

'Captain Tanqueray.'

'Wounded or missing?'

'Killed.' He shook his head. 'Makes you think.'

'Yeh. It makes me think that they'll go on getting a good time whenever they come here. I don't care about all these shortages. One thing we *can* do for 'em is to give 'em food and drink and clean sheets for as long as we're able.'

She took the rest of the mail and went back to her room, leaving the door open. Presently she heard someone come clattering through the front door, and Starr asking brusquely, 'Here! Whose things are those, mate?'

'Officer and a lady,' a Cockney voice answered. Then another, younger voice, Canadian, said, 'Good morning. My . . . wife and I would like a room, and a private sitting-room.'

Starr replied, 'I'm very sorry, sir. We're full right up.'

Louisa heard a girl's 'Oh!' of disappointment, then the Canadian asking, 'Look, we don't know anyone in London. If you could recommend . . .'

'Well, sir, I'm afraid all the hotels are booked up these days. It isn't easy to find accommodation in London now, and what with being short-staffed everywhere . . .'

'Oh, Ian, what are we going to do?' asked the girl. Her English voice was light and very young.

Louisa, who had just been scanning a letter, got up and went out, just as the Canadian was saying resignedly, 'Don't worry, Fay. I guess the cab-driver will help us find somewhere. It was just that we'd heard so much about this place.'

He had addressed this last to Starr, who turned to see Louisa approaching. The Canadian proved to be a young officer, gaunt-featured and thin and quite probably a good few years younger than he looked. The girl beside him was a pretty blonde, expensively dressed. asking brusquely, 'Here! Whose things are those, mate?' She could not have been a day over eighteen Louisa thought. She also thought that she had seen her before. When Starr had introduced them she said bluntly to the girl, 'I know you, don't I?'

The pretty eyes widened. 'Oh, no! I'm sure you don't.'

'Mm! I don't often forget a face.' She turned to the officer, who was regarding her nervously. She could feel tension radiating from him.

'On leave from France, are you, Captain McLean?'

'Yes. We just had to travel up to Scotland for a day or two, but we planned to spend the rest of the week in London.'

Louisa's glance had taken in their baggage. It was expensive, hers as well as his. She smiled suddenly, wanting to dispel the anxiety from his look. She waved the letter she was holding at Starr.

'Just in the nick of time. Commander Davies has had to cancel. Number Seven.'

'You'll like it,' she told the young couple, waving aside their effusive thanks. 'Lovely sitting-room and bed. Just what you was asking for.'

So it proved. And they got more than they had asked for: while they were unpacking, Mary came in with an ice bucket and a bottle of champagne, 'with Mrs Trotter's compliments'.

Merriman should have taken up the wine by rights, but he was being interviewed in the parlour. There had been menace in Louisa's eye when she had told him in the kitchen that she would see him later. Now he stood before her in the knowledge that something had occurred to make her extra angry. Although it had not concerned him, he would no doubt be made the scapegoat.

Just after the newly arrived couple had gone upstairs, with Starr carrying their luggage, Louisa had seen a spreading trickle from Fred's basket. The old animal, unwilling to risk a further sortie into the cold, had tried to ease himself secretly, and had failed. He looked up pitifully as Louisa loomed over him furiously. Barely managing to control her language in the hearing of the young strangers, she called up to Starr to get back immediately he had finished and put his dog into the yard.

And now, Merriman knew, the tongue-lashing he would have to endure would be all the more stinging.

'That bloody dog!' she breathed. 'As for you, Merriman, I do not expect staff to come downstairs later than guests, understand? I don't care if you are decrepit, or you was kept up late. It's no excuse.'

He sniffed. 'There is a great deal of extra work, madam. Especially with the Major away just now. I have to . . .'

'Listen—I'm paying you good wages. A damn sight more than you got before the war, or what you'd get anywhere else. If you're not up to the job any longer— and to my mind you haven't been for donkey's years— then just let me know, and you can clear off.'

He knew as well as she did that she couldn't hope to replace him if he took her up on this. He was very, very old, but he had been in the job for decades. So long as his legs and arms would work he could carry out his duties automatically. And he had nowhere else to go if he left the Bentinck. He had always known it would be his last home.

'I'm very sorry, madam,' he said. 'I'll make sure Mr Starr gives me a knock in future.'

'Yes. I'd be glad if he'd start putting the hotel's concerns before that bleedin' dog's . . .'

At that moment the world seemed to disintegrate.

Louisa had been so preoccupied with her grievances, and Merriman was so deaf, that neither had registered an approaching roaring noise, as if a taxicab were being driven across the hall towards the closed parlour door. What they heard now was a rising shriek, like the whistle of an express train tearing non-stop through a station.

Moving with remarkable speed, Merriman lurched round the desk, crying, 'Get down, madam!' He grabbed the astonished Louisa by the shoulders and forced her head down below the level of the desk top, and bent his own back to put his head down as he stayed between her and the window.

It all took only a split second to happen. It was followed at once by a tremendous explosion, a flash, and more whistling noises, though the explosions which followed them were less close. There were other sounds in the immediate aftermath: the crash and tinkle of falling glass, a woman's scream repeated several times, men's shouts, and running feet.

Louisa straightened herself up. Her desk top was covered with splinters of glass. The letters which had been on it were strewn all over the room. Her old waiter, whose waxen face was whiter than ever, was examining a rip in the sleeve of his coat and the shirt underneath. A little blood was seeping through.

'Bloody 'ell!' Louisa exclaimed. She jumped from her chair and whipped from his other arm the white napkin which was as a much part of his costume as his tail-coat. She forced it round the cut and tied it un-gently.

'Come on,' she ordered. 'Mary's got her first-aid things.'

She propelled him, tottering, to the kitchen, past anxious guests whose words she ignored, though she heard the word 'bomb' several times, and someone said it had been aeroplanes, not Zepps. Mrs Cochrane was just about to mount the stairs as Louisa guided Merriman down. Ethel was sobbing noisily in the background.

'Oh, Mrs Trotter!' Mrs Cochrane cried. 'The kitchen

door's blown in, and Ethel's having hysterics.'

'Never mind her,' Louisa ordered Mary, who was trying to calm the maid. 'Merriman's got cut by glass. Come and bandage him proper.'

'What about my cellars?' the old man moaned, staring round. There was no time for anyone to answer. There came a rush of heavy feet down the stairs, and Starr appeared. He took one look at the shattered kitchen door, lying inward on the floor, with a pile of rubble behind it in the yard.

'Oh, my God!' he cried, rushing to the doorway. 'Fred! Fred?'

He stood in the yard, surrounded by fragments of masonry from which dust rose slowly and looked round wildly for his dog. There was no sign of Fred.

Dazed and fearful, Starr went to where lay a whole heap of rubble which had been an outhouse. He bent to start throwing the pieces aside when a voice hailed him from over the area wall.

'Here! Mind what you're doing! Don't touch that!'

Starr looked up, to see one of the local special constables. He was a lugubrious, bespectacled little man, a bank clerk in St James's, and he was widely disliked for his evident enjoyment in catching black-out offenders.

'Don't touch that rubble, whatever you do,' he warned again.

'Why not? My dog might be under it.'

'Because I'm ordering you not to.'

'Here, what's all this?' Louisa demanded, coming out to see wuat was going on.

Starr appealed to her, 'Madam, it's Fred. I'd put him out here as you ordered. I've got to clear this lot to find him . . .'

'And I'm ordering him not to,' interrupted the special.

'Oh, are you? Well, he's my porter, and this is my yard. So just you hop it!'

'Madam, I must ask you . . . In my opinion, there is an unexploded bomb under there.'

They both stared at him. He had the advantage.

'It was a raid by German aeroplanes. I happened to see the bombs dropping . . .'

Louisa tried, 'Thanks very much for warning us, then,' but he was able to reply smoothly, 'There was no time. Now, I am in charge of this incident, madam, and I must ask you and your porter to evacuate the yard.'

'Unexploded bomb!' Starr exclaimed, eyeing the rubble with less than conviction. 'I don't believe it.'

'There was one in Fulham only last week. I heard these coming down, and there were more of them than there were explosions.'

'It could be anywhere!'

'And it could be there. I'm taking no chances. I shall report to the proper army authorities. Meanwhile, madam, if you are the proprietress, I would recommend that you evacuate this hotel.'

'Oh, yeh? And where do you "recommend" everyone should go?'

'Some other hotel. Or there's a rest centre some volunteer ladies have set up behind Harrods.'

Louisa laughed harshly. 'Just the place for a dowager duchess, a couple of generals, a honeymoon couple, and half a dozen officers on leave from France. How long d'you reckon they should all stay there, then?'

'You and your staff, too, madam. Until the army send some trained personnel to locate the bomb and make it harmless.'

'Well, the army can do what it likes, but I'm not going anywhere. As for the staff and guests, it's up to them.'

Louisa said this with unmistakeable finality. Having written something in a notebook and promised threateningly to report her attitude, the special constable went hurriedly. Starr moved towards the rubble again, but Louisa said, 'Better not touch that.'

'But, madam, that special's just a bank cashier.'

'I daresay he don't know no more about bombs than I do, Starr. All the same, we mustn't put other lives at risk. If it is a bomb, and it goes off, it could bring the whole bloody hotel down, and kill everyone in it.'

She went in to galvanise the others into clearing up the debris, and then to go upstairs to tell her guests the situation and ask if anyone proposed leaving. Most of them replied by asking her the same question, and when she said it would take more than one probable bloody unexploded bomb to shift her from the Bentinck, all said that, in that case, they were staying, too.

Starr lingered in the yard, unable to take his eyes from the pile of broken bricks and shattered tiles and wood. He went carefully as close to it as he could, and bent down, cocking his ear to it.

'Fred!' he called gently. 'Fred, old son!'

But all he could hear was the murmur of a gathering crowd in the roadway, and men shouting orders to them to stay clear. Starr reached out a hand, wondering if by moving just one or two pieces he might be able to see down into the pile, or hear Fred crying. He withdrew the hand without touching anything. He didn't care about himself, but there were too many other lives he might endanger.

After listening for a while longer, he turned and went into the kitchen, and tried to obliterate his fears by joining in the general cleaning-up.

# CHAPTER SEVEN

'Of course we want to stay,' Captain McLean's young wife answered when Louisa reached the couple's room with her enquiry. 'Don't we, Ian?'

He turned from the window where he had been standing looking down into the busy street. Louisa could see that a twitch at the corner of one of his eyes was working fast.

'I . . . don't know,' he said hesitantly. 'I mean, if anything happened to you, darling . . .'

'Oh, Ian, how can you? It's so nice, and we were going to enjoy ourselves so much.'

'Yes, but an unexploded bomb, honey . . .'

Suddenly, and unexpectedly imperious, his wife turned to Louisa and said, 'We're staying!'

'Got you!' Louisa exclaimed. 'That's more the manner I knew. You're Bushy's girl!'

'No! I mean . . .'

'Sir Rodney Bush. He brought you here to tea, two or three years ago. You and your brother. Proper little horrors, you was. Bossing poor old Merriman about, till I had to speak to your dad.'

Fay was thoroughly alarmed now. 'You won't tell him—will you?'

'I dunno what there is to tell him yet. You livin' in sin?'

'No!' A white arm was thrust out sharply, the fingers of the hand stiffly extended. A wedding ring and an engagement ring gleamed on the third. 'We're on our honeymoon.'

'I thought so when I met you in the hall. Always look at their rings in this business. They put on a wedding ring carefully enough, some of 'em, but it's the engagement one they forget. Not that I care a toot,' Louisa added, sitting down, 'only when it's daughters of friends, and they look as if they're young enough to be at school . . .'

'I'm eighteen, Mrs Trotter.' A smile appeared on the pretty face. 'And I assure you I'm not spoiled any more. Neither is Tommy, my brother. He's in a battleship.'

'Der Gawd! And the last time I saw him you was both arguing ding-dong who should have the last of my special éclairs. Anyway, why are you afraid of your dad knowing, if you're married?'

'Because he doesn't know. You see, soon after the war began I was sent to Scotland to stay with an aunt, as soon as the first Zeppelin came over London.'

'Yes,' her husband intervened. 'So you'd be safe. That's why I say . . .'

His wife overrode him again. 'Ian's grandfather went to Canada from Scotland, so when Ian was posted to England he came up to his grandfather's old village to look for the family. We met in the church. He was searching through parish registers, and I helped him, and . . .'

'So you fell in love. And then what? You didn't ask papa, eh?'

Fay shook her head. 'Ian wanted to, but I knew he'd never consent. I know how against . . . wartime marriages he is. Anyway, he had two or three possibles earmarked for me.'

'That sounds like old Bushy, all right.'

'So as soon as Ian came back on leave from France this week I went to Gretna Green and he met me there. Now, you see how it would spoil everything if he found out we're here? We've only this week together before Ian goes back. We were starting to pretend this lovely little suite was our own home—just for this week. And now, the bomb makes it perfect.'

This remark surprised Louisa. She glanced again at

the Canadian. She had not noticed him smile during Fay's telling of their romantic adventure. He was still not smiling.

'Don't you see?' his wife was going on. 'Now we can share the danger together.' She turned to him. 'And when you go back to the trenches, I shall know exactly what it's like.'

Louisa noticed what his wife did not appear to do: that when she said "trenches", he shuddered.

She got up. 'All right, love. If he does put two and two together and guess you might be here, I'll make a point of not receiving his letter till you've gone. I'm glad you're staying. Oh, by the way, we shan't be able to serve lunch today. Too much glass and dust all over the kitchen.'

For the first time Captain McLeod showed some animation. He roused himself, as if determined to make an effort, and said brightly to his wife, 'In that case, I'll take you to the Ritz.'

Louisa wrinkled her nose. '*That* place! Well, at any rate I'll be able to make up to you for it at dinner.'

In the kitchen the staff worked hard to clear the mess. But the cloud of dust had settled everywhere, filming every surface and exposed utensil. There was nothing for it but to wash the lot. Starr found that the back door was not so badly damaged that it would not be re-hung temporarily. While he was doing it he went out again and again to put his ear to the pile of rubble. He could hear nothing.

'Perhaps he's run off,' Mary suggested. 'The gate's broken. He could easily have been frightened and run off.'

Starr answered doubtfully, 'He'd have come back by now. This is his home. Has been for most of his life. Still, I reckon I'll take a few minutes off to wander round the streets near here, if nobody minds.'

They wished him well and he went, to return a quarter of an hour later looking even gloomier.

'Not a sign. He wouldn't have gone far, even if he went at all. I reckon he's under that pile out there.'

A sudden knock at the door made the jumpy Ethel scream and drop a handful of spoons.

'For heaven's sake, pull yourself together,' Mrs Cochrane scolded. 'See who it is.'

The girl went apprehensively to the door, expecting the bomb to go off as soon as she opened it. It didn't. She found two soldiers standing there. One was a middle-aged sergeant with a drinker's face, two rows of medal ribbons on his chest, and a vast paunch. The other was young and decent-looking. He wore shapeless khaki overalls without insignia. He smiled politely at Ethel.

'Afternoon,' said the sergeant. 'Just come to have a look at your spot of bother.'

Mary came forward. 'Come to shift the bomb, have you? That will be a relief.'

But he shook his head. 'Not quite as simple as that, I'm afraid. I have made my examination of the reported location of the bomb, but it is not visible to the naked eye. Therefore, I cannot ascertain what kind of explosive device it is. Now, if it was visible I could assess the situation and take appropriate action. As it is, I shall be obliged to notify the experts and request them to have a look at it before taking any action.'

Mary, slightly bewildered by his jargon, asked, 'But . . . how long will that take? Mr Starr—our porter—his little dog was out in the yard when the raid happened, and he thinks he might be buried alive under that stuff.'

The younger man frowned unhappily and turned his head to look at the rubble. The sergeant said, 'Very unfortunate, I agree. 'Course, if it was a human being, I might have to take the risk myself. But for a dumb animal . . . Where there's other humans' lives to consider if anything went wrong, then I cannot rely solely on my own judgement. Not that I wouldn't mind putting myself in danger, even for an animal . . .'

'You must be very brave to do your job,' Mrs Cochrane

said from behind Mary and Ethel. 'Come inside, and I'll make you both a nice cup of tea.'

The sergeant puffed out his chest and strode in. The younger man followed him diffidently. He gave Ethel another little smile. She smiled back.

'I suppose you have to volunteer for this kind of work?' Mary asked the sergeant.

'*Some* do.' Then he looked at his subordinate. 'Some don't.'

'Still, I wish you could set Mr Starr's mind at rest, one way or the other. He's so attached to that little dog.'

'Well, I'll tell you what I'll do. I'll expedite matters as far as possible. You know, though, it's amazing how long a dog can last buried alive. One of our officers up at the Front had a terrier that was in a trench that had a direct hit from a shell. Know how long it was before we dug that poor little brute out? Three weeks. Three *weeks*, and not a scratch. Meanwhile, I'll take full responsibility for that bomb while I'm here.'

He turned to the younger man. 'Get out there, and board up that back gate. And take care to do it quietly. Vibrations might set the bomb off.'

'Yes, sergeant.'

Ethel pointed out, 'He hasn't had his tea yet.' But the young man had got up obediently and was making for the door.

'It's all right,' he said.

'At least take a bit of cake with you, then.'

But the sergeant intervened. 'I'm not having him eating on duty, if you don't mind. Go on. Get on with it!'

The man went out. Mrs Cochrane said, 'You're a bit hard on the poor boy, Sergeant. What's he done?'

'Him? It's not what he's done. It's what he hasn't. He's a Conchie.'

'One of them . . . those conscientious objectors?' Mrs Cochrane said, 'But he's in uniform.'

'Of a sort.' The sergeant tapped his own Royal Engineers shoulder badges proudly. 'Not like this, though.

111

They put him in the non-combatant corps—stretcher-bearing, bomb-clearance, etcetera. That's how I come to have the pleasure of his company.'

'And he looking such a nice boy!' Mary exclaimed. 'I think they're a disgrace.'

'I agree with you, miss. They give 'em classes, you know—the peace movement people. Tell 'em what to say for themselves. Set up mock tribunals to teach them how to swing the lead.'

Merriman came in with a basketful of broken bottles. The women jointly relayed the information to him. He merely sniffed.

'They should be sent to prison, the cowardly lot of them!' Mary exclaimed. 'When I think of poor Davie lying out there . . . My brother, you know,' she explained to the sergeant, who was now drinking tea and cramming cake into his mouth. 'If Mrs Trotter knew what that chap is, she wouldn't have him on the premises.'

'No more she would,' Mrs Cochrane agreed. 'There's no one in this hotel, sergeant, that isn't heart and soul in the War Effort.'

'Very glad to hear it, missus,' he said, when he had swallowed down the contents of his mouth. 'By the way, Mrs Trotter being the proprietress, I believe . . .'

'Proprietor,' Mrs Cochrane corrected him. 'She doesn't care for the other.'

'Well, whatever she is, I'd better go and explain the situation to her before I report back to headquarters.'

When he had swigged down the rest of the tea, had another cup and another piece of cake, and wiped his mouth with the back of his hand, he followed Mary up the stairs.

'What're you huffing about, Mr Merriman?' asked Mrs Cochrane, when they had gone.

'If you ask me, that sergeant knows a cushy billet when he finds one. Tea and cake! You won't find him moving on before he has to.'

'You shouldn't say such things! Didn't you notice

all those medals he was wearing?'

'Yes, I did. And I know what they are. Showed he went through all those campaigns knowing enough to keep himself out of harm's way.' He picked up his basket of shattered glass again. 'Just look at these. Some beautiful wines gone. Ruination!' He went away, shaking his head.

Two days later the bomb experts had still not arrived. The sergeant meanwhile took his ease in the kitchen by day, and the non-combatant, Clive Baker, kept watch in the yard all night. There was no invitation to sit by the fire for him. The women only spoke to him if they had to. Merriman was no conversationalist anyway; and Starr, who did have the occasional few words with the boy, was preoccupied with worry about Fred, who had still not come home.

The Sunday night was bitterly cold. Mary had gone to chapel. Mrs Cochrane was having her day out. Ethel, recovered from her shock, sat alone beside the kitchen range fire, reading a cheap romance magazine. There was a knock at the back door and Clive Baker came hesitantly in, carrying a billy can and his pack.

'D'you mind if I boil up a kettle?' he asked. 'It's freezing out there.' His accent was provincial, though not heavily so.

'Suit yourself.'

'Thanks.'

As usual, a kettle was on the stove, near to boiling point. He advanced it on to the grid. While it was coming to the boil he got a packet of tea and a tin of condensed milk out of his pack.

'You can use that teapot,' Ethel said magnanimously, glancing up from the magazine.

'Thanks. Would you like a cup?'

'No, thanks.'

She went on reading. After some moments he asked, 'Where's Mrs Cochrane and Mary?'

'Out.'

'Oh. I see.'

Ethel would have left it at that, but an appropriate barb sprang to her lips.

'Mary's gone to chapel to pray, because she's lost one brother at the Front and she's afraid for her other. And Mrs Cochrane's gone to a Spiritualist friend, because she's got a nephew missing—like a few other people.'

'Ethel . . .' he ventured.

She bridled. 'Miss Pettifer, if you don't mind.'

'Sorry. But don't you think it's right that I'm doing what I think is right?'

'Ho! You're right, and all the rest of us is wrong. Is that it?'

'Not everyone. There was this Mr Bertrand Russell I heard speak. And Clifford Allen—he's chairman of the No Conscription Fellowship. They went to prison for what they believe. Hard labour. They must have thought they were right, too.'

Clive had made her a cup of tea, after all. She took it hesitantly, unused to abstract argument and suspicious that he might be trying to get round her.

'Why didn't you go to prison, then?'

'I agreed to serve as a non-combatant. I offered to. It was never that I wanted to get out of the war, only . . .'

'What sort of things do they ask you at those tribunals?' Ethel had put her magazine down when she had taken her cup and was now giving him her full attention. He was a nice-looking chap, she thought. Clean and respectable in his manners, unlike that sergeant, whom she found uncouth.

Clive said, 'They asked me if I went to church. I said yes—well, chapel, that is. So they said, well, the bishops said we ought to fight, so what about that?'

'What did you say?'

'I said, I can't help what the bishops say. I have to follow my own conscience.'

'All I can say is there must be something wrong with

your conscience, then. The Germans are our enemies, aren't they? They started all this.'

'When you say the Germans, you take in the whole lot of them—millions. Haven't you ever thought how many of them there must have been who were against the war from the start? And millions of them who'd give anything to stop it now? If you ask me, there's more of them would be willing to make peace tomorrow than go on fighting.'

'Not if they was winning, they wouldn't. Just because it's all stalemate . . .'

'Stalemate. Exactly! Both sides just fighting for the sake of it. Neither can win, and both are losing every day. All those men being killed and maimed for nothing. If people here who think like I do, and Germans who think the same, could only get together . . .'

Ethel surprised him by exclaiming exasperatedly, 'Oh, why do you have to be different? It's complicated enough without that. Why can't you just be like all the others, and . . . and . . .'

'And go out there and kill Germans?'

'All right, yes! If you want to know, I reckon it's because you're a coward.'

He put down his mug swiftly and to her alarm picked up a big kitchen knife. She was about to scream as he came towards her, but he had reversed it in his hand and was offering her its handle.

'Take it,' he said calmly.

'What?'

'Take it. Stick it in me. Stab me. Go on!'

'You're mad!'

'No. You think I ought to go killing people you think are wrong. Well, you say I'm wrong, too. Then, you kill me.'

Ethel had not taken the knife. She kept her hands down and shrank back in her chair.

'I couldn't.'

To her great relief he put the knife back. 'Neither could

I,' he said. 'Now you know how I feel. If they put a rifle and bayonet in my hands and told me to stab a German in the stomach, I'd stab myself first.'

He seemed to sag. He sipped his tea, and said lamely, 'The worst of it is I often think to myself that being a pacifist is just an excuse. Some chaps haven't any doubt how they feel. Maybe they're the ones who'll do hard labour for it. Maybe I really am a coward.'

Ethel was surprised to hear herself protest, 'You're not! I know you're not.'

They had not heard Louisa enter the kitchen.

'What's all this?' she demanded, coming down the stairs, staring with hostility at the young man. The sergeant had made a point of telling her what he was. 'I thought you was supposed to be out guarding that bomb?'

'Yes, madam.'

He gathered up his things hastily and went. Louisa turned to Ethel.

'I'm ashamed of you, hob-nobbing with a Conchie. Drinking tea in my kitchen, indeed!'

'He thinks what he's doing is right, ma'am. He says there's others think the same. There's a Mr Russell and another gentleman in prison doing hard labour . . .'

She was interrupted by Louisa's sharp laugh. 'Bertie Russell doin' hard labour? Not likely! He asked for special treatment, and he got it. He's sitting in there as comfy as you please, having his own food brought in and writing his books. I reckon that young man of yours . . . Here—he hasn't been up to anything, has he?'

'No! He's got lovely manners. And he really believes in what he says.'

'I dare say he does. Sitting here in a cushy billet while better men than him are getting killed. Well, I shan't need you any more tonight. You'd better clear off to bed.'

'Yes, madam.'

The third day of the bomb dawned. Starr began it

116

like all the others by looking in the yard, then doing a quick tour of the neighbouring streets. Again he stopped any local policemen, specials and doormen he knew and asked the same question. Again they shook their heads. No one had seen Fred.

Starr went unhappily back to the Bentinck and joined Mary and Mrs Cochrane in the dispense for a pre-breakfast cup of tea. Mary was unhurriedly opening the crumpled envelope of what proved to be a letter in untidy writing on lined paper. She only glanced at it, then returned to the subject she and the cook had been discussing.

'I was saying to Mrs Cochrane, Mr Starr, that I'm not sure it is a good thing, this Spiritualism.'

'Some of them are no better than crooks,' he agreed. 'Taking money under false pretences.'

'My friend isn't like that,' Mrs Cochrane said. 'She never makes a charge. It's just that she has this gift, and with so many people grieving . . . Anyway, I don't say I'm too sure about it, either.'

Mary returned to the letter, frowning over the bad handwriting of one of her aunts in Wales. She was only half listening, as was Starr, wrapped in his own thoughts, as Mrs Cochrane rambled on, '. . . Though I can quite see it must be a comfort to get a last message from a loved one. Just a little something to make up for reading that awful telegram . . .'

'My auntie's writing gets worse and worse,' Mary grumbled. 'I can hardly read what she's scribbled on the back here. "I am . . . afraid I have some . . . bad . . . news which has only just come. Your . . ." Oh! No! No!'

Mary burst into wild sobs. Starr and Mrs Cochrane sprang to their feet. Mrs Cochrane put her arm round the girl's heaving shoulders. Starr's eyes were on the letter clenched in her hand. Louisa hurried in.

'What's all the row for? What's up with her now?'

'It's a letter from Wales, madam,' Starr told her. 'Some bad news.'

Louisa jerked her head. 'Go on, hop it, you two. I'll see to her.'

They hastened out. She pulled a chair next to Mary's and sat on it. The Welsh girl was her oldest friend, but it was little more than a harmonious working relationship.

Between sobs Mary managed to tell her that her other brother, Gareth, had just been reported killed.

'First Davie, now Gareth!' she cried. 'It's not fair!'

Louisa tried some clumsy comforting.

'I'm ever so sorry, Mary. But, let's face it, you didn't really ever see much of either of 'em, did you? I mean, it's a blessing you weren't really close.'

'No it's not! That's the worst of it. When I heard Davie was dead I thought "I never really knew him, and I won't let this happen with Gareth. When he comes home on leave I'll spend some time with him. He's my brother, and I ought to get to know him". And now he's dead, and I'll never see him again.'

'No, it don't seem right,' Louisa added awkwardly, 'But I suppose, if you look at it that way, they're sort of together now.'

Mary cried harder again. Not knowing what else to say, Louisa tried the only kind of comfort she ever lavished upon herself.

'Come on, love, it's no good upsetting yourself like this. I know it's very hard, but life has to go on.'

The bitterness of Mary's retort took her aback.

'Is that what you'd say if Lord Haslemere was killed?'

They looked at one another, equally shocked. Then Mary said, 'Oh, I shouldn't have said that. I'm sorry.'

'That's all right, love. I can tell you, every time I see a telegram envelope I feel afraid.'

She got up and went to a cupboard. 'Now, I'm going to give you a glass of brandy, *which* you're going to drink, and then I'm packing you off to Wales for a few days.'

'Oh no! How could you manage?'

'Leave that to me. You can see the family, have a good cry, and get it all out of your system. Anyway, you're tired out. You've been doing everybody else's work as well as your own.' She had a sudden inspiration. 'Besides, I know just where to go to get a bit of temporary help while you're away. Now, drink this up, and no arguing.'

Mary was sent off that same day. In the evening, Louisa stood at the foot of the stairs to the hall, watching the prettiest, best-bred maid the Bentinck had ever seen coming down with a small tray of coffee things.

'There you are,' smiled Fay McLeod happily. 'That's all the hot-water bottles in the beds. And I took Mrs Peterborough her camomile tea. She hadn't her glasses on, so she tipped me.'

She handed the tray to Louisa and dipped in the pocket of the apron she was wearing over her flowered dress. She took out a coin and put it on the tray. 'There. You'd better have it for the staff.'

'All right, thanks. It is good of you to help, dear.'

'Oh, it's the least we could do, when you fitted us in so kindly. Anyway, we're enjoying it.'

'Well, I must say your hubby's not a bad assistant waiter.' She led the way into the dispense. Ian McLeod sat there with a bottle and glass. 'You see?' Louisa went on. 'Half buffy. It's a common fault among waiters.'

'I'm not buffy,' the Canadian captain objected. 'I've had a few drinks, that's all.'

'Well, shove the bottle over. We'll all have a glass.'

Louisa could tell that he was a little tipsy. But the twitch was not there. He and his little wife had fallen in eagerly with the idea that they might help her with just a few duties, with the rest of the staff fully extended. She noticed that he had drunk most of the bottle, though. She opened another. He drank eagerly.

'Funny,' he said.

'What's funny, darling?'

'Funny to think this time next week I'll be in France. You have to laugh—huh?'

Fay looked at Louisa, who gave her a knowing look

119

back.

'That's right,' Louisa said. 'The worse things are, the more you got to laugh. You'd never get through 'em otherwise.'

He seemed not to notice that she had spoken. He went on, 'There you are, in the forward trench, stooping along, trying to keep your head below the parapet, because you're scared to death of getting it shot off . . . That's funny, huh? Scared to death of death.'

Louisa saw that Fay was about to reach out her hand to stop him rambling, and restrained her unobtrusively.

He said, '. . . And there's this soldier leaning against the parapet, and you knock into him . . . and he falls over. But the fellow behind is shoving you along, so you tread on the soldier, only your foot goes right through him, and there's this awful smell . . .'

'Oh no!' Fay cried, heedless of Louisa. But he ignored her, took another copious drink, and went on: 'D'you know, we looked out one morning, and there was a fellow caught in the barbed wire. I suppose he'd been out on a raid during the night. Only, the trouble was, he wasn't dead. And the more he tried to free himself, the more he got tangled up in it. You know what we did? We laughed. Poor devil, we laughed at him. So, you wonder whether you'll get caught up next time, and whether the other fellows will try to rescue you, or just laugh . . .'

He finished his drink, looked at the empty glass, then remembered his wife and Louisa. They were staring at him with horrified eyes. He said in a now very slurred voice, 'Sorry. Not supposed to mention things like this at home. Shouldn't talk about them in front of Fay.'

He reached for the bottle, but Louisa pulled it away from his hand. She got up, holding it.

'Don't worry about her,' she said with a forced smile. 'She's old Bushy's girl. Tougher than she looks. Now, go on. Off to bed with you. I'm not having my staff getting blind drunk in the dispense.'

Ian laughed as he got up unsteadily. 'Mrs Trotter,

you're a trump!' He wove his way out of the door, holding on to one of its posts as he passed through. Louisa held Fay back by the arm.

'Take this,' she said low, giving her the bottle of brandy from which she had given Mary a tot that morning. 'Don't give him too much, and have a bit of a swig yourself. Just . . . hold him in your arms. Can't you see? He's frightened to death of going back.'

She watched Fay catch up with Ian and take his arm to help him upstairs. Then she went to her parlour, shut herself in, and took down the latest of several photographs of Charlie. She looked at it for a long time.

At the back gate, Starr, watched sympathetically by Clive, who sat huddled in his cape and a groundsheet, stood at the gate and called, 'Fred? Fred, boy?' But there was no answering sound.

# CHAPTER EIGHT

Starr slept badly again that night. By the next morning he felt ready to crack. There was that fat sergeant, seated proprietorially at the end of the kitchen table, eating a breakfast of bacon, egg, toast and tea, with a copy of *John Bull* propped up in front of him. There was his Conchie offsider, standing near the dumb waiter, drinking tea and never taking his eyes off Ethel, who seemed never to take hers off him, either. But where was poor little Fred all this time? The usual morning round of the doormen and policemen elicited no information. Was he under that rubble, dead or alive? Starr felt by now that it would not matter either way, if only he could *know*.

'How are you getting on, then, Sergeant?' he asked pointedly.

The soldier raised his eyes from the paper and asked vaguely, 'Eh?'

Starr jerked his head in the direction of the back door. 'Out there. How are you getting on?'

'Oh. Ah, well, unfortunately there's been a big demand for the bomb experts. Not many of 'em, you know, and what with the Zepps, and now these Gotha bombers . . . Very unexpected, they was. Got everyone on the hop, I can tell you.'

'So when do you expect somebody to come? It is the centre of London, after all.'

'True, true. But from what I understand, our brave boys at the Front have to come first . . .'

The sergeant let his sentence tail away and returned to his reading and eating. Starr had a sudden suspicion, an

123

echo from his own soldiering days, that the man was swinging the lead. He knew there was no bomb; had probably been told so by now, but knew when he was comfortable and intended to make it last as long as possible. Starr thought suddenly of calling his bluff; of going out there and tearing that rubble apart himself, to search for the truth. The only thing that had stopped him so far— he was not afraid for his own sake—was consideration for the other people on the premises, should he set off an explosion, and for Fred, who, if he were under there, might yet be dug out alive, but would certainly be killed with the rest of them if a bomb went off.

He was startled by a clattering sound from the yard, and a cry from Ethel, rushing past him.

'Clive!'

Even the sergeant had been galvanised into action. He had leaped from his chair to the door and was shouting, 'What you doing out there?'

The bewildered Starr noticed now that the young Conchie was absent from the kitchen. There were sounds from the yard of bricks and wood being thrown about. He hurried to see.

'I'm looking to see if there *is* a bomb,' Starr heard the boy reply.

The sergeant yelled, 'No, leave it alone! I order you to leave that alone.'

'I'm not taking your orders,' came the determined reply. 'I'm not a soldier. You've told me that often enough.'

The sergeant almost ran back into the kitchen. Without hesitation he dived under the solid table and stayed there, crying as he went, 'The damned fool will have us all killed!'

'Ethel,' Mrs Cochrane ordered, 'fasten that door. We don't want no explosions in here.'

But Ethel stood there, watching Clive working on the rubble. Mrs Cochrane gave Starr a sharp push.

'Get upstairs, can't you, and tell Mrs Trotter. She

ought to warn the guests to take cover, in case . . .'

He obeyed. His instinct had been to go and help the boy in the yard, but there was this other duty to be done. He hurried off to tell Louisa. Instead of rushing around her rooms, though, she stormed at once down to the kitchen, demanding to know what was going on in her hotel without her consent.

She and Starr were faced by a dusty, grim-faced Clive. He was just coming in through the back door, clapping his hands together and banging dust out of his clothing.

He said dully, 'It's all right. There's no bomb. Just a lot of bricks knocked down in the blast from the others.'

To Louisa's surprise, the sergeant crawled out from under the table, saying, 'Might be one underneath that mess, all the same.'

'There isn't,' his assistant told him. 'I've been right down to the cobblestones.'

'Oh, that's a relief!' Mrs Cochrane cried, but the young man didn't look at her. His eyes were on Starr.

'I'm sorry, Mr Starr. I'm afraid your . . . little dog . . . It wouldn't have made any difference if we'd found him at once. He must have died instantly. I . . . put a piece of tarpaulin over him. P'raps you'd like me to . . .'

Starr shook his head and said heavily, 'No thanks. I'll see to it. Me and Fred, we've always looked out for each other.'

He went slowly out, watched silently by the women. The sergeant spoiled the moment by shouting at Clive, 'You might have got us all killed! I'll have you court-martialled for this.'

Ethel gasped, 'Oh, Sergeant, you won't really, will you?'

'No.' It was Louisa's iciest tone. 'I don't reckon he will. After all, we'd all have to give evidence, wouldn't we?' She looked hard at the sergeant. 'I'd be prepared to give any of my staff time off for that. In fact, it'd be a real pleasure.'

He began to mumble fast about being willing to

reconsider the matter; regarding Baker's action as due to excess of zeal . . .

Starr heard none of it. He was standing outside the back door, looking down into the strewn yard, his eyes concentrated on a very small tarpaulin bundle amongst the broken bricks and the dust.

A few days later Ethel came out into that same yard, now cleared, swept clean and washed down. She opened a dustbin and stuffed into it a brown paper bag of feathers from a goose she had just finished plucking. A few of the small white plumes escaped and drifted up out of the area. One of them was deftly caught by a young man, in the act of opening the gate and coming down the steps.

'This for me?' Clive Baker asked with a grin.

Ethel coloured up and said, 'No, it isn't! I've just been plucking a goose.'

He looked at the feather in his fingers and then stuffed it into one of his uniform pockets and buttoned it safely away.

'All the same, I'll keep it as a souvenir. Nobody else's given me one.'

'Oh, Clive . . . I didn't mean . . . Anyway, what're you doing here?'

'I came to see you.'

'Me?' Ethel's cheeks flushed even deeper.

'I just wanted to tell you I've volunteered for France.'

'You never!'

'Oh, only for digging out mines and shells, or stretcher-bearing. I can't kill anyone, Ethel. I can't really.'

'I'm glad you can't,' she said. Another white feather floated down and she made a successful grab for it, saying, 'I'll keep one to remind me of you, then.'

He came closer, bringing something from his pocket.

'Will you keep this with it?' he asked, holding out a little box. She saw a small jewelled ring.

'It belonged to my Gran,' he explained hastily. 'She brought me up. It came to me when she died, and . . .'

'But . . .'—she was floundering—'it's . . . an engagement ring . . . I mean, it'd mean we're engaged . . .'

'Yes, it might—mightn't it?'

'You're not pulling my leg?'

He came close to her and said, 'No, Ethel. I'm not pulling your leg. Only . . . there is something you ought to know.'

She had known from the first instant that there was some trick to it.

'What?' she asked.

'That if I should get . . . ill, or anything . . . in France, I don't get a pension. On account of being a conscientious objector. Refusing active service.'

Ethel felt a great relief. 'Oh, Clive!' she cried. 'You and your blooming conscience!'

She hurried into his arms, not pausing to think that they had never so much as kissed or even held one another before. Hundreds of thousands of other young men and women had become united in this precipitate way in those years, and for many the first kisses had been the last.


Upstairs, in the hall, Louisa was bidding farewell to Ian and Fay McLean. Mrs Peterborough, a censorious lady who invariably found fault with the Bentinck's arrangements but would not dream of staying anywhere else, interrupted them.

'It isn't good enough, Mrs Trotter. The service here is not what it was.'

'Oh. Sorry about that, Mrs P. I haven't had anyone else complaining.'

'The way staff come and go . . . There was such a nice little chambermaid served me the other morning, and I haven't seen her since.'

Wearing a new fur stole and a stylish hat, Fay McLean went unrecognised, but she and Ian had difficulty in suppressing laughter. Louisa said, straightfaced, 'Oh, she was only temporary. Wouldn't stay 'cos the tips wasn't good enough.'

The old lady mumbled something and went off upstairs. The three laughed together. Mary, who had returned the day before, approached with Merriman, carrying a hamper between them.

'Here you are, Ian,' Louisa said. 'This is for you. Don't let anyone drop it. There's a couple of bottles in it.'

'Say, thanks, Louisa. I've had the most wonderful leave a guy could ask for.'

'Glad to hear it. You're looking well on it.'

'Sure thing. But we must be getting a move on. If I could just have our bill, please?'

'There ain't no bill. There's no charge.'

'Oh, Louisa . . .!' Fay protested.

'I can't start charging my staff for staying here. I really ought to pay you some wages.'

They all laughed again, and both kissed Louisa on the cheek.

'Thank you,' Fay said. 'And . . . if there's a baby, I hope you'll be godmother.'

'Not quite suited for that,' Louisa said, shaking her head, as if to shake the topic away. 'Where you going when you've seen Ian off?'

'Back home to Scotland. I have to face the music some time.'

'Well, give my regards to your pa. Oh, and if he asks why I didn't answer his telegram, say it only arrived this morning.'

'You mean he . . .?'

'Four days ago. They do get delayed sometimes, though.'

They parted company. As Louisa was making for her parlour, Mary reminded her, 'Time for the ceremony, madam.'

'Eh? Oh, that. I 'spect so.'

Starr, Mrs Cochrane and Ethel appeared from the kitchen region. The others went with them to the wall nearest Starr's chair. A small Union Jack hung there,

with a cord attached. At a nod from Starr, Louisa stepped
forward and pulled the cord. The Jack was drawn aside,
revealing a little plaque of the type put up in streets
where people had been killed in the air raids. The
inscription read:

**In memory of Fred, killed by enemy action, 1917,
R.I.P.**

**He died for his country.**

Starr stepped forward and on to a hook which had been
attached to the lower right-hand corner of the plaque
he hung Fred's collar, with its own little Union Jack.
Starr stood back and saluted. A little sob escaped Ethel,
and Mrs Cochrane wiped her eyes with the back of a hand.

There was an awkward silence. Then Louisa said, 'Yeh.
Well, that's it, then,' and they dispersed. Mrs Cochrane
took Ethel's arm to detain her, though, and said to
Louisa, 'Could I have a word with you, madam—with
Ethel?'

Wondering what new staff crisis had arisen, Louisa
motioned towards her parlour and they all went in.
'Well?' she demanded, noting that Ethel was almost
guiltily avoiding her gaze. 'What's it all about?'

'Go on,' Mrs Cochrane ordered the girl, who gave
Louisa a furtive glance and said, 'Please, madam, I want
to give in my notice.'

'You what? You can't leave me now, when maids are
so hard to get.'

Mrs Cochrane nodded fierce agreement. She said,
'She's decided to go into munitions.'

'What? You must be mad, Ethel. What on earth do
you want to do a thing like that for? And after all the
trouble I took making sure everyone in this hotel would
be exempted. We're doing important work here, looking
after officers on leave, and generals and admirals having
meetings they don't want all Whitehall to know about.
Why should you want to leave all of a sudden?'

It was Mrs Cochrane who answered again.

'She's got herself engaged.'

'Who to? Oh, no, don't tell me!'

'That young Private Baker.'

Louisa looked as if she might shake Ethel. She told her scornfully, 'You wanting to go off and work in munitions, and getting engaged to a Conchie!'

Ethel showed animation at last. 'He's not a Conchie. He's a Conscientious Objector. And he's volunteered for the Front, so I want to help get the war finished quick, before anything can happen to him.'

The point went home. Louisa had often wondered to herself how much longer the slaughter was going to go on; how the law of averages was becoming an increasing threat to Charlie's survival.

'Yeh,' she conceded. 'I still think you're more useful here, but if you've made up your mind . . .'

'I have, madam. The minute he spoke to me.'

'All right, then. Let me know when you want to go, and I'll get your wages made up. I . . . might even give you a bob or two extra as an engagement present.'

Ethel smiled her gratitude. 'Thank you, madam.'

'But, as you're still here, you've got work to do. Go on with you!'

The girl scurried happily away, Mrs Cochrane following more sedately. Left alone, Louisa picked up Charlie's photograph and gazed at it with new apprehension.

'That was a nice thing to do,' Mary said, coming in.

'Eh? Oh, well, if she's leaving, she's leaving.'

'I meant the plaque,' Mary said. 'I know Mr Starr appreciated it very much. Poor little Fred!'

Louisa put the framed photograph carefully back in its place.

'Yeh, well . . . If there's one good thing that bomb did, it was getting rid of that bloody dog. Never could stand him meself.'

She jerked her head up suddenly as they both heard an unmistakable sound from the hall. The two women looked at one another in astonishment, then went to the door of Louisa's room to stand and look out.

Starr was placing a puppy in Fred's basket. It was obvious to them, from its black, brown and white markings, that it was destined to grow into the very image of Fred.

Starr reached up and took the collar from its hook on the plaque. He bent to show it to the puppy, as it sat and quivered in its unaccustomed surroundings.

'Now, Fred,' they heard him say, 'this collar's too big for you now, and you haven't earned the right to wear it yet. But I hope in time you'll grow into it and prove yourself worthy.'

He hung the collar back in its place. Louisa turned away from her door, back into the parlour, with a heartfelt groan.

'Oh, Gaw' blimey!'

# CHAPTER NINE

Major Smith-Barton returned, bringing with him the news that he had been appointed a King's Messenger.

'A what?' Louisa asked.

'King's Messenger. Rather an honour, actually. Besides, it'll help keep me young.'

'What do you have to do?'

'Sort of glorified postman. Buzzing back and forth between the War Office here and Haig's headquarters at St Omer. Important despatches, you know. All the secret stuff. Have to have it chained to my wrist in case I fall asleep or get buffy, or something. And I get a compartment to myself however I travel.'

Louisa grumbled a bit about everyone deserting her, when things were difficult enough already. And things were difficult, in 1917. Domestic servants were at a premium, as women, revelling in their release from this form of slavery, worked at men's jobs in factories and offices. The German U-boat blockade had caused a growing shortage of coal, bread, sugar, potatoes, and other staple items. Butter and margarine were things of the past on most tables, though not at the Bentinck; men in high places or with personal influence whom Louisa had befriended over the years showed their gratitude by finding her things denied to others. She was quite unscrupulous about pulling her many strings. The rationing scheme introduced by Lloyd George's Ministry of Food was only voluntary, and she chose to ignore it. Her guests—and particularly those who were serving officers on leave—came first with Louisa Trotter. The fields of

France had been liberally sown with millions of wooden crosses; and for every one there were several dead without graves. The thunder of massed guns on both sides of the lines could be heard even in London, more than a hundred miles away.

The one loss Louisa had heard of without regret was that of her own husband. A letter from his sister had given the news that he had died suddenly of a liver complaint—'And we know what *that* would be,' Louisa remarked to the Major—leaving no property. There had been no address on the notepaper, and Louisa had made no effort to locate Nora, for any reason whatever.

The Major went off on his first mission. He returned a few days later, his uniform rumpled with travel and lines of tiredness about his eyes. But his air was brisk with the satisfaction of doing something useful for his country again.

'Letter from old Charlie for you,' he told Louisa, giving her it. 'Saw him for a minute or two at H.Q. He's near Ypres.'

Louisa was scanning the brief note eagerly. She laughed out loud. 'He says he'd like to line up all politicians, profiteers, pacifists, newspapermen and the four or five thousand red-tabbed half-witted staff officers at Fourth Corps's headquarters and chuck them in the River Wiser.'

'Yser.'

'Who cares? Crikey, the censor must have turned a blind eye when he read this.'

The Major winked. 'No censor. I brought it in the diplomatic bag.'

'He sounds fed up to the teeth.'

'I'm afraid they all are now.'

Louisa put the letter down beside her scrapbook, on which she had been working.

'Three bloody years, and not a thing to show for it. More than half our friends gone, Major. The old 'uns, as well as the young. This country's a place for women and

134

children only, now. And on top of it all, I've got to close this place.'

Major Smith-Barton was shocked. 'You mean . . . shut up shop?'

'Yeh.' Louisa indicated the temporary repairs to the windows and a wooden prop between the floor and the ceiling. 'On account of this. A nosey little devil from the Council came poking about the other day. Said as it was a "public place"—the Bentinck a "public place", I ask you!—it wasn't safe, on account of what the bomb did. The builders will have to come in, and it'll be seven or eight weeks' work. Everyone's to get out meanwhile.'

The Major frowned. He had been told that he would not be required to undertake another mission for at least a fortnight; the pool of former officers available for the responsible work was large, and many were younger than he. It meant that he, too, would have to look for somewhere else to stay temporarily.

'I know,' Louisa replied when he told her. 'Me, too, and the rest of the staff. I wish you could smuggle me across in your diplomatic bag to see Charlie.'

They both laughed, but the Major said, looking at her thoughtfully, 'I might just be able to wangle you a pass . . . If we could say that you were going over to do some important war work.'

'Such as what? Go up the dugouts and cook for 'em? And I'm sure General Haig's got himself a nice French chef.'

The Major took a chair and said seriously, 'I stayed in Boulogne yesterday before catching the mail boat. It's full of stores' dumps and hospitals and transit camps— all pretty well organised, I gather. But there's one thing that struck me. You see the men coming on leave from the Front in trains and buses and carts, and Lord knows what else, and they're just dropped at the quay, waiting for the next boat. They have to wait all night sometimes, and there's no canteen . . .'

'You mean they don't get nothing? No tea? No food?'

'Nothing at all, except what they're carrying. It's a sort of gap in the organisation. Now, if someone like you were to go over there and start something up . . .'

Louisa was striding to the door. She jerked it open and bawled, 'Starr! Stop messing about with that blooming puppy and get me Mary and Mrs Cochrane up here. In double-quick time.'

She came back to the Major. He could see the gleam in her eyes. He had made his suggestion only tentatively, as an unlikely possibility, but she had seized upon it with typical impulsiveness.

'Would there be any premises handy, though?' she asked.

'Actually, there is a sort of old waiting-room buffet place with a bit of a kitchen behind. It's in pretty bad order, but bang on the quay. They shelter in it when it rains. I looked into it while I was waiting—but I must confess I never dreamed that you . . .'

'You reckon you could wangle it for me to take it over?'

'I have, ah, one or two highly influential friends in the Quartermaster-General's department. I won't tell you their names, because I promised not to—but I can tell you that some of the supplies you've been able to get in recent months have been due to them. They've fond memories of you and this place. I'm sure they'd work it for you.'

'Then I'm on.'

Mary, Mrs Cochrane and Starr had entered. Louisa ignored Starr and went to stand in front of the two women, who were wondering just how they had managed to displease her this time.

'You're both going to volunteer for service abroad,' she told them straight out. 'It's your chance to do something for the war.'

'Not me,' Mrs Cochrane answered. 'I'm not going abroad.'

'Yes you are. You and Mary and me are going to hop across to Boulong for a little holiday and open a canteen.

It's either that, or sit on our backsides somewhere while this place is done up.'

'Can I go, madam?' Starr asked, but she shook her head.

'No. You've saddled yourself with that new dog, and the poor little blighter'll need looking after. Besides, someone's got to caretake here, with workmen all over the place. You and old Merrilegs can keep an eye on 'em together and make sure they don't drink all the wine and nick half the contents.' She turned to the women again. 'Now, I don't want no arguin'. You're volunteering, and that's that. We'll fill the 'bus up with stuff, and the Major will fix us passes and drive.'

She turned to see him goggling at her. 'It was all your idea,' she reminded him. 'I'm only obeyin' orders. Now, pass me the Army and Navy catalogue, Mary, and let's start making lists.'

It was one thing, thought Mary, to hear the guns from London, like the low growl of distant thunder; it was very much another, though, to hear them from the quay at Boulogne. It was dusk when their boat docked there, and the sky seemed charged with constant lightning, in keeping with that unremitting roar. She was frightened by it, and by the awesome feeling of being in a foreign country, an experience she had never had before.

Not that Boulogne appeared all that foreign, where the quay was concerned. The dockers who unloaded the Bentinck 'bus as it came down in its rope sling gabbled in French and smoked a pungent sort of tobacco. There were a few French soldiers, and a couple of men whose uniform, which she had seen depicted in magazines, told her they were gendarmes. But almost everyone else was British, or at least British-speaking. English Tommies, Scots, Welshmen, Irishmen, Canadians, Australians, New Zealanders, even little Indians, swarmed everywhere. They were distinguished from one another in only one major way: those who were clean and neat, and silent and glum, were the ones who had come on the same boat as the Bentinck contingent, and would be going on immediately to the Front. Those who were dirty, red-eyed, strained-looking, clad in a strange assortment of garments which in some instances included spiked German helmets, were joking and singing: they were going on Blightly leave.

When the 'bus had been unroped, the Major tried to start it. Nothing happened.

'Damp, I'm afraid,' he apologised to Louisa.

'How far we got to go?'

'Oh, only just over there.' He pointed to a small, derelict-looking railway building.

'Come on,' Louisa ordered Mary and Mrs Cochrane, who were standing looking apprehensively on. 'We'll all shove.'

She put her shoulder to the vehicle as an example. But there was no need. Some of the tired, cheerful men from the Front saw their difficulty and came and pushed the 'bus for them. One of them gave Mary a kiss on the cheek, which made her blush, his mates cheer, and Louisa grin. The soldiers went off, waving, to await their orders to board the ship.

Major Smith-Barton led the way into the building. What they saw did nothing to raise Mary's spirits, or Mrs Cochrane's. It had obviously once been a waiting-room and bar-buffet combined, but had been disused for years, perhaps since the outbreak of war. Marble-topped tables were thick with dust. Chairs were strewn everywhere, some of them lying on their backs. The big counter bore at one end a boiler of antique design, and had behind it a cracked, fly-blown mirror. An iron stove stood in the centre of the floor, surrounded by debris. A good deal of the plaster had fallen from the ceiling, but at least there seemed to be no holes right through the roof. There were empty cigarette packets galore, match-boxes, tobacco tins, ration tins—every kind of litter.

Louisa spotted a swing door beside the counter and pushed her way through it into what had been the kitchen.

It was as derelict as the rest of the place, but her quick eye took in the excellent capacity of the big stoves, boilers and sink. She turned a stiff tap. Brown water spluttered out and after a few moments became a steady, clear stream.

'Lovely,' she declared. 'Just what we was looking for, wasn't it, Mrs C.? Right, then—let's get cracking, else the war'll be over. Major . . .?'

'Yes, my dear?'

'Just go out and fetch a few of them nice lads to help us unload the 'bus and help tidy up a bit. Give 'em something to do while they're hanging about.'

In no time at all, it seemed, the place had been cleaned up and put straight. There had been no lack of willing help from the troops: many who had offered it had had to be turned away, with thanks. Louisa, helped by a Royal Engineer, had got the boiler going safely. Two tea urns she had brought with her were on the counter and filled. Cakes and sandwiches had been laid out. It was late night by now, and Mary and Mrs Cochrane felt ready to drop, but Louisa insisted on serving all the men who had helped, and then sending them to tell their mates on the quay that the place was open for business.

A long queue quickly formed. The hut, which had been almost a ruin a few hours before, resounded to happy chatter, the clink of cups and saucers, and the hiss of the urns. Mary was in charge of them, while the Major, with a white apron over his uniform, presided over the food. The men looked curiously at his badges of rank; but such was the informal atmosphere that they accepted him in the role in which Louisa had cast him, as a mere counter hand. A box with a slit in the top constituted the only system of charging. It bore the request, 'Pay what you can. Minimum, 1d.'

Not surprisingly, the stock they had brought from England was sold out within two hours. Reluctantly, Louisa asked the last of the queueing men to leave, and put a *Closed* notice outside the door, which she locked.

'Cleaned out!' she exclaimed. 'Blimey, talk about the ravening hordes . . . Here—who're you?'

She was addressing a very young soldier, who was drying crockery for Mary and Mrs Cochrane, who were side by side at one of the big sinks.

'He offered to help, madam,' Mary explained.

'Can I, ma'am?' the man asked anxiously. His accent was lowland Scots. A thick jam sandwich lay close to him, from which he had evidently been taking large bites. He was thin and pale.

Louisa had tipped out the contents of the contributions box on to a table top. He nodded towards it. 'I'd just started as a ledger clerk in the bank before I joined up. I'll count it for you, if you like.'

'All right,' said Louisa. 'Nice to have an expert.'

The man prepared to finish drying the present pile. He said, 'I was a volunteer. I'm not a conscript.'

Louisa looked at him curiously. He had seemed unusually anxious to tell her that. He struck her as edgy, defensive.

'You're not going on leave, then?' she asked.

'No, ma'am. I'm an orderly up at the transit camp.'

'Too young to fight, eh?'

'I've done a bit of that.'

'Oh. Wounded, or something?'

'Only a scratch—but it went a bit bad. I've a pretty nice cushy job here, so I can come down and help a bit each day, if you want.'

He dried his hands, picked up the sandwich and devoured it with an eagerness which surprised Louisa. If he had a cushy job she'd have thought he would be well fed. She nodded thanks for his offer, then turned to the Major, who was beginning to stack crockery.

'I'll do that Major. You get out there and on to that boat before it goes. Oh, don't goggle at me like that. You know you can wangle anything you want. Somebody's got to go for more supplies, and I'm not letting Mary or Mrs C. loose amongst all them men. I'll write you a list.'

Give it to Starr or Merriman, and they'll get the stuff brought round to the Bentinck.'

'But Louisa, think of the cost. I'm sure the Quarter-master's department will arrange to supply you.'

'Yeh, after a few weeks of red tape and form-filling. Look, while I'm running this place personally, I'm paying —right? They can arrange it how they like when I've gone back—only I bet the grub won't be half as good. Now, fifty dozen potted meat. One hundredweight best flour. Ten bags porridge oats . . .'

'But they'll never load the 'bus aboard tonight,' the Major protested feebly.

'Never mind the bloomin' 'bus. It isn't working, any-way. Pull a few more strings with your friends. You'll need a couple of lorries at least.'

She returned to her list-making. The Major glanced at Mary and Mrs Cochrane. Despite their tiredness they were smiling their admiration of their formidable mistress. Major Smith-Barton smiled back, took off his apron, and went off into the night with the list.

The Scots soldier—Jock, he told them he was known as—finished the counting, which he had done with dexterity, and reported, 'Seventeen pounds eightpence three farthings, some foreign coins, four buttons and one cap badge.'

'Bless their little hearts!' Louisa exclaimed. 'If the guests at my hotel paid up like that I'd be a millionaire by now.'

'What'll we spend it on?' Mrs Cochrane asked.

'Giving them more scoff, of course. Something cooked —fried eggs, sausages, porridge . . .'

Mrs Cochrane let out a sigh of exhaustion. Louisa packed her off to the side room which they had com-mandeered for communal sleeping-quarters, with camp beds and a canvas field wash-stand. Jock filled up the big stove with coke. Then Louisa told him, 'Come on, now. High time you was back at your camp, or you'll be on a charge. Mary, off to bed.'

Jock seemed to hesitate. Then he said goodnight and went. Louisa locked the door behind him, watching him through the glass as he wandered slowly away, as if going nowhere. Then she turned away and forgot him. She had just discovered how tired she was.

A signboard with LOUISA'S painted on it adorned the building now. The canteen had been in operation for more than a week and was already a talked-about institution wherever men who had passed through Boulogne met. Despite Louisa's insistence that she was going to pay her own way, supplies had mysteriously kept arriving which had certainly not come directly from London. She asked no questions, and was glad of them; the volume of business was far too great to have been sustained entirely by her own importations.

A coffee urn had joined the tea ones. Mary was serving from it one morning, with Jock beside her dispensing the food. Louisa and Mrs Cochrane were cooking and baking in the kitchen behind.

'Cup of coffee, please, miss.' It was just another voice making the same old request, but something about its clipped correctness made Mary glance up. She saw a tall officer, in a British Warm coat, with a muffler half-obscuring his face. Her immediate instinct was to say, 'I'm sorry, sir. We don't serve officers.' Then she stared and said, 'Lord Haslemere!'

'Hello, Mary. You're looking well. Thriving on hard work, eh?'

'Thank you, sir. Yes.'

'Where is She?'

'In the back, m'lord.'

He nodded and went to the swing door. He passed through it quietly, finding both women with their backs to him. Mrs Cochrane was pushing a vast consignment of sausage rolls into an oven. Louisa was frying a great many eggs in a huge pan. Without turning she said, 'They aren't ready yet. Don't come fussing me.'

Attempting an imitation of Mary's Welsh, Charlie said, 'I'm ever so sorry, Mrs Trotter.' He stepped forward swiftly and kissed her neck.

She jerked her head round, staring.

'Here!' she accused. 'You didn't half give me a turn. Mrs C., just finish these eggs off for me, will you?' Mrs Cochrane beamed and took over, giving a little bob in Charlie's direction as she moved to do so. He smiled back at her.

'Well, fancy you!' Louisa exclaimed. Her original wish to come to France had been in the hope of seeing him, but the furious activity into which she had plunged herself had driven the thought from her mind.

'I work over here,' he reminded her. 'Didn't you know?'

'So do we, don't we, Mrs C.? Fifty-dozen eggs I've fried this morning. Over four thousand sausage rolls, Mrs C.'s turned out this week so far, not to mention sandwiches, porridge, chips by the hundredweight, and enough tea and coffee to float the Home Fleet.'

'Mad as ever, but magnificent, Louisa. You're the talk of France. I couldn't wait to get a chance to come and collect a fresh detachment from the holding battalion.'

'When they come, they'll come in here. The whole army does.'

'Yes, well, it won't be till tomorrow, so I'm putting up at the Hôtel Louvre. I was hoping you'd come and have dinner with me there.'

Mary had come through the swing door and had heard this. She heard Louisa answer, 'Sorry, Charlie. I can't get away from this place. We go on half the night when the poor blighters miss the leave boat and get stranded here.'

Mary said boldly, 'Go on, now. We can manage for one evening. Some of the Salvation Army people are coming in, anyway.'

It had been arranged already that when Louisa's time came to return to England, the Salvation Army would take over the canteen. A few of them were already helping, to learn the ropes.

'Anyway,' Charlie said, 'I've already ordered the taxi to come and pick you up. Seven, sharp—and that's an order.'

'Bloomin' cheek! But I ain't got nothing to wear—and I smell like a frying-shop.'

Mary smiled. 'It won't be the first time I've been your lady's maid,' she reminded Louisa. Lord Haslemere smiled his thanks to her, and left them to concentrate for the time being on dishing up for the waiting queue outside.

Late that afternoon, when the Salvation Army lasses had taken up their duties, Mary bullied Louisa into letting her wash her hair for her at the canvas basin. She heated towels on the stove and managed to do a creditable job on those still richly auburn locks, which she twisted and pinned up into a coil on top of Louisa's head. Louisa had managed to get a thorough body-wash, and had found a clean blouse and skirt, devoid of the smell of cookery. Mary held a hand-mirror for her, and she was pleased with what she saw in it. Mrs Cochrane came in to say that the taxi was waiting, and stayed to admire her.

'Remember the last time you did this, Mary?' Louisa asked.

'I said you looked like a duchess. Well, you still do, madam.'

'More like a housemaid on her night off,' Louisa muttered; but she was feeling elated and excited. She pinned her jewelled Coldstream star on to her dress.

One other luxury she had brought with her was her fur coat. It had proved of practical value already, for sleeping in when the nights were extra cold. She put it on now over her clothes. The overall effect was splendid: she might have been dressed for an evening out in the West End.

'Have a nice evening, madam,' Mrs Cochrane said.

Louisa thanked her and went. Mary emptied the

water from the field-basin into a pail. They heard a cheer
and some admiring whistles from the troops outside as
Louisa sallied forth. Mrs Cochrane asked, 'When was
that, Mary?'

'What?'

'The last time you told her she looked like a duchess?'

But Mary wasn't answering. She remembered it
vividly, although it had been something like sixteen
years ago, and that time, too, they had been about to
dine alone.

# CHAPTER TEN

'Merci,' Charlie said. The old, lame waiter, who had poured coffee and brandy for them, bowed and limped slowly out of the bed-sitting room in the Hotel Louvre. A rich aroma hung in the air.

'Nice dinner,' Louisa said. 'But then, the Frogs know a thing or two about it. One thing I'll tell you, I don't think I'll ever be able to look a fried egg in the eye again.'

Charlie handed her her glass. She stood up and surprised him by saying, 'Turn out the lamp a minute, love.' She saw his look. 'Nothing shocking . . .'

He obeyed. She went to the blacked-out window and raised the blind. The view was at once terrible and magnificent. The rooftops and chimneys of Boulogne were silhouetted against a background of orange flame in the far distance, as the war burned on like some inextinguishable fire. The glow alternately intensified and died. Lightning-like flashes tinged it with blue and white; and the rumble of the guns never ceased.

'Where's all that going on?' Louisa asked Charlie, close at her side.

'I should think it's Bethune way. Our gunners were starting a bit of a show before I left, and the Boche are countering.'

'How's far's that?'

'Forty miles. Forty-five, maybe.'

'Looks like a forest fire. Gives me the shivers.'

'It seems somehow worse from here than it is up there. A fire's right, though—and nobody seems to want to put it out. "We're here, because we're here, because we're here . . .".'

Louisa pulled the blind down. Charlie re-lit the lamp with his pocket lighter. She sat down again.

'Is that how you really feel about the war these days?'

'We all do. There's no point in it any more. Just a huge, idiotic waste of life.'

'No more the knight in shining armour, eh?'

'Oh, he went west, together with his white horse, in a great big black cloud of high explosive somewhere near Ginchy last September. The day we lost fifteen hundred officers and four hundred men, just to gain one insignificant little hamlet on a slope. I'm known as Grandpa now—the Old Survivor.'

'Then I reckon you've earned yourself a nice safe billet back home.'

'Perhaps. But I couldn't leave—not while I'm all in one piece. And I haven't cracked up yet. I hate it, but I couldn't walk away from it. The battalion's the only real thing to me any more. Even during dinner I thought several times what might be happening up there . . . whether the rations got up all right . . . how Billy Knowles is doing . . .'

'Who's he?'

'A young officer. Just out. He's going on his first raid . . . just about now.'

'Is it all in aid of this Spring Offensive the papers keep going on about?'

'I suppose so. The papers always seem to know more than we do. No one tells us anything.'

'Perhaps it's only a rumour, then?' Louisa said it hopefully, but he disappointed her.

'Oh, no. There's always an offensive in the Spring. Like snowdrops, you know. Nothing like being shelled like hell and sprayed with machine-gun bullets to get the winter stiffness out of your bones. "Good for morale," says the General. Oddly enough, it is. We're all feeling chirpier already. Anything is better than sitting in the cold, shivering and getting sniped at, and cursing the news.'

'. . . And politicians, and profiteers, and pacifists . . .'

'And bishops. They're the latest hate. Especially the one who talked about death in battle as The Great Adventure.'

'Why don't you write to him and give him a bollocking?'

'He wouldn't understand. He couldn't'

'You write a good letter, Charlie. Always have.'

'But not about this sort of thing. I couldn't even talk to you like this in London. It's only because this place is . . . a sort of No Man's Land for both of us.' He paused, and then went on, 'I suppose I'm talking about it now because life has suddenly become rather . . . precarious. Every second seems so important. Damn it, I can't tell you how I regret what a stuffy, useless fellow I used to be.'

'You wasn't.'

'I was, really. Everything I did was for my own enjoyment.'

'I was just the same. I knew what I wanted out of life, and nothing and no one else mattered.'

'Unselfishness: that's what's taught me my lesson. It's pathetic, though, that it's taken a brutal, stupid war, and scores of my own men killed and terribly wounded, to show me what incredible endurance and courage there is in people . . . and unselfishness. It's their example that's kept me going when things have been really bad.'

He broke off again, and smiled weakly.

'Sorry—jawing on like this. More brandy?'

Louisa shook her head, surprisingly. It was not like her to refuse another drink.

'Coffee, then?'

Another shake of the head.

'You're tired, I expect. You work so hard at that canteen.' Charlie looked at his watch. 'The taxi will be here in a few minutes, anyway . . .'

But she was shaking her head yet again. There was something mysterious in her eyes.

'There won't be no taxi,' she said, almost challengingly.

'I told it not to come back.'

For long seconds there was silence between them. Charlie was staring at her, as the implications of what she had said sank in. She returned his look levelly. At last she said, 'I can't exactly read welcome on the mat.'

'No . . . I mean . . .'

'I won't stay if you don't want.'

'I do. I want you to stay very much . . . Only . . .' It lacked conviction. He stumbled on, 'I just thought that, long ago, we'd agreed . . . well, to be great friends. To . . . "frame our love," was how you put it then, so that we'd have it to treasure always and look back on.'

Louisa answered quietly, 'Yeh, well, you can always take things out of frames and dust 'em down. When I said that, it seemed the best thing at the time, considering the situation we was both in. And it worked for a time. What I didn't bargain for was that you'd turn out to be like a toothache—something that's always there. I can't get rid of the thought of you, Charlie, love, much as I've done my best. And now, like you said, when every second's precious, and we're here on Tom Tiddler's Ground . . .'

He came over to her and kissed her tenderly. Then he held her face and looked closely into her big blue eyes.

'We must have been completely mad,' he breathed. 'Wasting all these years . . .'

'No. We had to wait. You did the decent thing and offered to marry me, but it wouldn't have been right then. You'd got your position, and I'd got my hotel filling me mind. We're different now, since the war came. I . . . know better, now.'

'You'll . . . marry me?'

There was a pause in which Louisa searched his face. Then she answered, 'Yeh. After. When the guns stop. If you still want me to.'

'I've always . . .'

'But have you thought? *Really* thought?'

'What about?'

'All them toffee-nosed country ladies in Yorkshire

saying "Poor Charlie's bought it again. Got hooked by a common cook from London, who's been after him for years".'

'You're jumping fences too far ahead, darling.'

'They've got to be jumped sometime.'

'Anyway, we don't have to live at Bishopsleigh.'

'Oh yes, we do. That's your home. You've got your duty to it and your family and all the folks on the estate. You're responsible for 'em.'

Charlie's habitual lack of determination seemed to leave him suddenly. He took her by both hands and gently but firmly drew her to her feet. They stood and kissed at length, no longer hearing the incessant pounding of the guns. Then he stood back and led her by one hand to where his small bed lay in the shadows beyond the lamplight.

'Just tonight, at least,' he said softly, 'let's stop caring what other people might say or think. Let's just do what *we* want to do—both of us.'

At length the canteen was closed for that evening. There were supplies enough to have carried on, but Louisa had at last seen the necessity of keeping to set hours, in the interest of her helpers' strength. When a boat was due in the middle of the night or the early hours, she would arrange to open specially; otherwise, eleven o'clock was the limit.

There was still work to be done behind the locked doors, though. Mary and Mrs Cochrane were finishing the seemingly endless task of washing up. Jock was counting the takings at the table. Mary could see, reflected in the mirror above her head, his fingers flicking skilfully at coins of different denominations, sorting them into neat piles.

'Nice lot of boys tonight,' Mrs Cochrane was commenting. 'Especially them Aussies. But their language! Would have made Mrs Trotter sound like a vicar's wife . . .'

But Mary wasn't listening. Something had shaken her. In the mirror she had seen Jock glance up, then slide one of the piles of coins off the table and into his pocket. She didn't believe he had seen her watching.

'She's late,' Mrs Cochrane went on.

'Yes,' Mary said dazedly. 'You go to bed. I'll shut up.'

'I hope she won't be too late. Can't be all that safe out at this time.'

Mary took a deep breath.

'If you really want to know,' she said in a low voice, 'I don't think she'll be back tonight.'

Mrs Cochrane gaped for a moment, then said, 'I knew he was . . . special. But I didn't know . . .'

'She had that look in her eyes tonight I hadn't seen for all these years.'

'So that's it. Well, good luck to them both, is what I say. I'll go, then. Good night, love. Good night, Jock.'

Jock bade her his cheerful good night. When she had gone he said to Mary, 'Sixteen pounds four shillings and threepence.' He swept it all into the money-bag, which he brought to Mary, who took it in silence, to lock away in the drawer to which she kept the key. He asked, with a change in his voice, 'Any chance of a cup of cocoa?'

'Of course. Might as well make use of the kettle while it's still warm.'

The big blackened kettle was constantly on. Mary mixed cocoa for them both in mugs and poured the steaming water in. Jock took his, sipped it, then said, 'I may not be able to get in tomorrow . . .'

'Oh?'

'No. In fact, I may not be back for quite a while.'

'You been posted, then?'

'Yes. Yes, that's it. I'm . . . off wi' a draft in the morning.'

'We'll miss you, I'm sure.'

They wandered through into the buffet and sat at one of the tables. The air was heavy with the masculine odours of sweat and tobacco. There was a long silence. Mary noticed how unhappy the young Scotsman was looking, for a change. He had been so cheerful since that first day. At last he said, 'You saw me tak' that money, didn't you?'

She nodded.

'I thought so. Honest, Mary, I've never stolen a penny in my life before.' He reached into his pocket and put some coins on the table. 'Five bob. Here it is back.'

But she pushed it towards him again.

'No. Keep it. You must need it, or you wouldn't have taken it, I know. I just wish you'd asked for it, that's all.'

'You're a saint, Mary,' he said, almost emotionally. 'You're the kindest girl I ever met. Only . . . I couldnae ask.'

'Why ever not?'

He seemed to glance round the empty room before replying, 'I'm a deserter.'

'You . . . mean . . . you've run away?'

'There's plenty do,' he told her earnestly. 'Honest—it gets to be more than a man can take. You don't know. You cannae know what it's like.'

Mary had been shocked initially. Her two brothers lost in action; Ethel's Conchie; Lord Haslemere soldiering on, when he could surely have got out of it honourably enough by now. And now a deserter . . . But there was something basic and honest about this man, she'd always felt sure. Perhaps it was a fellow-feeling between two Celts. At any rate, she said, 'What happened, then? You can tell me, Jock.'

He gave a great heaving sigh, as if relieved to be able to speak at last.

'We were in one of the new divisions. Got pushed into the Somme battle last July. We were pathetic. Had tae go and hold a wood—that was the orders. We'd hardly set off towards it before they shelled us like hell. Our officer was killed and it was bloody chaos . . . raining and misty, too. We got into a trench on the edge of the wood, with dead Jerries and our own dead all over the place. Anyway, an officer comes along and says we're tae hold the line. There was only three of us, and a sergeant groaning and moaning in the trees. We had tae go out and get him, but he was so bad hurt he said tae shoot him. We couldnae do that . . . and just then there was a crack, and my mate Hamish caught it here . . .'

He touched his forehead, just where the top of the nose met it.

'I legged it back then, and just ran and ran. I was in a real panic. I didnae know where I was or what I was doing. When light came, I was awa' back among the old lines, without my rifle and most of my kit. I just sat there. They'd told us the rule—"Desertion in face of the enemy. Court Martial. Firing Squad. No excuses".'

Mary was appalled. 'Is that true?'

'It's true, all right. They're shooting them every morning, up at the Bull-ring. If you listen for it, you'll hear 'em. I was a bloody idiot, Mary. If I'd gone tae an officer then and there I might hae got away wi' it . . .'

'What did you do?'

'I just went on back . . . each night. It was easy enough. I worked for an old French biddy on her farm for a few months—there's no men left on the farms now. Then the police got nosey, so I came here. I thought, where there's a crowd of us . . .'

'Can't you get on a ship, or something? Get back home?'

Jock shrugged. 'That's what most of 'em try to do. They get caught, though. They're alive to it at Folkestone and Dover. Anyway, it's too late. The bloody Military Police picked me up today, wanting tae see my paybook. I said it was up at the camp. I've got tae report to them tomorrow with it—but they've got my number meanwhile.'

With a forefinger, he flicked at the telltale identity tag, tied with a cord round his neck. 'So, I've got tae run for it.'

'But where? Where will you go?'

He shook his head helplessly. Mary sensed that he had lost the energy and the will to run any further; that if he could have done, he would willingly have worked twenty-four hours a day in their canteen, so long as he was saved from the mess into which a moment of panic had got him. She recalled again Ethel's Conchie, and thought how alike these two men's reactions to war had been, yet how different at the outset.

'Jock,' she said, 'I think you'd best spend the night here. You've nowhere to go. The more you run, the worse it will be for you. Look, you'll be safe here for tonight. In the morning, when the Major comes back from St Omer, we'll ask him. He'll know what to do for the best.'

'He's an officer,' Jock replied dully.

'Not an ordinary one, he isn't,' Mary said, and spoke more truly than she realised.

Dawn broke slowly; almost imperceptibly because of the constant flare in the sky. The guns' rumble continued.

Louisa slid carefully from the bed. It had a goose-feather mattress, a welcome change from the roughness of her own camp bed. Charlie lay full length, motionless except for his breathing.

She dressed with the utmost caution. Luckily, the floor didn't creak, though she guessed it would take more violent noise than that to wake him. When she had got all her things on, and her fur coat over them, she went to the table where she had noticed writing things the night before. She took a pencil and paper and scribbled a note.

*'Don't come to say goodbye. Bless you, my*
*only love—L.'*

She tiptoed across to where he lay without having moved. She looked down for long moments at the slim, strong shoulders, half revealed under the sheets. Then she kissed the paper, placed it on the blanket over his legs, and crept silently from the room, holding her handkerchief to her nose.

'No, Mary,' Major Smith-Barton told the Welsh girl emphatically, 'there is absolutely nothing I can do. I'm sorry.'

'You could see him,' she pleaded. 'At least talk to him. Listen to him . . .'

'All right, my dear. Since you ask me. But I promise nothing.'

She led him to a cupboard, where she had concealed the young Scot for the night on a bed of provision sacks. When she opened the door he came out, scrambling and blinking. As soon as he saw the Major he came to rigid attention before him. The Major looked hard at the pale young face, which he had never paused to examine in detail before.

'How old are you, Jock?'

'Eighteen, sir.'

'Quite sure? That's the truth?'

'Sure, sir. I can prove it.'

'So, when you joined up you were . . .?'

'Not quite seventeen, sir.'

'Hm. Well, that's to your credit. If you were under-age when you enlisted . . .'

'Volunteered, sir.'

'Quite.'

'Major . . .' Mary began, but he motioned her to silence. He wandered away, one hand behind his back, the other holding his chin, deep in thought. They watched him like a pair of children. At last he came back to them. He addressed Jock firmly.

'Now, listen carefully. You will get on the leave boat this morning. I'm going on it myself, and you may carry my luggage and follow me up the gangway. If you're questioned, say you're my soldier servant. If the questioning goes deeper than that, then I'm afraid you're on your own. I shan't know you. I shall have to let them conclude you're an impostor or a thief. Understand?'

'Sir.'

'When you get to Folkestone, go straight to the recruiting depot and enlist. Give them your name and true age. Once you've sworn the oath, tell the officer the truth. Everything.'

'Everything, sir? But . . .'

'Hold nothing back. Make it quite clear you were under-age when you enlisted first. You should have been found out at the time and never permitted to come out here. There have been a number of such cases where blind eyes have been turned, but it doesn't shift the responsibility away from the recruiting people. With any luck there'll be no more than some brief sort of enquiry, and they'll give you the benefit of it.'

Jock said eagerly, 'That's all I ask, sir. A second chance.'

The Major regarded him watchfully. 'It's pretty certain you'll find yourself back . . . up *there*.'

Jock swallowed. 'I'll no' let anyone down, sir. I promise.'

'Good boy. Well, I'm embarking at eleven. My things are in the kitchen. Good luck to you.'

The Major stumped away. Then he came back abruptly and asked Mary, 'Where's Mrs Trotter this morning? Don't seem to have seen her.'

'She was . . . out very late with Lord Haslemere, sir. She went for a bit of a lie-down, and said not to be disturbed.'

'Oh. Ah. Very well, then. If I don't see her before I go, tell her I'll be back the day after tomorrow. Give her, er, my love.'

'And mine, too,' said Jock, as he parted from Mary with a little kiss two hours later. Louisa had still not appeared.

When she did come out, very late that morning, she announced that they were winding up the operation immediately. As it happened, a note had come from Starr to say that the builders were moving out of the Bentinck the following day. For Louisa, it could not have been more timely.

Her departure from France was something of a ceremonial occasion. The boat in which she, Mary and Mrs Cochrane were to travel was at the quayside, her complement of leave-bound troops already embarked. They

157

lined the landward rails, causing the vessel to list quite perceptibly, in their eagerness to see the fabled Duchess of Duke Street hand over the canteen keys to a grey-haired Salvation Army captain. A cheer arose at that moment. Then a Salvationist bandsman, quite uninstructed, raised his cornet and sounded the key for 'For She's a Jolly Good Fellow'. For once, the sound of the guns was swamped, as a thousand voices chorussed together.

'Now, I call that really nice. Really nice, that is, madam,' Mrs Cochrane said.

They were back in the peaceful haven of the Bentinck Hotel. All the staff were crowded into Louisa's parlour. Merriman was busily uncorking the first of a brace of champagne bottles and filling glasses for them all.

The object of Mrs Cochrane's admiration was a parchment scroll which Louisa held unrolled between outstretched arms. At the head of it were representations of the Union Jack and the Tricolor. Below, meticulously penned, were thanks to her and her staff from the Allied commandants of Boulogne for their sterling services to the welfare of the Forces.

'Shows what women can do, when they put themselves to it,' Louisa said.

'Poor Jock helped,' Mary reminded her. They had heard that the Major's plan for him had worked. He had been accepted back into the army immediately, without punishment, and sent back to France.

'And the Major,' Mrs Cochrane added.

'Eh?' he demanded, bustling in just then. 'What's that about me?'

Louisa handed him a full glass. 'We was just saying what a marvellous man you are, Major. You may not be able to pick a nag, but you're worth all the bookies at Epsom.'

'Thank you, my dear!' He leaned over to examine the scroll. 'I say, that's a handsome tribute—and well deserved, if I may say so.'

158

'You may. And thanks for all your help, too.'

'Not at all. Not at all.'

'Back to normal, now, eh?' Starr commented. 'Fred'll be pleased about that—won't you, lad?'

The puppy craned its neck to lick the back of Merriman's hand. He withdrew it fastidiously. 'Normal? Ruination, the way things are going.' He drank his champagne, then blew his ever-leaking nose.

The Major was making shifty noises in his throat. Louisa looked sharply at him and asked. 'What now, Major? What you trying to say?'

'I, er . . . Only that your achievements in France seem to have impressed the powers-that-be at G.H.Q. I've, ah, been requested to approach you—by the Chief of Staff in person, I hasten to say—to ask if you'd be willing to allow part of the hotel to become a home of recuperation for wounded officers . . .'

He looked down at his boots. Louisa Trotter was the least predictable of women. She might explode at the notion of anyone presuming to suggest to her how her premises might be used. On the other hand . . .

'Why not?' Major Smith-Barton was relieved to hear her ask. He looked up. She was glancing round her staff, her eyes shining with yet another of those enthusiasms which kept her going like a dynamo. 'Why not, indeed? We've done our bit for the Tommies. Now let the officers have their turn. Poor dears, the way their casualty rate grows and grows . . .'

She stopped speaking abruptly and applied herself to her glass. The Major and Mary noticed, and glanced at one another. The others appeared not to have done. But the Major took no chances. Usurping Merriman's position, he went over to where the second bottle of champagne lay waiting and quickly opened it, relieved to hear behind him a rattle of conversation which he hoped would wash away, for the moment at least, the thoughts which he and Mary alone knew were foremost in Louisa Trotter's mind.

# CHAPTER ELEVEN

It was August, 1918, and after four years of the most calamitous war in history the tide had turned once and for all against Germany. The eighth—that day which the Supreme Commander, General Ludendorff, would later term 'the black day of the German Army in the history of the war'—had passed. The surprise Allied attack launched on it, on a 14-mile front, had numbed the minds and will of the High Command. It was as if, after weary rounds of battering one another in a ring, one of two punch-drunk fighters had delivered the unexpected, desperate blow which was enough to sap the last of his equally exhausted opponent's ability to retaliate yet again.

Many more men on both sides would die or be maimed in the few weeks of fighting which remained. Ones who had almost miraculously got through four full years of it, when countless comrades they had known had long since perished or succumbed, would lose their luck in those last weeks, and their fate would seem all the more bitter to their mourners.

Charlie Haslemere had not reached August 1918 unscathed. Still a captain in the Coldstream—a regiment which, despite its many losses, did not share the practice of many others of giving its officers rapid promotion out of proportion to peacetime practice—he had been wounded in the head by a shrapnel splinter. He had spent many weeks in hospital in France, and then in a convalescent home in England, far from London. Louisa had wanted to go and see him, but had been told that it would be a

161

little while yet before it would be allowed. This had puzzled her. He had written to say that his brain, his eyesight, his looks, were intact, and that the wound was not serious at all. But she had obediently kept her distance, comforting herself that he was now out of the fighting, possibly for good, and proud that he had been awarded the Distinguished Service Order, the second highest decoration for gallant conduct.

Since the welfare expedition to Boulogne, life for Louisa and her staff had felt flat. The Bentinck had been fully repaired, but it would never, it seemed, be its old self again. Louisa clung to her principle of accepting officers only, preferably young and wounded. She cossetted them with as good food as she could contrive from the limited rations and what she could obtain on the side, although the latter had dwindled as the number of her benefactors had decreased due to death from old age or in battle. She dispensed drinks liberally 'on the house', and was as casual as ever about presenting bills for accommodation or meals.

Many young men had cause to be grateful to her for restoring them at least enough to be able to go back and face their hell again. Yet the process of doing it had given the Bentinck almost the air of a convalescent home, rather than an hotel. Some of its occupants spent much of their time merely sitting about, in the hall or in their rooms, brooding, remembering, unable to restrain their tempers at the least imagined slight. The sharp clatter of a dropped tray or even a glass was enough to set men shaking for hours, before they could manage to drive again from their minds the memory of near-fatal shell-bursts. Moments of true jocularity amongst them were few.

Louisa had tried to distract them by having a platform placed at one end of the hall. A piano was on it, for anyone to play who felt like doing so. Others gathered round it to sing. Sometimes someone would do an impromptu cabaret act, which might evoke a little applause and a few ironic comments. Stars of the theatre and music hall who happened to be friends of Louisa's took to dropping in whenever they were passing and had half an hour to spare, and would do a little act without thought of fee. Even members of the staff got up and performed, dragooned into it by Lieutenant Tommy Shepherd, who, with the red-haired widow, Daphne, now his wife, had figured prominently in the disreputable affair of Louisa Trotter versus the Royal Yacht Club, Cowes.

And Louisa was sitting for her portrait in oils. Many artists had wished to paint her, but she had never wanted to be bothered until Collinghurst put in his request. It was not that he was fashionable and expensive, both of which he undoubtedly was, but that he had luckily chosen a formula of words which so blended flattery with persuasion at a moment when she had chanced to be feeling jaded and in need of some new distraction, that she had agreed. Daily of late she had had herself driven to Highgate, four miles from the central London hub of her life, and four hundred feet above it. There, in his small, cluttered studio, she sat still, for a change, while the twinkling, rotund little man in his early fifties worked behind a large canvas, painting, scraping out, repainting, and all the while keeping her amused with the kind of scandalous gossip which she enjoyed hearing but seldom passed on.

He paused, this warm August afternoon, took up his big magnifying glass, and scrutinised keenly the detail upon which he had just been working. He said, with regret in his tone, 'I think the end's in sight.'

Louisa relaxed so far as her habitual stiffness of posture permitted.

'Thank God for that. You've taken long enough.'

'Patience, dear lady.'

'Oh, that's all right for you. I'm a busy woman.' Actually, she had been enjoying the experience, and he knew it.

He smiled. 'For any fashionable painter to catch the

163

face you present to the world would not be difficult. But I'm after something more than that.'

'Ho! So that's why you've changed me face fifty times, is it? Hoping you'd stumble on the right way by luck?'

She got up and came round to peer at the latest version.

'So that's it, eh?'

'I think so.'

'Well, I still think me mouth's too big.'

'Deliberately. An essential feature of you, my dear.'

'Oh, ta!'

'No, the hands were my biggest challenge.' He took them in his and studied them. 'Hands that have known the rough and tumble of the kitchen, and yet retain a delicacy. Artist's hands.'

Louisa withdrew them; only one man was privileged to touch her more than briefly.

'Yeh. Well, I can't hang about here all day. Will you be dropping in later, for a nightcap?'

'I may, I may,' he answered abstractedly, examining the portrait again. Louisa relented a little.

'Here, you know, I shall miss my sittings with you, Colly. You take me mind off things. Half the time, I feel like a ship without a rudder.'

The artist helped her into her light coat and held out her hat for her.

'But soon, alas, you'll no longer need me,' he said gallantly. 'Your warlord will be returning. I should like to meet him when he does. I'm grateful to him.'

'What for?'

'For enabling me to paint you at your most beautiful and characterful. If he hadn't survived his wound, I should have had a tragic face to paint, and that would have been a pity. How is he, by the way?'

'All right, thanks. Says he's still got to take things easy. I reckon his D.S.O.'s been a real tonic to him, though.'

'Yes, of course. Do you know, I should like to paint all the V.C.s and all the D.S.O.s, just to see what they have in common?' Collinghurst took yet another look at

164

his work. 'Do you think the mouth really is too big? I tell you what—come again tomorrow, and we'll have another try.'

'Oh blimey, I think you do it on purpose! All right—for the sake of me mouth, then. But it's the last time, Colly. I mean it.'

He bowed and took her to the door. He was a man who valued his solitude, but not when he had just spent a few hours in Louisa Trotter's company.

While she was on her way back to the Bentinck, a rough-and-ready rehearsal was going on there for a concert the staff were to give that evening. Tommy Shepherd, the producer, was trying to drill Starr and Major Smith-Barton for their parts in a song of tribute to Louisa which her staff had with much difficulty written between them.

'I'm really not much of a hand at this,' the Major apologised, having blundered to a halt at the same place in the same line, three attempts running. 'Can never remember the words, you know.'

Starr scratched his head. 'I reckon Fred could do it better than me,' he admitted, and stroked his dog, now almost the image of his predecessor.

'Oh, come on,' Tommy cajoled them both. 'It's all written down for you.'

'In *your* handwriting?' remarked an ironic voice at his elbow. They all turned, to see Charlie Haslemere standing there in his uniform. A bandage was round his hatless head, and he was very pale and thin in the face; but he was smiling with his eyes as well as his lips.

'Is this the convalescent home for wounded officers?' he asked.

Starr snapped to attention. 'Welcome back, my lord.'

'Charlie!' the Major exclaimed.

'Old bean!' cried Tommy. 'Marvellous!'

He retrieved a walking-stick which had been lying on the corner of the platform and limped off smartly towards the dispense. He was back in a few moments with a drink, but Charlie waved it away.

'Not allowed it,' he explained. 'Is Louisa about?'

The Major explained about the portrait session, then went on apologetically, 'I'm afraid, old chap, since we didn't know when you'd be back, I've put some people in your sitting-room. It was either that, or turn 'em away. But I'll soon get rid of 'em now.'

'No, no. So long as my bedroom's still free?'

'Oh, yes.'

'That'll do for now, then. I just couldn't stick that hospital a minute longer.'

'My dear fellow—the devil, these head wounds.'

Charlie nodded. 'They certainly last. But I'm fine, really.' He turned to Tommy Shepherd. 'What happened to you, though?'

Tommy blushed ruefully. 'They got down to the dregs and called me up. First day in action, guts wobbling with fear, got shot in the arse by one of my own men— or so they told me. Painful as hell. Can barely sit down.'

Charlie laughed. 'Louisa wrote that you'd been shot, but spared me the details. Could have been worse, though.'

'Oh, yes. So Daphne and I are trying to make our-selves useful here. Anyway, you're just in time for tonight's show. We've cooked up a little surprise for . . .'

He broke off abruptly and looked past Charlie, who turned round, to find Louisa looking at him from just inside the swing door.

'What you doing here?' she demanded, though smiling her pleasure.

'You going to send me back, Louisa?'

'Course not!'

She stepped briskly forward to take his arm. Charlie nodded to the other men.

'Excuse me, gentlemen.'

He went off with Louisa into her parlour, where they kissed, long and hard, behind the closed door.

Then they gossiped, and had tea, and gossiped still, and Louisa had some champagne, though Charlie refused; and still they gossiped. Louisa brought out her scrapbook at his insistence, though she had not wanted to risk depressing him with its memories of so many lost friends.

'Poor Evelyn!' he exclaimed over the photograph of a young Grenadier subaltern. 'They were next to us. The next trench. The whole lot wiped out—the day I got this.' He tapped his temple gently. 'Practically all our old friends seem to be in here, Louisa. What'll happen to us?

'We'll concentrate on the living, Charlie. It's the only way.'

She took the book off his lap and put it on her desk. She was about to lower herself on to his knee in its place, when there was a tap at the door and Tommy Shepherd looked in.

'Sorry to interrupt, old things, but we're ready to begin.'

'Oh, your bloomin' concert. Not tonight, thanks, Tommy. You just carry on.'

Seeing Tommy's dismayed look, Charlie got up, saying, 'I'd like to hear it. Come on, Louisa.'

She went with him reluctantly, and was surprised to find the hall filled and most of her staff on the platform. Starr came forward and conducted her and Charlie to seats in the centre of the front row, with RESERVED labels on them. Then he remounted the platform and stood in line with Mary, Major Smith-Barton and Merriman. Tommy and Daphne Shepherd stood at the side. A woman unknown to Louisa sat at the piano, and when she began to play an introduction it was obvious that she had the professional touch.

Applause followed, then Tommy held up his hand.

'Ladies and gentlemen, the staff of the Bentinck Hotel, and friends . . . We proudly present a little song, composed by all of us here, in honour of Mrs Louisa Trotter.'

Under the loud applause the pianist was seen to be

playing. The tune which eventually emerged, as the tumult died, was 'Oh, Mr Porter.' There was some uneasy glancing at one another by the lined-up staff and a disreputable piece of paper was seen to be handed hastily by Tommy to the first in line, Starr, as the ensemble sang an opening chorus:

> *'Oh Mrs Trotter, what shall we do?*
> *We wanted to write a song to show*
>   *we think the world of you—*
> *But when we came to write it,*
>   *we couldn't make it rhyme—*
> *Oh Mrs Trotter, isn't it a bloomin' shame!'*

Great applause and cheering greeted this effort, and the pianist had to go on vamping for several bars until it died down. Charlie glanced at Louisa and her eyes met his. She was smiling, full of happiness to be sitting there beside him.

It was by now tolerably quiet. Starr cleared his throat quickly and sang alone:

> *'First the major had a go*
> *Which didn't get us far . . .'*

He thrust the paper into Mary's hands. She sang pipingly,

> *'Then we passed the duty on*
> *To Fred and Mr Starr . . .'*

And so it continued down the line, the continuity broken only by the Major, who managed to get the words wrong, even holding them up to his eyes. Merriman came to the rescue, with surprising aplomb and a voice unexpectedly strong, considering the great number of years it had been in use. And then the final chorus was reached:

> *'Finally we decided it was all beyond our means,*
> *So we all sat down and had a drink*
>   *and thought of other things,*
> *Felt a pang of sad regret*
> *The Major he had lost his bet,*
>   *But still we're here to sing,*

168

*Oh Mrs Trotter . . .' etc.*

Tommy Shepherd waved his arms at one side of the audience and his wife waved hers at the other; but they needed no urging to join in lustily. For those few moments, every person there in the Bentinck's hall forgot pain, anxiety, worry, fear, as they united in singing a noisy, thrice-repeated tribute to Louisa. When they had done, they applauded and cheered themselves, then called unanimously for her to make a speech. She stood up and faced them.

'Very nice. Thank you very much. Now Charlie and me'll give you a song back.'

This was a popular decision with everyone except Charlie Haslemere, who hesitantly allowed her to lead him to the piano, amidst renewed applause.

'I'm hopelessly out of practice,' he hissed.

'Never mind. What shall we give 'em? I know—can you manage "Let the Great Bit World keep turning"?'

He fumbled a few exploratory notes, then committed himself. After the brief introduction Louisa filled her lungs and let go with:

> *'Let the great big world keep turning,*
> *Never mind if I've got you.*
> *For I only know that I want you so,*
> *And that no one else will do . . .'*

She turned her eyes to Charlie, but he did not look up. He was frowning deeply, holding his face close to the keyboard, evidently concentrating fiercely. Louisa sang to him:

> *'You have simply set me yearning,*
> *And for ever I'll be true.*
> *Let the great big world keep on turning round,*
> *Now I've found someone like . . .'*

But she didn't complete the line. Charlie's hands had sunk on to the keyboard, making a blur of notes. His head drooped, and he was grimacing with pain or distress.

'I'm . . . sorry . . .' he muttered thickly, and raised a

hand to his head. The hand was shaking violently.

Louisa hurried to him and so did Starr, to a buzz of concern, sympathetic but knowing, from the Audience. One or two officers rose to come to help, but Tommy Shepherd waved them back to their seats and motioned the professional pianist towards the piano stool, from which Louisa and Starr had now raised Charlie. As they walked him away towards the stairs, the pianist struck up 'Keep the Home Fires Burning', and Daphne Shepherd sang it, gesturing to the audience to join in.

Major Smith-Barton joined Charlie's escort; but by now he seemed to have recovered from whatever attack he had suffered. He gripped the banister rail and started to mount the stairs slowly, saying, 'It's all right. I can manage.'

'You sure?' Louisa demanded.

'Yes. Sorry about that. Eyes just went out of focus. It happens now and then. It's why they kept me in so long.'

He went on up, but the others followed him, a watchful escort. Louisa opened the door of Charlie's permanent suite. The sitting-room was rank with cigarette smoke. The three nerve-wrecked young officers who had camp beds there, Pryce, Spedding and Reynolds, were playing cards; they never showed themselves downstairs.

Louisa turned on the Major. 'What's this lot doin' here?'

'I'm sorry. My fault. I didn't think Charlie was coming back yet, and we'd nowhere else to put them.'

'I don't care about that. Get 'em out.' Louisa was ruthless when it came to enforcing her priorities.

The three stared at her, like scared schoolboys caught smoking in the dormitory.

'No,' Charlie countermanded with quiet authority. 'Let them stay.'

'Now, look here, Charlie . . .'

'Let them stay in here. I'll go into the bedroom.'

Louisa was going to protest again, but Starr murmured, 'Captain Dean is leaving tomorrow, madam. We can transfer these gentlemen to his room after breakfast.'

'All right.' She addressed the three, who had risen sheepishly. 'But you can tidy up before you go. This ain't a bleedin' barracks.'

She followed Charlie into his bedroom. The Major, hanging back, gave the young officers a secret smile of reassurance. They didn't return it; they never smiled.

In the bedroom, Louisa told Charlie, 'I think we ought to get you back to that hospital.'

'Oh, no! For God's sake don't send me back to that loony-bin.'

'Loony-bin!'

'Well . . . not exactly. I'll be all right, Louisa. Just too much excitement, that's all.' He raised her hand and kissed it. 'I'm so glad to be back, my dear. Back with you. Don't worry. I'll sleep now, and you'll see I'll be as right as a trivet tomorrow.'

She left him. On her way through the sitting-room she paused to warn its occupants, in a low, fierce tone, that if they made any racket and disturbed his lordship's sleep, they'd be out on their arses in double-quick time.

Her stricture had evidently had its effect, she thought, as soon as she saw Charlie coming downstairs next morning. He moved briskly, without depending on the banister, and smiled happily. But as he reached the foot he blundered into Mary, who was coming towards the stairs carrying a pile of books for a bedridden officer who had been injured in an aeroplane crash. Louisa, standing in her hat and coat, waiting for the Major to bring the hotel 'bus round to drive her to Highgate, saw clearly that the collision had been sheer misjudgement on Charlie's part. Thousands of people passed one another in London's crowded streets every day, with scarcely ever a bump. Yet Charlie had had all the room in the world to avoid Mary.

He had helped Mary pick up the books, with a graceful

apology, and she had gone on her way. He came across to Louisa.

'Morning, Louisa. Where are you off to?'

'Colly's place. You sleep all right?'

'Like a top. Who's Colly?'

'Collinghurst, the painter. Final sitting for me bloomin' portrait. I wrote and told you.'

'Ah, yes. I'd forgotten.'

'Major's taking me in the 'bus. Feel like a ride?'

'Of course.'

Louisa looked at him more keenly. 'I was hoping you'd be sensible and stay in bed all morning.'

'Nonsense. I'm fine. Never felt better. Look, there's the 'bus. Come on.'

The Major ushered them into the 'bus, ageing now but still immaculately painted and polished, and drove them up from the stuffy, claustrophobic atmosphere of the West End to the clear air of Highgate, the northern approach to London, where Georgian houses nestled in a village setting and lucky ones commanded vistas of Hampstead Heath or thirty miles or so to Epping Forest and beyond. With a little imagination, as she stood at the artist's window in Southwood Lane, Louisa could fancy she could see as far as the Essex home at Wanstead from where she had set forth on life's adventure to become assistant cook to Lord Henry Norton, in whose house she had first met Charlie, his nephew, and from which appointment all else had sprung.

Charlie, an amateur artist himself when he had had time for it before the war, proved entranced by Collinghurst's portrait of Louisa.

'You've captured her completely!' he told the beaming little man with the red cheeks and diffident manner. 'I'm lost in admiration. Congratulations!'

Louisa put in, 'There's been a bit of controversy about the mouth.'

'The mouth's perfect. And the colours of the dress, against that background . . . Perfectly judged, Mr

172

Collinghurst.'

'I'm overwhelmed, Lord Haslemere. Thank you.'

'So?' asked Louisa, defeated over this matter of aesthetics. 'What's going to happen to it now?'

'I shall exhibit it, of course.'

'And I shall buy it,' Charlie declared promptly.

'Hang rather nicely in the hall, won't it?' Major Smith-Barton suggested; but Louisa protested, 'Oh no! Don't want to keep seeing meself all day long.'

Charlie agreed. 'It's for me, not the hotel. I shall have it in my rooms, above the fireplace.' He asked the artist, 'May we take it now?'

'No. Give me a day or two to tidy it up, will you? And Lord Haslemere . . .'

'Yes?'

'Will you sit for me, when you can find the time? It would give me the greatest pleasure to paint you.'

If Charlie had only noticed it, Collinghurst had been studying him quite intently while he had been examining the portrait; watching, in particular, his face.

'Go on, Charlie,' Louisa said. 'Tit for tat. I might even buy yours, if it's any good.'

'Oh, well . . .all right.'

The artist's smile broadened. 'Excellent! If we could start soon, I could hold off any other work. A day or two, say?'

Charlie nodded. 'Perhaps we'd better. I might have to go back to France. Depending . . .'

'They're not havin' you back yet awhile,' Louisa told him firmly. 'Not while I'm lookin' after you. Don't worry, Colly. I'll send him up to you.'

The artist shook Charlie's hand.

'Goodbye, Lord Haslemere. Such a pleasure.'

Again neither Charlie nor the others noticed it, but his expert inspection of Charlie's features was keen—especially something about the eyes.

Louisa's portrait had been hung over Charlie's sitting-room fireplace. His suite was his own again now. The morose casualties had been transferred to another room, their cigarette fumes dispersed through opened windows and with bowls of fragrant pot-pourri, and everything tidied up in their wake. It was quite like old times again, Mary Phillips remarked in the kitchen; only she and the others knew it was far from like them. The bandage was still wrapped round Lord Haslemere's head, and there were several disturbing manifestations of his condition for them to report to one another.

'Keeps bumping into things,' said Starr. 'Almost trod on poor little Fred's tail, as if he hadn't even seen him sitting there.'

Merriman sniffed. 'Couldn't find his knife and fork properly at dinner. Picked up the fish knife for his soup at first.'

Mary added unhappily, 'He got so upset over a book he was reading. Kept looking closer and closer at it, he did, then threw it down on the sofa beside him and started rubbing his eyes with his fist. I'd have felt awful if he'd seen me watching, though.'

This information reached Louisa via the Major. Both of them had items to add to it as well.

'Problem is,' said Major Smith-Barton, 'one can't get Charlie to admit anything's wrong. If you'd agree, dear lady, I think we ought to take it into our hands to act for his own good.'

''Course I agree. Only, I'm not getting in touch with that hospital to come and fetch him back. That'd be betraying him.'

'No question of that. But I do happen to have a surgeon friend. At school together, you know? Sir Ernest Horsfield. I'm sure he'd have a look at him.'

'What sort of surgeon?'

'Well, er . . . brain. Harley Street. Top man.'

'I see,' Louisa answered slowly. 'All right, then. Get him here.'

Major Smith-Barton, whose range of acquaintance had never ceased to amaze Louisa in all the years she had known him, produced the surgeon the very next day. He proved to be elderly, watchful, with an air of utter professional omniscience but a dry sense of humour, which he soon needed to deal with an irate Charlie when the Major showed him into the suite.

'My dear fellow,' Sir Ernest assured Charlie, 'I just happened to be downstairs . . .'

'Like hell you were! This is ridiculous. Absurd. Quite unnecessary. Someone's inveigled you here under false pretences.'

The surgeon was unmoved. He had in his time faced every prevarication known to reluctant patients.

'I was chatting with my old friend Toby Smith-Barton here. He was telling me about your heroic deed—your wound. He happened to mention these dizzy spells. I know it might not be quite professional etiquette, but I said I'd be only too pleased to take a look at you without formality, if you wished. If you insist, though, I'll go at once.'

The suave manner had won over far more obstinate patients than Charlie, who apologised. The surgeon waved it away.

'Think nothing of it. I find myself flying off the handle more and more, these days, and I've been no nearer the Front than Boulogne. The strain, you know. Tells on us all, in our different ways.'

Charlie nodded. 'What . . . do you want me to do?'

Sir Ernest glanced at the Major, who took the hint and left them alone; then he turned back to Charlie.

'Just sit down, will you? Thank you.' He sat, too, and unclasped his bag, to bring out various instruments—a small magnifying loupe, a pocket torch, an ophthalmoscope. 'Now, these dizzy spells . . .?'

'They warned me at the hospital to expect certain minor . . . reactions.'

'Quite. Any pain? Headaches?'

'Not to speak of.'

Sir Ernest picked up a newspaper he had seen lying

near him. He held it up to Charlie's eyes. 'Read the headline, will you?'

'"Bapaume captured". About time, too.'

'And beneath it?'

With slight hesitation, Charlie managed, '"35,000 prisoners and 270 guns taken . . ."'

'Good. Very good. What's the time by your mantelpiece clock?'

Without hesitation Charlie answered, 'Seventeen minutes past four.'

'Excellent. Now, I'd like you, please, to get up and walk across to the piano.'

Charlie obeyed. While his back was to him, Sir Ernest quietly moved a small table to impinge upon the track he would take if he came back the same way.

'Now, walk back to me, please.'

Charlie did so. He caught his left leg on the corner of the table. He frowned down at it, puzzled.

Sir Ernest requested him to sit again and proceeded to examine his eyes closely through the magnifying loupe, illuminating them with the small torch in his other hand. As he worked he asked, 'Do you ever experience any . . . visual hallucinations? Flashing lights, rings, colours, unformed objects?'

'Nothing like that at all.'

'No, as it were, pictures? A field; a landscape; a lady beside a stream . . .?'

'Good Lord, no!' Charlie laughed. He indicated the portrait over the mantelpiece. 'That's the only lady I have visions of.'

'Oh. Is that Mrs Trotter?'

'Just painted by Collinghurst.'

'I see. Now, I want you to look into my right eye. Concentrate on it—and tell me how many fingers I'm holding up on my hand to one side?'

'Three.'

'Now?'

'One.'

'Now?'

'Three again.'

'Thank you.' Sir Ernest did not inform Charlie that he had held up four that time. Instead, he asked, 'Do you ever get sensations of weakness in your hands and legs?'

'A spot of pins and needles occasionally. But I thought my eyes were on trial.'

'Of course,' the surgeon smiled. 'May I look at the wound?'

He unbandaged it and peered.

'McKinnon, I see.'

'How on earth . . .?'

'We know one another's work pretty well. Don't you know the story of the surgeon who was examining a patient he thought he'd never met before, for an operation on his piles? Soon as he felt 'em he said, "I remember you now, Mr Robinson. 1912, wasn't it?".'

As Charlie laughed, Sir Ernest Horsfield was re-packing his bag. He explained, 'We're a pretty inhuman lot, in my business. Forget a man's face but remember his piles. It's the same with recognising one another's handiwork. I fancy I can spot a McKinnon whenever I see one. Bit obstinate about healing up, though, I see.'

'That's what I'm beginning to think,' Charlie agreed. 'But I don't know how long these things take.'

'No. Quite.'

Sir Ernest paused in the act of packing his bag and produced the ophthalmoscope, as if as a casual afterthought. But there was nothing casual about the examination to which he subjected Charlie's eyes through it.

He explained to Louisa and Major Smith-Barton, over a glass of sherry in Louisa's parlour shortly afterwards: 'It's hard to be exact, on the strength of one brief examination, but I'm afraid certain things are apparent. The head wound *has* impaired the sight. I think there could still be a tiny fragment of splinter buried in there. The optic disc at the back of the eye where the nerve fibres lead to the brain has atrophied . . .'

177

'What's that mean?' Louisa asked abruptly.

'Well, looking on the bright side, it could stabilise. His sight could remain as it is now—for the rest of his life. Or there could be . . . further deterioration.'

The Major asked quietly, 'You mean he could go blind?'

'I'm afraid so, Toby. It's a possibility we . . . he will have to face up to.'

Louisa asked, aghast, 'But can't you do an operation on him?'

'I could—in time. But there would be too many risks at present, so soon after the original operation. We have to wait.'

'Just watch it get worse?'

'Not necessarily. As I say, there is hope. But there's really no choice for the time being. He can lead a normal life. You must keep an eye on him, though, Mrs Trotter. He finds distances difficult to judge, which means he could be a danger to himself—out in the street, for instance. And I particularly want you to let me know, *at once*, if you notice any weakness in his limbs. A slight paralysis of the hand; a limp . . . anything like that.'

He got up.

'I'll see him again in a fortnight. He's a proud man, isn't he? Strong will. So he might try to deceive you. Be vigilant, for his sake. Goodbye, Mrs Trotter, Toby.'

The Major saw him out, then returned. He couldn't recall having seen Louisa ever look frightened of anything. She was frightened now, though. The expression on her pale face, her tense posture, and the look in the big eyes told him all too plainly. She licked her lips and said, in a low voice, 'I don't want no one but us to know about this, Major. The staff . . . *no* one. Understand?'

The Major understood.

# CHAPTER TWELVE

Charlie had invited Louisa to dine with him that evening in his sitting-room, the scene of the most momentously-shared time in their lives. Merriman, who had been on duty on that same occasion, presided over the arrangements. As he lit the candles on the round table, the room lights dimmed, as Charlie switched them off, one by one.

'So, what did Mrs Cochrane manage to come up with in the end?' he asked.

'Some trout, my lord. Eggs, asparagus, and strawberries.'

'To begin, though? Hors d'oeuvre?'

'Not permitted these days, my lord. Order of the government. Even Mrs Trotter can't get all the way round food rationing.'

'It must be an extremely long way round, then. Anyway, thank you, Merriman. We'll eat at nine o'clock, on the dot.'

'M'lord.'

The timeless old man withdrew. A moment later Louisa came in. She was at her radiant best. She wore her most expensive evening gown, his presents of the Coldstream Star and jet necklace at her breast and neck respectively. Her coiled, auburn hair shone and the big blue eyes glowed.

'This is a nice surprise, Charlie,' she remarked, looking round.

'More than you deserve—getting that eminent headtester to see me. Tell me, did he confide his mumbo-jumbo to you afterwards?'

'Course not. There's something between doctor and patient, isn't there?' She accepted the cocktail he handed her. 'I wouldn't have understood, if he had.'

'Mm! That makes me think he tried. But I'm quite well, you know.'

'Can see you are. In the pink.'

The reservation in her tone wasn't lost on him.

'Well . . . these things do take time. You should've seen some of the other poor blighters. I'm one of the lucky ones. And in future, Louisa Trotter, if you don't mind, *I'll* be the judge of whether I need anyone to examine me. That understood?'

'Aye, aye, Captain.'

Louisa went to the sofa to sit down with her drink. It was gin-based. She preferred wine or brandy, but sipped it without complaint. Charlie came to sit beside her. She couldn't help noticing how unusually abrupt he had become in all his movements.

He said, 'So that's enough about my state of health. Now let's talk about us, and the future. I don't think the war can last much longer. Bapaume's been taken, and with Foch in command we should break through the Hindenburg Line in the next month or so. And that should be the end of it; which means, my dear, that if we stick to our agreement to get married the moment the guns stop . . . then we'll be married by Christmas.'

So fast was his talk that Louisa, still hesitant about marriage, even to him, exclaimed, 'Here! Hang on a minute!'

'What's the matter? You do still want to marry me?'

'Yes . . . 'Course I do. Only . . . just need time to take it in, that's all.'

Charlie stared at her uncertainly for some moments, then said, 'I see what's on your mind. It's the Bentinck, isn't it? The idea of inactivity appals you. Well, there's no need to close it down. We really don't have to spend much time at Bishopsleigh. We'll make this place our home—make a separate flat for ourselves . . . Louisa? What's the matter? You're shivering.'

She was, though she didn't know why. She took his hand.

'I'm all right, love. Let's meet our problems when we come to 'em, eh?'

Later that same evening she confided her real worry to the Major. She had not enjoyed the dinner. Charlie had eaten little, so neither had she, and she hated being the only one drinking. He had chattered on about all sorts of things, but nothing concerning *them*. It was the subject she had for so long been glad not to think about, even; only now that she needed to talk it out, and he was anxious to do so, she found she couldn't face it. She was aware that she had disappointed him by not enthusing over marriage plans, and they had found themselves at cross-purposes and unable to have a constructive discussion.

At length, Charlie had said he felt a headache coming on rapidly. He had gone to bed. It was only eleven o'clock. Louisa was glad to find the Major available for a drinking partner. Her guests were either in their rooms or crowded in the hall, where the comedian Harry Tate, who had called in after a theatre performance, was making them roar with his droll monologue sketches.

'Have another brandy,' Louisa urged. They were sitting in her parlour, with the rise and fall of the laughter reaching them. 'Go on. Help yourself.'

The Major obeyed willingly enough. He still wore his uniform, but his shoulders were no longer so defiantly stiff as they had been when he had first put it on again at the beginning of the war. The years of attrition had had their effect on his resilient spirit, too.

He sighed. 'So you think it's all an act of bravado he's putting on? Convincing himself that all's well?'

'I dunno. I mean, he must know it isn't. He spilled the wine twice.'

'A lot of men's hands shake nowadays, Louisa.'

The Major held one of his own out, palm down and fingers spread; but he put it down again when he saw Louisa looking at it, and knew she was noticing how steady it was compared with Charlie's. She said, 'It's not that. He missed the glass completely. Poured it on the tablecloth.'

There was a silence. Then Major Smith-Barton asked, 'D'you think he noticed your anxiety?'

'I tried hard not to let on.'

'No, I mean about the whole question . . . of marriage. Rather tricky now, I mean to say.'

'You don't think I'd chuck him, just because he's goin' blind?'

'Good Lord, no! But it does put a different slant on things—from his point of view. He won't like the feeling of being dependent on you.'

'He's going to have to be dependent on somebody. It might as bloomin' well be me. Anyway, we don't know how much he knows, do we?'

'No,' replied the Major. 'But if the worst comes to the worst, and he does go . . . blind, without warning, he's not going to thank anyone for not letting him know.'

'That's just what I was thinking. I reckon he ought to be told the truth. It's his right to know.'

The Major nodded unhappily.

'The question is, who's going to tell him—and how?'

'I nearly did tonight—only I hadn't the heart.'

'I know how you felt. Louisa, my dear, shall we agree between us, as his closest friends here, that if the right moment offers itself to either of us, we'll take it?'

Louisa nodded agreement, shivering again as she did so. She drained her glass abruptly.

'Let's hope it's soon. Give us some more brandy, will you? My inside's like ice.'

Next morning, once more, Charlie came downstairs seemingly as fit as a fiddle. His spirits were further raised by a letter from Buckingham Palace, fixing the date for his Investiture. His D.S.O. ribbon was on the breast of his uniform.

'Off to Highgate this morning,' he told Louisa in the hall. 'Your friend Collinghurst, remember? He telephoned that he'd like to start sketching me, if I'm free, and I said I am. Care to come with me?'

'I'd like to, Charlie, but I really have to stay in this morning. Mrs Cochrane's off ill, and there's a couple of special lunches.'

'Ah, well—pity. I thought I'd get the old car out. See if it still works. It's spent the war in that garage in Albany Street.'

Major Smith-Barton, who was seated nearby reading *The Times,* put down the newspaper when he heard this and cleared his throat.

'Er, sorry, Charlie—couldn't help over-hearing. Look, I've got to go out to Hampstead myself. Promised to visit an old . . . cousin. Taking the hotel 'bus, so I can easily drop you off and pick you up again.'

'No, no. That's the other side of the Heath.'

'No trouble. Few minutes away, that's all.'

'Thanks, but I rather fancy driving myself.'

The Major glanced helplessly at Louisa. She said firmly, 'You're not ready yet, Charlie.'

'What do you mean?'

'Just that.'

'Who says I'm not?'

'Sir Ernest Horsfield, if you want to know.'

'What twaddle. The question of driving's never come up. At least, not with me. Has he been talking behind my back?'

'He . . . asked us to look after you.'

'That's it,' the Major hastened to add, coming over. 'Told us you might get impatient or over-confident, and we're to put the brake on you if you do, old chap.'

'Well, damn that!'

'Come on, Charlie,' Louisa coaxed him. 'Be a good boy now—for me.'

'Well . . . Well, all right, then, this time. But when I go to the Palace, I go under my own steam!'

'Of course, of course,' the Major agreed, glad to be able to temporise. 'Now, whenever you're ready will suit me. The 'bus is outside.'

They set off together a few minutes later. Charlie sat up in the front beside the Major, but said little throughout that journey of contrasts: fashionable, dignified Albany Street; slatternly Camden Town and Kentish Town; then up the steep curving sweep of West Hill to the Georgian enclave that was Highgate Village. The Major dropped Charlie in Southwood Lane, lingered to make arrangements with him and Collinghurst about what time he should return, then drove off slowly down Hampstead Lane, past Kenwood and the Spaniards, on his non-existent errand. He parked the 'bus on the edge of the Heath and went for a long walk until it was time to drive back to Highgate.

They descended once more to the levels of London. As they approached Regent's Park, the Major, whose feet were quite tired enough already, summoned up his resolution and asked Charlie casually, 'Care for a stroll in the park? Lovely day.'

Charlie agreed. He was in a more affable mood now. The cheerful little artist had his way with tactiturn sitters, and it had worked. The 'bus was parked again and the two men went strolling slowly towards the large lake. There were many rowing-boats out, this warm day of high summer. Cheerful badinage came across the water from young men, and screams of exaggerated fear from the girls as the inexpert rowers rocked and splashed them. Many people lay inert on the grass, thankful just to rest in peace and quiet. A lot of them were men in hospital blue.

The Major said, 'I'd like to hear about your little show sometime, Charlie. They don't dish out D.S.O.s for nothing, even now.'

Charlie smiled. 'When I was in hospital, Toby, I made

184

a vow not to spend the rest of my life boring people with my war reminiscences.'

'Quite right, too. But you can make an exception for an old soldier, can't you? Awfully frustrating, don't you know, living this war at second-hand. Getting no nearer to it than a brief spell of King's Messengering. Living off titbits of gossip.'

They were approaching an empty bench. Charlie moved towards it. The Major noticed with alarm that he was limping slightly, and that when they sat down he rubbed his left thigh vigorously.

'Pins and needles,' Charlie said, 'Comes now and again. Soon pass off. As to my "little show", it was a bloody great mess. Bungled orders. No heroics. Just panic and mess, and I did what I did to save my skin and one or two others. That's all. Anyway, that's enough of it. Can you even imagine war on a day like this?'

But for the wounded soldiers, and those strolling in uniform, it was hard to do so.

'God mocks in a mysterious way,' Charlie added.

'Almost over, if we're to believe the newspapers,' the Major ventured. 'Then what, I wonder? You, er . . . and Louisa . . . You'll get married?'

'She's told you, has she?'

'Hints. Rumours amongst the staff, don't you know?'

'They're right. When the guns stop, is our pledge. I've been living for that day.'

'Congratulations, old boy. Only . . . Look, Charlie, there is something . . .'

The Major's tone made Charlie turn his look towards him in that apprehensive way which a man might use if he sensed his best friend was about to tell him something disagreeable about his girl. The older man's face was grave.

'I have a difficult task,' he said, dry-lipped. 'Horsfield spoke to us . . . to Louisa and me . . . after your examination. The fact is, I'm afraid the news isn't too good . . . about your sight. Nothing definite, of course. Things could stay as they are, he emphasised that. Only . . .'

Charlie spared him with a gentle touch on his arm.

'Thank you, Toby.'

'You . . . knew already?'

'I'd guessed. There are times when I fear the worst, and others when I believe in the best. Just now, I can see you perfectly clearly. That couple over there . . . absolutely distinctly. Most things, most of the time. Then, suddenly, for no reason . . . Dammit, they said at the hospital it would soon pass. They *told* me it would. I didn't say anything to Louisa, because I've been expecting it to go and I didn't want to worry her in the meantime. Only, it hasn't yet. If anything, it's happening more frequently.'

'My dear chap . . .!'

'What did Horsfield say? I want the truth, Toby, please.'

The Major shrugged. 'I've told you all I know. He isn't sure.'

'Did he mention . . . any period of time? Months? Weeks . . . before . . . ?'

'Not at all. I told you, it's not certain.'

Charlie was shaking his head. 'It is, though. It's getting worse, day by day. Would you expect Louisa to marry a blind man?'

'She'd marry you tomorrow, whatever your condition,' Major Smith-Barton retorted promptly. But the blunt directness with which Charlie had spoken had shaken him.

Charlie was getting up. 'Come on,' he said. 'Let's go home.'

He walked away, noticeably limping.

When they got back to the Bentinck he went straight to his rooms without a word to Starr in the hall. Louisa went up to him soon afterwards. She found his door locked, and he wouldn't open it for her.

Their relief was great next day when Merriman, carrying Charlie's breakfast tray, was admitted. He stayed in the room only long enough to set the tray down on the table, and heard the door locked behind him as soon as he went out again; but at least he was able to report to an anxious Louisa that his lordship was shaved, and seemed quite himself, and was evidently going to eat breakfast.

Louisa decided to leave Charlie alone to have out his fit of the blues. The Major had told her all about the conversation in the park, and she thought she could understand the reaction it must have caused. But when the whole of that day and evening passed with Charlie still refusing to let anyone but Merriman come and go, and would not even talk to Louisa through the door, she began to worry more. She consulted the Major yet again.

'Had we better ask old Horsfield to come?' she suggested.

'He's in Manchester all this week, remember?'

'Oh, that's right. What're we goin' to do?'

'I've been thinking about that, Louisa. If you don't mind taking one more person into our confidence . . .?'

'Who?'

'Tommy Shepherd.'

'That daft young ha'porth!'

'Tommy's not so daft as he makes out. It's his pose. Being a marquis without a bean humiliates him, and this is his way of trying to act devil-may-care about it.'

'But what could he do, anyway?'

'He's not a peer for nothing. He has his friends in various places. One of them's Ian Fraser.'

'Who?'

'He was blinded quite early in the war. Captain, I think. He and a chap called Arthur Pearson set up a charity for blinded Servicemen. Its H.Q.'s in Regent's Park, in a house an American financier fellow called Otto Kahn has let them have for the duration of the war. They've taken their name from it, in fact—St Dunstan's.'

'You reckon they could help somehow?'

'From what I've heard Tommy say, their chief

187

function is teaching men how to come to terms with their condition. Show 'em how to start life again in a new way. Convince 'em everything isn't over.'

Louisa took a deep breath.

'I'm game. You want me to go and see this Fraser?'

'No need. I'll get Tommy to take me. See if we can persuade him to send one of his helpers along here to talk to Charlie.'

'*If* he'll even let him past his door.'

The Major said, with a humourless grin, 'I fancy we can surmount that little problem.'

Captain Ian Fraser readily agreed to send a blinded officer back to the Bentinck with the Major and Tommy. He summoned a young man in his mid-twenties, whom he introduced as Captain Mason. He gave him brisk instructions and handed him a case containing certain equipment. Tommy carried the case for Mason, who declined a helping arm as they went to the 'bus, but tapped his way expertly with a heavy white walking-stick.

At the hotel the Major sent for Merriman and gave him orders of his own. The old man went off to the dispense and came back shortly with a tray of tea things. There were two cups and saucers on it. He led the way upstairs, followed by Captain Mason escorted by the Major. Merriman knocked at Charlie's door and called, 'It's Merriman, my lord. Your tea.'

Charlie had been playing the piano softly. He stopped and they heard him unlock the door. Merriman went in and the blind officer, with a deftness the Major admired from outside, slipped in after him.

'Who the devil . . . ?' the Major heard Charlie demand angrily. Merriman answered, 'Captain Mason, my lord. From St Dunstan's, Regent's Park.'

'Roger Mason,' the officer said. 'Sorry to barge in like this.'

Unseen to the Major, he held out a hand. To the Major's relief, Charlie evidently took it, for he heard him say, though not exactly welcomingly, 'Sit down, please.'

Merriman came out and closed the door. He nodded to the Major and winked. They went off downstairs together.

In the room Charlie, whose hand had been forced out of common courtesy to a blinded brother officer, poured tea for them both. He knew it was no coincidence that there were the two cups and saucers, and recognised that he had been tricked; but he was compelled to hear Mason out, and that young man proved to be a shrewd salesman.

'Ian Fraser's friend Lieutenant Shepherd told him about your spot of trouble,' he explained. 'Fraser asked me to come and say how delighted he'd be if you'd consider giving us a helping hand.'

This approach was quite unexpected. Charlie asked, 'How could I help? I'm afraid I don't see . . .'

'Neither do I—in a different sense of the term,' Mason answered with a grin. 'I got mine at Arras. Instantaneous. The shock's greater that way, initially, but at least it's over and done with without waiting for it to happen. But do you know about St Dunstan's? We've had quite a splash in the papers recently.'

'I've heard about it, of course.'

'Let me show you some of our literature, then.'

Mason groped for his case. He could have put his hand straight on to its handle, if he had chosen, but by seeming to have lost it he forced Charlie to pick it up for him and pass it over. It was a step towards cooperation.

Mason unlatched it and took out leaflets, a book about the teaching of Braille, the printing system for the blind, and a Braille watch.

'Now . . .' he said, leaning forward; and he was gratified to sense that Lord Haslemere was leaning forward, too, giving him interested attention.

While this interview was taking place, Louisa was at Highgate again. The artist, Collinghurst, had telephoned and asked to see her soon. She had refused, but he had repeated the request, and something uncustomarily serious about his tone had persuaded her to go.

He laid his sketches of Charlie before her. She examined them, then looked at him curiously.

'You know, then?' she said, wonderingly.

He nodded. 'The very first time I saw him. I have to confess it's why I wanted so urgently to get him to come and sit for me. A man in the process of going blind is a rare catch for a painter. Something about the eyes one could never encounter in anyone else. I hope you'll forgive me?'

Louisa shrugged. 'What d'you want to see me for, then?'

'I wanted to tell you . . . in case you didn't know and weren't prepared. Only I see you are. The other question is, do you want me to continue?'

'I want him as he was. Do your own thing for yourself if you must, but I want the Charlie Haslemere I've always known. If you can do that for me, I'll be grateful.'

He nodded. 'If you can let me have photographs, I can do it.'

'All right.' She indicated the sketches. 'Only, for pity's sake don't let him see these. They're too clever by half.'

He promised.


'So,' Roger Mason said to Charlie, 'I need hardly tell you how much your name and connections could help us. We're an entirely self-supporting charity, you know. Always looking for ways to raise money. And morale. Tell a man he's afflicted, and, he'll believe it. Convince him he isn't—that he's just a bit different from other people, but that the world's still his oyster—and he'll accept that equally. All sorts of careers open—the church, farming, teaching, crafts and manual trades . . . How about coming over to see our workshops? Meet Ian Fraser and Arthur Pearson? I think you'll get on splendidly with them.'

'You're very persuasive, Mason,' Charlie said. The

younger man could hear the smile in his voice, and smiled, too.

'It's my job. Tell you what, most mornings before breakfast we go for a row on the lake. Young shopgirls volunteer to cox our boats. Great way to start the day. Why not come out for a row tomorrow, and breakfast with us after, then I'll show you round?'

'The blind leading the to-be-blind, eh?'

'Something of that sort. Will you come?'

Charlie's mind was suddenly made up. 'Yes. I'd like that.'

'Splendid! Seven ack-emma, then?'

They shook hands warmly. When he showed Mason out, Charlie took him down to the hall personally and handed him over to the Major to be driven back to St Dunstan's. To the relief of the watching Starr, he didn't go straight back upstairs. He lingered to give Fred a pat, then sent for Merriman and ordered him to arrange for dinner in his room with Mrs Trotter that evening.

Captain Mason had done his work expertly. Louisa found Charlie full of new hope, eager to visit St Dunstan's and enthusiastic to involve himself in its good work. Mason had left the Braille watch with him. Charlie showed it to her like a boy proud of an expensive new toy. She could have cried, but exercised all her self-control and covered up her anguish with rallying chatter. They laughed a good deal, he naturally, she with contrived effort. She was pleased to see him so cheerful and relaxed, of course, but too much was weighing on her mind to make it possible for her to be the same.

He went to bed early, as his custom had become, and for once Louisa decided to get in an early night, too. But she had only just finished the long process of brushing her hair and had settled down into bed when there came an urgent knocking at her door. It was Mary Phillips.

'Oh, madam!' she said, her eyes wide. 'It's his lordship. He's shouting and swearing terribly. I can hear him right through his door.'

'A nightmare, I expect,' said Louisa, struggling out of bed again.

'It's terrible,' Mary insisted, unconvinced. 'I never heard anything like it.'

Louisa put on her dressing-gown and together they hurried to Charlie's suite. Louisa could hear his voice well before they reached the door. He was roaring out, as if trying to make his voice heard above some great din.

The door was unlocked. They went in and closed it behind them. They crossed the sitting-room and went into the bedroom. Charlie's bed looked as if it had been torn to pieces by Furies. He was threshing about in the midst of the disorder, clawing at sheets, sweating copiously, gasping.

'Sergeant?' he yelled. 'Where the hell are you? What the hell's going on? I gave you an order, and I want it obeyed. Are you deaf, man?'

His voice rose to a crescendo. He suddenly sat upright, his eyes wide open. One hand clutched his temple. The other pointed into a dark corner of the room.

'You men, there! We're lost! Can you tell us the way to . . .? The *way*, damn you! We've lost our *way*!'

Louisa and Mary hastened forward to hold him, both frightened that he might tear off his bandage and reopen his wound. But he struggled with them, not recognising them.

'What are you doing? Why are you shovelling earth on me? You're trying to bury me! Stop it . . .!'

'Charlie—Charlie! It's me—Louisa.'

'Louisa? They're shovelling earth on me, Louisa. Don't let them . . .'

'Quiet, Charlie, love. It's a dream. Only a dream.'

'No. No dream. It's . . .'

But he suddenly ceased to rave. He sat for some moments, panting heavily, supported by the women, one at either side of the ruined bed. Then he slowly turned his gaze on Louisa, focusing his eyes with obvious effort.

'What . . . what's happening?'

'It's all right, love. A nightmare. Just lie back now.'

Mary picked up his flung pillows and placed them for him. Louisa eased him down on to them, while Mary quickly restored order to the sheets and blanket and eiderdown.

'Shell burst,' he murmured. 'Quite near. Like an explosion in my mind.'

'There, Charlie. Hush!'

The hands Louisa reached out to hold were clammy and cold for that warm August night; yet sweat trickled down his face and neck.

'Click—in my head,' he muttered.

'Shall I get Starr to fetch a doctor, madam?' Mary whispered. Louisa shook her head. She knew that Sir Ernest Horsfield was still away. In any case, she believed it had been a bad nightmare, nothing more.

'You go to bed,' she said. 'I'll stay with him. I can always telephone somebody if he gets worse.'

Mary went away doubtfully. Louisa turned to Charlie again. His eyes were closed. He was rambling drowsily, 'Field . . . hedgerows . . . Young corporal had his hand blown off . . . Something he said . . . do you remember? Blackberries. That's it. Tongues, lips, stained with the juice . . . faces like squashed fruit.'

He opened his eyes suddenly.

'Louisa?'

'I'm here. What is it, love?'

But he looked at her wildly, fearfully.

'You shouldn't be here! It's not safe! Can't you see the sky lit up? No place for you to be, Louisa!'

'You aren't out there any more, Charlie. You're home. There's no fighting.'

'No . . . When the guns stop . . .'

'Yeh. They've stopped for you, Charlie.'

'Home . . .?'

'That's it.'

'Not . . . not that hospital . . . please!'

Louisa didn't answer. She didn't wish, later, to be accused of having betrayed him.

He closed his eyes again. The drowsiness returned to his voice.

'Louisa . . . will you come with me tomorrow? Rowing on the lake?'

She had no need to answer this time. He was breathing steadily, quite asleep. She wanted to mop the sweat from his face, but didn't dare risk waking him.

He slept peacefully, watched by her constantly. It was not until six in the morning, with the sunlight brightly rimming the closed blinds, that she tiptoed away to her own room, to wash and dress. She felt utterly drained.

Half an hour later, Starr looked up from tethering Fred to his chair in the hall, and saw her coming downstairs, pale but immaculate.

'Good morning, madam,' he greeted her.

'Morning.'

'I was just wondering about his lordship's call, madam. He asked me to call him so he could go rowing with Captain Mason on Regent's Park lake. Only, Mary told me about last night, and . . .'

'Don't bother him. He's sleeping. I'll telephone St Dunstan's.'

'Very good, madam.'

Somehow Louisa got through her day's tasks. She had known exhaustion before, had nearly died of it, but for Charlie's having saved her. But this time felt different. She was frightened, not resigned. She felt a desperate lack of mental reserves to draw upon.

She looked in on Charlie twice that morning. He still slept. After lunch she yielded to Mary's insistence that she have a lie down in her bedroom. The next thing she knew it was five o'clock. She straightened her hair and hurried to Charlie's room.

To her surprise and relief, he was sitting in an armchair which he had turned to face the window. He wore his

194

dressing-gown over his pyjamas. He had not shaved, but his hair was brushed neatly.

'No need to creep in, Louisa,' he smiled.

'Hello, Charlie! How are you?'

'Very peaceful. Did you have a nice rest?'

'Longer than I meant, thanks. Here—how did you know?'

'Mary told me. She looked in, and I was awake, so she brought me some nice scrambled eggs and tea. I'm sorry about last night.'

'That's all right, love.'

He said abruptly, 'Do you think I should go back to hospital?'

Although it had been her thought, she had not the heart to admit it.

'Don't be silly.'

'I'm not being. I don't want to, of course, but I don't want to be a blight on this place. What was I saying last night?'

'You was . . . ramblin' a bit. About the war. Just a nightmare.'

'Extraordinary. I can't remember a thing about it now. Could you light me a cigarette, please? My hand seems a bit . . .'

He held one hand up. It was quivering in every part. He let it fall hopelessly. Louisa got him a cigarette, placed it between his lips and lit it with a match.

'I had something to do today,' he said, furrowing his brow. 'What was it?'

'You was going rowin' on the lake with Captain Mason. Doesn't matter. I telephoned him. Go when you like, he said.'

'They want to help me, you know. Not *me* help *them*.'

'Bit of tit-for-tat, I daresay. It's a good idea.'

He took a long drag at the cigarette and removed it from his mouth with violently shaking fingers. Then he made another of his startlingly sudden changes of subject.

'I was thinking about Lottie last night. There's a look

195

of her in your portrait. Have you noticed?'

He continued staring out of the window while Louisa looked at the now-framed oil, hanging over the mantelpiece. She could see no resemblance to the pert, hostile child she had encountered so fleetingly in Yorkshire. Charlie was saying, 'Amazing what you can see, if you close your eyes. Vividly. I can see her exactly. I can see every detail of Bishopsleigh, too. Even paths joining in the garden.' He sighed. 'This room's getting so small.'

Louisa made a great effort.

'They're not taking you back to no hospital, love. Mary and me'll look after you. She knows about nursing, and I'm not so bad at it. You know, Charlie, it's a funny thing —all we've been through together, we've never been on an even keel, have we? I mean, either you're pickin' me up, or I'm pickin' you up. Like a couple of old drunks. Remember the second time you saw me? You comin' home from some ladylove, and me staggerin' back from market and collapsin' in your arms, five o'clock in the morning? What a way to start somethin', eh? Tuppeny bloomin' romance! Well, from now on, I don't care what anybody says, we're goin' to do things in style. Start off with a bloomin' great wedding, just like we promised each other. Then we do this place up, so's we get a bit of privacy. Then go up to Yorkshire for a bit, and we'll entertain all them county ladies and give 'em a dinner they'll never forget. And then . . .'

She stopped. She had been gazing out of the window while she had been speaking, seeing nothing but the future in her imagination, not noticing that he had not responded with a word or even a sound of approval. A dreadful chill surged through her as she turned fearfully to look at him. His eyes were open, but blind now. The cigarette had fallen to the carpet and the acrid smell of singeing reached her nostrils.

She knew, from his stillness and his silence, that Charlie was dead.

# CHAPTER THIRTEEN

After the euphoria of rejoicing which attended the Armistice of November 1918 a heavy feeling of anticlimax settled over all Britain. The war years had been exhausting, dangerous, worrying, unsettling. They had also been dramatic, full of movement, noise and alarums. Suddenly, all that was at an end. To nerves which had been kept stretched taut for several years the peace was unexciting, bewildering in its intangibility as opposed to the reality of war. Like the aftermath to a feverish illness, listlessness and depression set in. There was to be a sunlit new life for all, the Prime Minister, David Lloyd George, had proclaimed; but somehow the sun failed to shine.

There was little of light and cheer in the Bentinck Hotel. Although she had taken Lord Haslemere's death with dignity and without dramatics, Louisa Trotter had clearly been shattered by it. The powerful spring within her seemed to have been allowed to uncoil to its slackest, and it appeared that nothing would ever wind it tight again. Instead of bustling about the place, noisy, bossy, interfering, she sat by the hour in her parlour, not troubling to switch on the light on even the gloomiest winter afternoons. With that silver-framed photograph held limply in her lap, she stared into the fire, but saw no fancied pictures in it.

She looked older suddenly. She was certainly thinner, for she ate scarcely anything. She was not always careful about her dress or her toilet. The will to do anything at all seemed to have left her.

Her attitude infected the others. The Major and

Merriman were old, worn men. Starr's boots no longer squeaked briskly when he moved. Mary Phillips, her Aunt Gwyneth, Mrs Cochrane, all were tired out, worried about their security, lacking enthusiasm for anything.

The hotel was old and tired, too. Since the repairs after the bombing nothing had been done to renovate it. Paintwork was worn and chipped; metalwork seldom gleamed; there was the smell of neglect in its passages, as there had been when Louisa and Augustus Trotter had bought it from its ailing owner years ago.

A visitor came to the dispense one dark December afternoon. She was Ethel, the maid who had married the Conscientious Objector, Clive Baker. She wore shabby black.

'Blown up carrying a stretcher,' she told them. 'Two days before the Armistice. Two days! I wondered . . .' she addressed Mary, '. . . if Mrs Trotter might take me on again?'

Mary looked at her uncomfortably. 'I'll ask,' she promised. 'Only, with the hotel being as good as closed— only the present guests, until they go, and no new ones wanted . . . well, there just isn't the work.'

'That's right,' said her Aunt Gwyneth, and promptly sneezed and blew her nose before she could go on. 'I've been expecting my notice for weeks. I was only taken on part-time and she's always saying I'll have to go.' She sneezed again.

'But I was kitchen,' Ethel pointed out. 'What's happened to the cooking—the parties?'

'You might well ask,' Mrs Cochrane said. 'She gets requests, but she turns 'em all down. Can't be bothered, she says. Soon, they'll all stop asking, and that'll be it.'

'I don't know what we're coming to,' Gwyneth went on. 'Not like the old days, it isn't.' Yet again she sneezed.

'Nothing is,' croaked Merriman. 'And you'd better go home with that cold of yours, Mrs Davies.'

'It's no cold. Just the dust from brushing the stairs.

They were thick with it. I could never stand dust, but I can't keep the whole place clean by myself.'

'I could help,' Ethel said hopefully. 'Honest, I don't care what I have to do. The money's nearly all gone, and I can't get work nowhere. Please, Mary.'

'I said I'll speak to Mrs Trotter, I'll have to wait for the right moment, though. She won't listen, otherwise.'

The bell from Louisa's parlour rang. Mary got up.

'There,' she said more brightly. 'Could be just the chance.'

She turned at the door as her aunt went into a paroxysm of sneezing.

'You have got a cold, Auntie. Go home to bed. Can we spare her a drop of brandy, Mr Merriman?'

'Anything to stop that sneezing and coughing around the place,' he agreed, and went to fill a small bottle of it.

Mary found Louisa with her light on for a change. She had a letter before her on the desk. She looked up as her assistant came in.

'You look washed out, Mary.'

'Just a bit tired, madam. And worried.'

'What you worryin' about now?'

'The bills, madam.'

'Bills?'

'Oh, I told you, madam—months of them. I've been working them out and my head's going round and round with the figures. There's ever so much owing.'

'Who cares?'

'Someone must. There's a very nasty note from Mr Foster, the butcher. I've never known him nasty before. Letting us have his best all through the war, he says, but six months outstanding is no joke, he says . . .'

'All right, all right. I'll pay him.'

'And there's a final note from the gas. They'll cut it off if we don't pay.'

'I've heard that one before.'

'But they will, madam. And we can't manage without gas.'

Louisa flopped back in her chair.

'Let 'em cut it off, then.'

'Oh, madam!'

'This hotel's finished. Finished. Everything I cared about is finished. I want to leave this place and never see another hotel as long as I live—which won't be too long, I hope.'

'Ma'am!'

Louisa waved a limp hand at the letter.

'There's a gentleman here wants a nice comfortable business as a sideline for his wife. Made his money in munitions or something. Well, his wife is welcome to this place.'

'You couldn't!'

'I'm going to, Mary. I've come to the end at last.

'But . . . all the rest of us . . . We've got our homes here.'

'I'll put in a word for you all.'

'No one would ever take old Mr Merriman on. The Major would never work for anyone but you. And Starr, and Fred . . . There's not many jobs to be found now. Servants are going out of fashion. There's . . . there's Ethel in the dispense wanting to know if you'd take her back because she can't get work.'

'Ethel?'

'Was our kitchenmaid. Married that poor Conchie boy. He got killed.'

'Oh, yeh. Well, tell her I'll give her a reference, but that's all I can do. Not today, though. She can come back tomorrow. Oh, for Gawd's sake, Mary, stop looking like a ghost. I'm sorry, but I'm sick to my death of looking after other people. I'm thinking about meself now, for a change.'

Mary turned unhappily to go. Louisa roused herself sufficiently to order, 'Don't go telling 'em no tales about this, yet.' She indicated the letter.

Mary retorted almost scornfully, 'Don't you think they've a right to know? It's all their lives.'

'Don't you cheek me, miss!' Louisa snapped back, with

one of her rare shows of spirit. Mary turned away and went out without answering.

'Auntie gone?' she asked in the dispense, where Merriman and Starr sat alone, moodily drinking tea.

'Yes,' Merriman replied. 'That cold's getting on her chest. I hope she hasn't brought that 'flu into the place. As if we hadn't enough to put up with . . .'

Starr interrupted to ask Mary, 'What was Mrs Trotter on about?'

'Oh . . . Just the bills.'

'Don't say she's thinking of paying them!'

'I wish she would, Mr Starr. Oh, they worry me so.'

He leaned forward. 'I'll tell you something, Mary. She's got enough money in that desk of hers to pay a year's bills. Maybe more.'

'What?'

'Cheques. Never cashed. All those officers coming here on leave, and she hasn't cashed a single one of their cheques. Not right through the war.'

'You've been spying, have you?'

'No. I happen to have a pair of good ears, that's all. I heard the Major and Mrs Trotter talking as they was crossing the hall. Fred and I was reading the paper, but we heard him say, "But you can't hang on to 'em for ever," and she said back, "I'll burn 'em before I'll cash 'em".'

Merriman sniffed. 'She would, too. Mark my words.'

'Oh, dear!' wailed Mary, more distressed than ever. 'Whatever happens to us all then?'


Louisa put on her coat and hat and went out. She got a motor omnibus going east. Within an hour she was letting herself into the little terraced house in Wanstead, Essex, from where she had originally sallied forth to make her bid for fortune and fame as the best cook in London. She seldom went there. She and her mother always rubbed one another up the wrong way, and her morose father's world-weariness depressed her. But she had kept her door key; it was the only link she had with her family.

She found her father on his own, sitting in the neat kitchen. He was in an armchair before the fire, with a blanket over his knees. He was dozing and had not heard her come in. He woke with a start when she entered the room, and she saw relief on his face. He glanced round. Several clocks, ticking in a variety of rhythms, told him that it was just gone six.

'Gawd!' he said. 'Thought it was your mum, and me with no kettle on ready. How are you, lass?'

Louisa shrugged. She moved the kettle from the side of the range to the hob. 'She at the hospital again?'

'Yes. Spends half her time there. There's nothing she can do about it. Only upsets Arthur, and that upsets her.'

Louisa's brother had rejoined the army in mid-war. He had not long been at the Front before a shell had burst in a trench where he had been resting. All his comrades round him had been killed by it. He had lost both his legs. The strong, bullish man had been reduced to a helpless, angry cripple. Louisa had visited him in hospital once only. He had railed at her cruelly from his bed, pouring out his resentment at the way life had treated him compared with her. She had felt that he would have attacked her if he had been able to move. The shell had damaged more than his body. She intended not to visit him again.

'You look peaky,' Mr Leyton observed. 'Cup of tea will buck you up.'

'I want more'n tea, Dad. I want the impossible.'

'What's that?'

'I want to go back to the way everything was—before the war.'

'Don't we all? Can't turn the clocks back, though.'

'Dad, I'm thinking of giving up the Bentinck. Selling up.'

She saw his quick look of alarm. It saddened her to know, as she did, that his first thought at the news was for himself. Louisa's parents had received fairly regular money from her over the years. Even this mild, sympathetic little man had his avaricious side; he had lost his own will to work and had allowed himself to depend on his prosperous daughter.

He swallowed and said, 'You don't want to give that place up. I mean, it's your life.'

'It's dying. I wish I was.'

'Oh, Louisa!'

'I feel as old as the hills. What have I got to live for?'

'You're still a young woman . . . Please, love, don't *you* give up. I know I'm a selfish blighter, but if you give up, what've I got left?'

She put out her hand impulsively and he took it, gripping it hard.

'Go on,' he said. 'Have a good cry. Do you good.'

But she shook her head. 'I'm past tears. I've got this lump in my throat, but I can't cry. All the time there's this lump—kind of stuck. Food won't go down, hardly.'

'Yeh. You've lost weight, that's a fact. Thin as a wand.'

They heard the front door.

'Here's your mum. Get the tea ready quick, love.'

Mrs Leyton came in. Her shoulders drooped. She had been quite a handsome woman, but sourness of spirit, together with care and strain, had aged her quickly in the last four years. She saw Louisa, but didn't smile at her.

'Oh. You're here.'

She dragged off her coat and hat and looked meaningfully at her husband.

'I'll have my chair, Ernest.'

He vacated it for her.

'When I come in, tired and worn out, I like my own chair. No tea made?'

'Just coming up, Mum.'

'Aren't you going to ask after your own brother?'

'How is he?'

'No better, no worse. What's going to happen to him? That's what I want to know.'

Her husband ventured, 'I suppose he'll have artificial legs. Soon learn to make the best of 'em. At least they do better than the old peg legs these days.'

'How can you say such dreadful things? Him, who was such a big, strong, proud man.'

'So were a lot of others,' Mr Leyton muttered. His wife turned on him savagely, 'You're hard. You're so hard!'

'You've always called me soft. Silly and soft.'

'Your own son!' She began to cry. 'He told me not to go again. Said he doesn't want me mooning over him. Said to forget he ever happened. How can I forget my own son? Oh, where the 'ell's that cup of tea?'

Louisa had it ready. Neither she nor her father made any effort to comfort her mother. They didn't like her, either of them; and they didn't like Arthur. There was nothing sincere to be said to her.

When she had at last sniffed away her tears of self-pity she asked Louisa ungraciously, 'Anyway, what do you want? You haven't been near us for donkey's years.'

Mr Leyton began to say, 'She just popped in for . . .' but Louisa over-rode him.

'I'm selling the Bentinck.'

'*What's* that?'

'I am selling the Bentinck.'

'Oh my God! One thing after another!'

'You won't go short, if that's what's worrying you.'

'Oh? "My lord" left you rich, has he?'

Louisa grabbed her coat and began to struggle into it. Her father urged her, 'Don't go, Lou. You haven't been here two minutes. Drink your tea.'

'No thanks. I might choke.'

Mrs Leyton said, 'Because I've come home—that's why she's going. Can't go to see her brother, and can't stay two minutes in the same room with her mother. Oh, you are a hard pair, you two.'

Louisa bent to give her father a peck on the cheek. Then she slammed out of the house without so much as a glance at her mother.

She had gone there instinctively, as a child runs home to its family when it has been hurt or bullied. Louisa had been genuinely hurt, and, in her fancy, bullied by life. The inborn homing instinct had worked in her and she had responded to it—only to be rejected. Now she felt worse than ever. All her lifelines seemed to have been cut.

She walked away from the little house, the little road. As she had done eighteen years before, when she had been twenty-one and ready for life's adventures, she turned her steps towards the open scrubland of Wanstead Flats. There was an omnibus service all the way from the pretty village now, but she chose to walk. Spots of rain began to fall. She paid them no heed, and did not even bother to turn up her coat collar against the cold.

Louisa had not gone far before hurrying footsteps sounded behind her. She did not trouble to turn. The thought of an assault never entered her mind. Then she heard her name called, and stopped and looked round in surprise. Her father came panting up, wearing his coat and muffler.

'Dad! What d'you think you're doin'?'

'I'm seeing you back to your hotel, that's what. I can't bear it to see you so upset.'

'I'm all right. Honest.'

'All the same, I'm coming with you.'

Louisa managed a little smile. 'You'll have Mum after you.'

With a spirit she had not seen in him for years he answered firmly, 'Look, all these years I've kept quiet and let her drain the life out of me. Then Arthur came back and started, too. Only, when you came to me tonight you was wanting help, and I didn't give you it.'

'Thanks, Dad. I know how things are. Only, you go home, please. You'll only make things worse for yourself.'

'I've told you, I'm seeing you home first. Please, Lou. I want to help you, only I don't know what I can do. But at least, let me do this.'

She tucked her arm into his suddenly.

'All right, Dad. Thanks. Let's go back to the bus-stop, shall we? I don't want you catching your death.'

They rode together to Piccadilly Circus along that same route the young Louisa had taken in the horse-'bus. They said little. Having made his impulsive gesture, Mr Leyton was back in the shell which was his personal prison. He knew what sort of reception would await him back at Wanstead—tears, recriminations, an endless recitation of self-pity. He could manage it, as he always did, by saying nothing and trying to close his mind as well as his ears. Just for an hour or two, meanwhile, he was free, an escaped prisoner at large. It was enough.

Major Smith-Barton, who had been pacing the hall agitatedly, unable to find anyone who knew where Louisa had disappeared to, greeted them with deep relief.

'My God, we thought we'd lost you, Louisa! Good evening, Mr Leyton. Has there been . . .?'

'She's all right. I wanted to see her home safe.'

'Go home now, Dad,' Louisa said, but he shook his head again.

'Not yet. I want to see you all right first.'

'Quite right, sir,' the Major said. 'I shall send Merriman into the parlour with some brandy, and it *will* be drunk. That's an order, I'm afraid.'

'Since when did you give the orders round here?' Louisa demanded. The two men were glad to see her flare up. Her father exerted his strength and steered her towards her parlour.

The Major joined them there shortly. Mr Leyton had stirred up the dozing fire. He accepted his brandy with pleasure and astonished Louisa by asking the Major if he had a cigarette.

'Don't smoke,' he explained, 'but there are moments . . . and I reckon this is one of them.'

The Major proffered his case. The cigarettes were Turkish, but it didn't matter to Mr Leyton. He only took a few puffs before throwing it on the fire; but it had fulfilled its purpose.

'Now,' the Major said to Louisa, taking an official-looking envelope from his inside pocket at the same time, 'this letter's come from Charlie's lawyer. The Will's been read.'

'I don't want to know.'

'You've got to. He wanted you to be there, but you wouldn't go, so he's written.'

'No.'

'But my dear . . .'

'I told you, no!'

'Louisa,' said her father. The brandy had affected him quickly, since he had not drunk spirits for years, and once again he was feeling that he cared nothing for any sort of consequence. 'Open that letter, and read what's inside. I'm not leaving until you have.'

She made no move. He added, 'I mean what I say, girl. Open it—or, by God, I'll fetch you one round your earhole.'

To their astonishment she gave a great wail and burst into torrents of tears. She cried and cried, her shoulders shaking, all of her quivering, tears dripping unheeded down on to her dress. They sat still and let her go on. Unwittingly, Ernest Leyton had burst the dam for her. He had spoken to her as he had not done since she was a child, and all the years of division between them since that time had been bridged by that common little threat of a father to a naughty infant.

Gradually, the crying fit subsided. The tears gave way to dry sobs, and they in turn to sniffs and little moans. Then at last Louisa fumbled for her handkerchief, rubbed her eyes, blew her nose, and sat upright once more.

The Major was quick to provide more brandy for them all. Louisa drank a lot of hers at a gulp. It was another good sign.

Her father put the envelope into her hand. She looked at it, and then at him. Then she opened it.

There were two pieces of paper inside. One was an official statement with figures on it. The other was a letter. The handwriting was Charlie's. Watched in silence by the two men, she read it to herself.

'*Louisa, my darling, whether the guns have stopped or not, when you read this letter, it is written to my beloved, whom I shall always think of as my wife, my love for all eternity.*'

At this point, Louisa's control broke down again. She cried for several minutes; but the tears were from a different source. It was not too long before she could resume reading again.

'*. . . I am thinking of you at our Bentinck as you read this—never despairing, keeping your pecker up through it all. Thoughts of you have kept me sane. I have sat out there in those tiny dugouts—wet to the skin—like a hunted fox, and I have heard your laughter and seen your bright eyes. You must never be defeated, my dear— never, for my sake as well as your own. You must use the money to redecorate the old place. Make it like new— like we did when we first went there. Remember how we bought the furniture at that auction . . .?*'

Tears overcame her once more. There was little more to read when she recovered again; just a conclusion and some parting endearments. She folded the letter carefully and tucked it into her dress, without offering to show it or read out any of it. Then she picked up the other piece of paper, and saw that the figure at the bottom, underlined, was forty thousand pounds.

There was a tap at the door and Mary came in. She looked distraught.

'Not now, Mary,' the Major said, but she ignored him and appealed to Louisa.

'Oh, madam! It's Auntie Gwyneth. I think she's dying.'

Louisa regarded her vaguely for a moment before asking, 'What d'you mean?'

Mary stared at the Major. 'Didn't the Major tell you?

She collapsed in the street, just as she was setting off home. Starr brought her back in here and we put her in my room. I think it's the 'flu, ma'am. She's ever so poorly . . .'

Louisa's colour rose. 'Why the 'ell wasn't I told?'

'I looked for you everywhere, ma'am, only you weren't here.'

'I'm sorry,' the Major mumbled. 'Quite slipped my mind with . . . all this.'

'Please, madam,' Mary begged. 'She says she wants to die . . .'

'*Wants* to?'

'Yes. With losing her job, and all, and nothing to live for any more. Oh, I'm sorry, ma'am, but I had to tell them all you were selling up. I know you said not to, but it was their right to know.'

Louisa sprang to her feet. 'She's *not* dying. She is not bloody dying. I'm sick of death and talk of death. Major, give me that brandy bottle. Now, come on, Mary. I'll give her dying, indeed!'

She stormed out with Mary following. Mr Leyton sighed.

'Can't think what came over me, speaking to her like a kid. Haven't seen her cry since she was a tot, and then hardly ever. Always was a tough little customer.'

'Did the trick, though,' the Major said. 'Have another brandy—oh, she's taken it. I'll get some more.'

'No thanks. I'd better be on my way. More tears to face at the other end, I'm afraid, but I don't care any more.'

The Major escorted him out to the hall, asked Starr to fetch a taxicab, and, as he was going off to do so, slipped money into his hand and told him to pay the driver in advance.

Up in Mary's room, Louisa stood over the moaning form in the bed and demanded, 'What's all this I hear?'

'Cruel . . .!' Gwyneth wheezed, and coughed.

'Cruel? I haven't started on you yet.'

'Taking away our work . . .'

'Help me sit her up, Mary. She'll do no good lying flat like that. Never clear the phlegm. Pneumonia before you can say Jack Robinson.'

They heaved the woman up and got pillows behind her, but she was not to be comforted.

'Go away. Leave me alone. I'd rather die.'

'No-one's dying here. Make up your mind to that, and it'll be easier for us all. Besides, I need you in the hotel.'

'. . . Die . . .'

'Best needlewoman I ever had. Really care about marking the sheets and towels. Now, you're going to drink this, and there'll be calves' foot jelly later on.'

Having administered to the bewildered patient, Louisa went briskly down to the dispense. A girl in black was sitting there, talking to Merriman. She stood up as Louisa entered. Louisa recognised Ethel.

'Ethel, isn't it? Look, go straight down to Mrs Cochrane and ask her to make up a tray for Mrs Davies. Calves' foot jelly, and all that.'

'Yes'm.'

'Then take it up to her in Mary's room.'

The girl seemed to hesitate. Louisa asked, 'I take it you *are* ready to start work now?'

'Oh, yes, Mrs Trotter.'

'That's the stuff. Get yourself a pinny, and get on with it, then.'

Louisa turned to Merriman, as the delighted Ethel bustled away.

'What you sitting there for, like an old codfish? I'll have a bottle of wine in my room—smartish. Might be two glasses—might be three.'

'Very good, madam.'

But when she got back to the parlour she found only the Major, lingering hesitantly.

'Your father went home,' he told her. 'Left his love.'

'Ta.'

'Er . . .'

'What!'

'Mary was saying . . . about the future of the hotel . . .'

'A man'll be coming.'

'Oh!'

'Yeh. I'll be on to him first thing in the morning.'

'I see,' Major Smith-Barton said heavily. 'This fellow who wants a sideline for his wife?'

'I didn't say him.'

'Oh? But I thought . . .'

'Too many people thinking what's best for Louisa Trotter.'

'Dear lady, we all wish what's best for you.'

'And for yourselves. Well, I can't blame you. Oh, cheer up, Major—it's not the man you think. The one I'm sending for's called Holdron. Holdron & Son—only the son's a daughter, I hear, 'cos the son was killed at Passchendale and the daughter's taken his place in the firm. Builders and decorators. Carryin' on regardless.'

Hope began to dawn in the Major's face.

'You . . . mean . . .'

'I'm havin' the place done up, that's what I mean. The way Charlie wants it. Expense no object. Ah, Merrilegs—just in time. Me dad's gone home, so the third glass is going spare. Fill yourself up as well. Right. And the toast is—Charlie!'

# CHAPTER FOURTEEN

Louisa sat straight-backed and motionless in the middle of the taxi's seat, as the big square vehicle nosed its way cautiously through the narrow country lane. Branches of blackthorn and may tapped and scraped at the windows, but she took no heed of their beckoning; her face wore the faraway look it often wore now, despite her renewed determination to keep going for Charlie's sake. When the taxi rounded a corner and stopped in the little cobbled square, the driver spoke to her twice before she came out of her reverie.

'This is where you wanted, Mrs Trotter.'

The square was deserted but for two men working on a wooden platform near the shrouded bulk of the War Memorial, and two young girls riding aimlessly round on bicycles. Louisa paid them no attention, but they stared frankly at her, as did the workmen. She was a startling apparition for rural Yorkshire, in her elegantly-cut suit, the skirt fashionably short, well above the trim silk-clad ankles. The black she wore from head to foot was not an uncommon garb these days, but it looked very different on her from cheap, mass-produced mourning. Her jewelled Coldstream Star shone against it. The great sheaf of flowers she held blazed with colour, the pinks and yellows of forced roses, purple iris, striped parrot tulips, the downy gold heads of mimosa, bronze and red wallflowers, nestling in a frame of delicate maiden-hair fern.

Glancing up at the church tower, Louisa walked briskly, her high heels clattering on the cobbles, towards the gates of Bishopsleigh.

In the private graveyard beside the family chapel, near the entrance gates, the grass was freshly cut and fragrant. Two new graves, one very recent, stood out from the older ones. For a moment her eyes rested on Margaret's stone; then she turned and knelt by the other, laying the flowers over it, hiding its raw look. Somewhere a blackbird was singing full-throatedly in wild sweet cadences. The sharp breeze brought country scents, a bright May sun shone from a brilliant blue sky dotted with creamy clouds. Louisa shook her head with a kind of anger. So much life, so much promise . . . it seemed impossible, ridiculous that she could be so near him, yet completely out of reach. She touched the earth with her gloved hand, as though it might warm under her fingers, but its cold clamminess seemed to have nothing to do with the vibrant person who lay beneath. What had he said, among his ravings the night before he died? 'They're shovelling earth on me . . .'

She got to her feet and looked across the grounds to the Hall. 'We don't have to live at Bishopsleigh', he had said. But they must, she had told him. It was his place, his village. Well, if things had been different she'd have been the lady of Bishopsleigh by now. Lady Haslemere, like poor Margaret had been, but, unlike Margaret, not accepted by Charlie's friends or his tenants because she had a common voice and blunt ways. What would have happened? Perhaps, for him, she'd have changed herself a bit. Talked more the way they did, which she knew how to do perfectly well; she only kept her rough speech out of inverted pride. For him, she'd have done anything, even that, and put up with the sideways looks and words whispered behind the hand, never so much as answering back with, "Oo the 'ell do you think you are?'

Come on, Louisa, snap out of it, she told herself. No good moanin' on about it.

But, as she walked through the dewy grass towards the Hall, her heart was heavy.

After the brightness outside, the house was dark and gloomy, ghostly shrouded furniture looming up out of the shadows, patches of sunlight filtering in to show up the dust that lay thick on floor and sill. Louisa following Nanny Ord down the hallway, sniffed.

'Smells damp.'

The little shrivelled woman looked up sharply.

'Damp? That it doesn't. Though I grant you Elsie Richards doesn't do 'alf she should. Always says she's "poorly". Must think I'm gormless, when it's well known as she's too fond of the . . .' She mimicked the raising of a glass. Louisa pulled impatiently at a drawn curtain, then gasped and leapt back as something flew out and blundered against her face.

'Whatever is it?' asked Nanny Ord.

'A moth—a bloomin' great big thing.' Louisa brushed at her cheek, ignoring Nanny's muttered denials that there were any moths in the place, or damp either. Crossing the room, now revealed in the full light in all its forlornness, she opened the clock that stood on the mantelpiece, wound and re-started it. Then she turned to the tall desk, and pulled off the dust-sheet that covered it, surveying the objects on it: silver ink-stand, letter-rack, blotter embossed with the Haslemere crest . . . She turned to Nanny.

'Mrs Ord, d'you remember a nice walnut box Lord Haslemere used to keep 'ere?'

'I do,' Nanny snapped.

'D'you know where it is? He wanted me to 'ave it.'

The old woman turned away, with an indignant snort. 'Well, I don't know about that. Don't like folk rummaging round in 'ere. Charlie won't like it, neither, poking round the house behind 'is back.'

Louisa looked after her, puzzled, as she drifted out, murmuring of the sadness of empty houses. From the hall, into which she had gone, there came men's voices and a hearty masculine laugh.

'Dear, oh dear, she's done it again. Nanny, you've left

214

the keys in the door, you batty old thing.'

Louisa recognised the voice. It was that of the Reverend Alec Bennett, the vicar whose impromptu music-hall performance had kept her and Charlie entertained—and Margaret, too. It was the last time Margaret had laughed . . .

'Are you coming to the service, Nanny?' he asked, coming in.

'Church service? I never go to church no more.'

The vicar laughed. 'I'm aware of that. But the Memorial Service is rather special.'

'You won't see me dead at no Memorial Service.'

'I notice you came to church when the visiting minister was here.'

'Aye,' Nanny snapped back, 'and I didn't like his sermon any more nor I like yours.'

Still laughing, the vicar came over to where Louisa stood in the shadows by the window. With him was a man in uniform. Louisa turned full face to them.

'Don't mind me, gentlemen. Nothing I like more than neglect.'

Bennett's face lit up with recognition. 'Mrs Trotter! I so hoped we should see you here today.'

'Good to see you, Vicar,' she said, meaning it.

He introduced his companion, Enfield, as a solicitor who was Charlie's executor. Louisa disliked him on sight, and ignored the smirk and the sizing-up glance he gave her. It was neither the time nor the place for that kind of thing, nor for his thoughtless gesture in lifting the cover off the grand piano, and running his fingers idly along the stiff keys, cobbling out a desultory tune. She turned her back on him, listening to the vicar, who was lamenting that he had let Nanny Ord go off with the keys again. 'I'd intended taking them—they should be in Mr Enfield's hands now. Heaven knows what sort of personal insult she'll make of it, though.'

'Her opinion of you don't seem to've improved,' Louisa commented.

'No, indeed. She helps me out at the vicarage now, you know, since her duties ended here. But I can't pretend she does it with much enthusiasm. And then, over the years, Nanny has become—what shall I say?—a little absent-minded. One of the facts she consistently overlooks is Lord Haslemere's death.'

'Oh.' Louisa understood now why the old woman had made that mysterious reference to Charlie as if he were living. She shivered, not entirely with the dank air of the room, and accepted gratefully Bennett's invitation to coffee at the vicarage. As they walked, he told her that his guest for the day was Lord Henry Norton. 'He's here to do the honours at the Service—standing in for the real heir, so to speak, who's somewhere or other. Where is he, Mr Enfield?'

'Canada, so far as we know.'

Louisa brooded. Lord Henry, her first employer, Charlie's uncle, in whose house she had met Charlie in such unlikely circumstances. As for the real heir; that would have been herself, if things had happened differently. Life played funny tricks.

The vicar glanced at his watch. The church bells were insistently loud, peeling their summons from the belfry only twenty yards away from his sitting-room. At the table Lord Henry, very bent and grizzled now, was short-sightedly studying his notes for the speech he was to make. Louisa, restless, wandered about the cluttered room of a man with a careless housekeeper and no wife, for Carrie Bennett had died many years before. Fossils, pebbles, sprays of dried flowers, all sorts of lumber. Louisa smiled. She lingered over a water-colour sketch, obviously unfinished, of heathers, the pink and purple clusters that grew on the moors and hills above Bishops-leigh.

'That's pretty.'

Alec Bennett was looking over her shoulder. 'Yes. You probably remember the artist—the child, Lottie Richards.

216

Dirty, cheeky young monkey she was when you were last here.'

Louisa was staring at the little picture. 'Well, I never. Yes, I remember 'er.' The stolen biscuits, her own scolding of the child . . .

'She comes to me for the odd class in botany, music, that sort of thing. She's a bright, lively young creature.' His tone was warm.

Louisa had been debating within herself. Now she said, 'As a matter of fact, Charlie asked me to keep an eye on Lottie. Now he's gone, and her father dead too, I must 'ave a talk with you about her sometime. Charlie always did 'ave a soft spot for the kid.'

'Yes, I remember. To tell the truth, I've sometimes wondered . . .'

There was a question in his eyes, but she did not meet them. The bells, which had stopped, re-started.

'Forgive me,' he said, 'but I really must get ready.'

She asked, for no particular reason, 'You was never tempted to marry again, was you, Vicar?'

'No. Losing Carrie rather took the heart out of me. Though it used to be a great sorrow to me that I had no sons. Now I thank God I had none to lose.'

The village square was crowded now. Everybody had turned out for the Memorial Service, Bishopsleigh's own celebration of its dead. Many women were in black, many men still in uniform; children stood silent and respectful, in their best Sunday clothes. On the platform by the shrouded Memorial a little string band was assembled, earnest-faced men, their hands blue with cold in the fresh wind, and by them was ranged the church choir, well-rehearsed and conscious of its importance in the ceremony.

Major Smith-Barton, who had come on from Harrogate after Louisa, stood beside her. They were all listening intently to the strong voice of their vicar, ringing out over the heads of the people to the farthest corners of the square.

'Let us commemorate and commend to the living memory of Our Heavenly Father, the shepherd of souls, the giver of life everlasting, those who have died in war for our country and its cause. May we especially remember the men of this village who fell, whose absence is felt by all of us here, and most acutely by their loved ones.

'Samuel Arkwright. David Butler. Philip Courtney. William Courtney and David Courtney. Michael Dawlish. James Gardiner and Peter Gardiner. Will Mackle. Stanley Pickering. And Captain Charles Wyndham Tyrrell, Viscount Haslemere.'

Louisa stood very straight, her face showing nothing of what she felt. The Major, beside her, was equally impassive. Lord Henry's lips were working in a last-minute rehearsal of his speech, his arm trembling under the weight of the wreath he carried. The vicar was speaking the lines of Laurence Binyon, *For the Fallen*, which would for ever epitomise grief for the dead in war:

'"*They shall grow not old, as we that are left grow old,*
*Age shall not weary them, nor the years condemn.*
*At the going down of the sun and in the morning*
*We will remember them.*"'

From the crowd came an echoing murmur. 'We will remember them.'

for them, eh? Nothing about how a man like Charlie might feel about losing the chance of happiness, the things he'd enjoyed, good food and drink, friendship and love. Oh no, they'd put him under six feet of earth and he could be bloody grateful for it. She felt her control beginning to crack, and was grateful when the crowd began to stir as the two minutes ended, and it was time for Lord Henry to move cautiously forward, to stand beside Alec Bennett. His old voice was surprisingly steady and strong when he spoke.

'It is my very considerable honour this day to unveil the Memorial stone which the people of this village have erected in loving and grateful memory of those men who never returned from battle.'

With measured dignity he pulled away the Union Jack that draped the memorial, revealing its new white stone, lettered in gold. At the foot of it he laid the wreath, saying 'The Legion of the Living salutes the Legion of the Dead.'

Alec Bennett said solemnly, his eyes on the gilt names, 'We shall not break faith with ye.' Then he turned to the musicians and gave them the cue for the introduction to *Abide with Me*.

It was a relief to hear the last words of the hymn, followed by the Blessing, and to move away. Louisa, on the Major's arm, had almost reached her waiting taxi when she heard her name called.

'Mrs Trotter! Mrs Trotter!'

She turned to see a girl, in a white dress and hat, running from the edge of the crowd towards her. Breathlessly her pursuer was saying, 'Mrs Trotter, I don't expect you remember me, but . . .'

Louisa sized up the pretty, animated face, with its hint of likeness. The girl would be about sixteen. There was no doubting who she was.

'Well,' Louisa said tartly, 'last time I saw you, miss, you was a right mucky little devil, that came up to me waist.'

'Never!' exclaimed the Major, his eyes dwelling admiringly on the girl.

'Yes,' Louisa went on, 'you've changed a sight more than I 'ave—but I remember you all right. Major, meet Miss Lottie Richards.'

The Major's little bow was gallant. 'Charmed to meet you, my dear.'

Lottie made an attempt at a curtsey, suddenly shy.

'Where's your mother?' Louisa asked.

'Oh—Mum doesn't like this sort of thing. It makes 'er cry.'

She was off again, darting into the crowd like a white swallow. But before disappearing she turned to look back. Louisa raised her hand, smiling, and got an answering grin.

It was impossible to get the girl out of her mind. She had looked well, had seemed sprightly enough. Nothing wrong with her that could be seen, and yet . . . Impelled by an instinct she could not fully understand, Louisa drove out that afternoon to Elsie Richards's cottage.

Her knock was not answered. Finding the door unlocked, she walked into the sitting-room.

'Phooo!' Her gloved hand went up to protect her nose from the stale smells of the place. There was dust, and the effluvia of unwashed human flesh, and the reek of stale beer and food. Louisa grimaced. The small room was untidy, littered, filthy, its one window permanently closed. There was a small bed in it—Lottie's, presumably, as the wall above was covered in pictures cut out from papers and magazines: fashion-plates, comic drawings, anything that had caught the child's fancy. Child? Nearer a woman. Oughtn't to be sleeping in a pigsty like this.

Elsie was slumped, asleep, in an armchair which badly needed recovering—and fumigating, Louisa guessed—beside the small empty grate, which held the ashes of a dead fire. At her feet in their shapeless slippers, lay an empty beer-bottle, overturned. Louisa marched forward and gave Elsie's shoulder a not particularly gentle shake.

'Ere! Come on, it ain't bed-time.'

Elsie was slow to rouse, and obviously still under the influence of the beer, but at last she realised where she was and that she had a visitor. Louisa hastily refused an invitation to a cup of tea, and perched herself fastidiously on the extreme edge of a hard kitchen chair to listen to Elsie's maudlin ramblings about the departed Will, from pneumonia, at the same time taking in with disgust every unsavoury detail of the room.

'Oh, I shall never get over it, an' that's a fact. Never. I feel it, 'im not bein' 'ere, all the time. An' then, Mrs Trotter, it makes life 'ard, don't it, to lose the bread-winner. An' me with a child still on mi 'ands.'

220

Louisa fancied the last remarks were made with intent. 'Lottie's hardly a child any more,' she said. 'Don't she work?'

'Oh, aye, she works. 'Up at t'Courtney's place, wi' the cows, milkin' and that.'

'And is she a good girl?'

Elsie's thick shoulders heaved with wheezy laughter. 'Good? When was our Lottie ever good? Little devil doesn't know what t'word means.'

She was covertly surveying the other woman: the silk of her dress, the shining shoes, the diamond brooch, the expensive hat on the fashionably-piled hair. Plenty of brass there. Was there any for Elsie, she wondered? Aloud, she asked if Mrs Trotter had come up for the Memorial Service.

'That's right.'

'Aye, I remember. You was an old friend of 'is lordship's.'

Louisa did not miss the sly implication, but said noncommittally 'Yes, I was.' Then, impulsive, she leant forward.

'Look, Mrs Richards, I want to do something to 'elp.'

Elsie's dull eyes lit up. 'It *is* terrible 'ard wi'out the breadwinner. Sometimes I 'ardly know where the next bite's comin' from.'

'Lottie looks a bright kid. Given 'alf a chance, what would she like to do?'

Elsie stared. 'What?'

'Lottie. What's she want to do with 'er life?'

'Nowt, so far as I know.'

Angry colour came into Louisa's cheeks, and her voice sharpened.

'Nowt?' she mocked. '*Nowt?* I bet you've never asked 'er. From the look of her I'd say she wants to dance like Maud Allan, act like Lily Brayton, maybe even cook like Louisa Trotter—set the bloody Thames on fire!'

Elsie stared, outraged. 'I'm sure I don't know what you're talkin' about!' She began to sniff. 'We've 'ad a

221

'ard life, Mrs Trotter, but I don't know what I'd do wi'out Lottie.'

Louisa was unmoved by this appeal. 'And what's going to happen to the girl if she stops here, may I ask?'

''Appen? What ought to 'appen?' Elsie snapped. 'She'll live, won't she, like the rest of us?'

Her flare of temper was brief. There was too much at stake. Had she already gone too far with this woman, who was certainly no lady but had plenty stacked away in that showy bag of hers? Elsie decided to return to pathos.

'There's nowt wrong wi' life that a bit more brass wouldn't put right,' she moaned.

'And there's a lot wrong with it that a bit of spit and polish *would* put right,' Louisa retaliated. Her round, she fancied.

The unconscious subject of this bickering was, meanwhile, sitting quietly at her lesson in the vicar's study. Today it was botany, the study of a dog-rose, Lottie carefully pulling the flower apart as Alec Bennett named its various parts. They were seated close together at the desk, and if Lottie was unaware of the affectionate, faintly disturbed look with which her teacher regarded her, Nanny Ord, coming in with a tray of coffee and biscuits, was not.

'Oh,' she said, setting down with a bang the tray with its one cup and saucer, 'I forgot you, young lady.'

'Don't matter.' Lottie was not sufficiently interested to look up. Nanny lingered, disparagingly looking over their shoulders at the work.

'I don't know what Lottie wants wi' all this, I'm sure, in 'er place,' she pronounced, with that peculiarly Yorkshire dedication to telling the truth, however unpleasant to the other party, though satisfactory to oneself. 'She'll end up neither fish nor fowl,' she added.

Lottie's cheeks and neck flushed painfully as she stared back at the old woman. 'I'm not goin' to stick 'ere milkin' cows the rest of mi life, if that's what you think,' she said defiantly.

'Oh? What are you goin' to do instead, madam?'

Lottie jumped up. 'First chance I get, I'm off!'

Scorning further comment Nanny tut-tutted and went out, muttering unintelligibly. Alec watched his pupil crunching a biscuit as if she had not eaten for weeks.

'You think there's some truth in what Nanny says, do you, Lottie?' he asked.

''Course not!' Lottie was trying to be airy. 'I mean, everything's different now, i'n't it, only nobody round 'ere's noticed. Oh well, four o'clock. I'd best go and clean t'silver at church.' With a nod, she was gone. Alec sighed, and sat down to examine her unfinished work.

It happened that just as Lottie was coming out of the church with her cleaning-bag Louisa was stepping into the cab which had waited for her while she visited Elsie Richards. Lottie waved to attract her attention, then ran to join her; a scene watched with dismay by Elsie, from the dirty window. Her horror increased as she saw Louisa hand Lottie into the cab and get in after her. The cab started, and they were lost to sight.

Elsie gave a loud train-whistle screech, and put down her half-empty stout bottle.

'The woman's kidnapped 'er! The thievin' cow's run off wi' 'er! Oooh! What am I goin' to do?'

What she did was to run out into the lane, in her slippered feet, shouting and sobbing, heading for the vicarage.

There, in the study, Alec and the Major were holding a fascinating discussion on the nature of romance and reality. Their peace was shattered by the sound of Elsie's approaching cries, and by her abrupt entrance, followed by Nanny, who had been drawn from the kitchen by the noise.

'Oh, Vicar,' Elsie was wailing, 'you must 'elp me, you must. She's been kidnapped! That woman's kidnapped my Lottie!'

Alec put down his pipe. 'Elsie, 'what *are* you talking

about? Do please try to be calm.'

'I saw it wi' mi own eyes! Pushed 'er into a big black motor-car, she did, and drove off wi' 'er!'

Nanny snorted. 'That's just the way she carried on when Will asked 'er to marry 'im and then changed 'is mind. She made such a wutherin' row 'e 'ad to ask 'er again for t'sake o' a quiet life.'

'Does she mean,' the Major enquired of his friend, 'that Louisa has kidnapped Lottie?'

'I believe she does, Major.'

'I sincerely hope she's mistaken. That cab's my only means of returning to Harrogate.' But as he said it, something attracted his attention.

'All's well,' he informed them from the window. 'Here they are—Louisa, Lottie, and the cab.'

The runaways entered, Lottie pink-cheeked with excitement, and both laughing.

'Took the girl for a spin in the cab,' Louisa told the assembled company. 'You'd think she was on the bloomin' moon, way she carried on.' Her smile faded as she took in the bedraggled and tear-stained Elsie, who immediately made a lunge at Lottie.

'My pet!' she wailed. 'My little luv! I thought you'd gone.'

'Gone where, Mum?'

'I thought that woman 'ad stolen you.'

Louisa's look was icy as her tone as she said 'I don't do things behind people's backs, Mrs Richards.'

'No? What was you doin', then, runnin' off wi' 'er like that, frightenin' the wits out o' me?'

'I didn't mean to scare you, Mrs Richards. I'm sorry,' Louisa said with unwonted humility, a little alarmed at the effect she had created unthinkingly. 'But you can see Lottie's quite safe.'

Elsie, encouraged, raised her voice to a screech again.

''Ow many ideas 'ave you put into that silly 'ead of 'ers? She's bad enough as it is.'

Lottie had gone to console her, but now, hurt, she

224

broke away, her loyalty strained. It had been so nice having the ride with Mrs Trotter, and no harm done to anybody; and now to walk into all this and be called bad names in front of people. The men, she could see, were sympathetic, and even Nanny was on her side, for once.

'Oh, Elsie! You always was a daft silly woman. Come on, you two, 'ome.' She urged them towards the door, where Lottie turned and gave Louisa the benefit of a brilliant smile.

'Thanks for the ride, missis!' she said.

Later that evening Louisa and the Major were still at the vicarage. High tea was over; the atmosphere was oddly strained, as if something must be said that was difficult to say. Out of a stream of casual talk, Louisa abruptly asked Alec, 'What sort of plans 'ave you got in mind for Lottie?'

He looked, for him, nettled. 'I? I don't have any plans for Lottie. She's hardly my responsibility, is she? Besides, I had the impression you were the one with plans.'

Louisa turned to him with a violent movement.

'I can't stand the thought of her livin' in that bloody pig-sty!'

He was startled. 'You exaggerate, I'm sure.'

'It *is* a pig-sty. And the old sow that runs it's drunk 'alf the time. I want Lottie out of there. I want her to come back to London with me.'

Alec stared from her to the Major, unhappy. 'I don't understand. There's something more to this than you've said, isn't there? Louisa?'

Louisa sighed. 'Yes.' She drank from the wine-glass at her side. The Major was lighting a cigar, with fingers that trembled a little. 'Yes,' she continued. 'You remember 'ow when Lottie was a little thing, just a few weeks old, it was Charlie brought her up 'ere for the Richards to take? I don't think nothing was ever said about where she was found. Or who's she was.'

Alec shook his head. After the slightest pause, Louisa

said 'She was ours. Charlie's and mine.'

'Ah,' he said without expression; then bowed his head on to his hands, like a man in despair, for a moment. Then he looked up at Louisa, angry.

'And so now, sixteen years later, you'd like to take her away again. This is her home, Louisa—whatever her blood, this is where her roots are.'

'I know,' Louisa snapped back. ''Ome, sweet 'ome. It's the sort of 'ome an animal has. A bolt hole. A place to stay dry in. It's the same old bloody argument, isn't it? Don't change. Be thankful for what you've got. Stay put. Well, if she stays put here I can't see much she'll 'ave to be thankful for, ten years from now.'

The Major put a hand gently on her shoulder. 'My dear, don't you think the young woman should be allowed to decide for herself?'

She whipped round. 'Yes, I do. But I don't want her to know who I am—not yet.'

She turned away from them, her hand to her head as if it ached. From beyond the slightly open door there was a flicker of movement, as though somebody who had been watching and listening in the hallway had heard what they had wanted to hear, and slipped away. Alec moved to Louisa.

'Aren't you just trying to ease your own guilty feelings?' he asked her.

'No, I don't think so. About Charlie? I don't feel guilty about Charlie. And it was all over, you know, years before I came up here to look after Margaret. No, I'm not sure why I'm so keen to 'ave her. And I'm sure why you're so keen to keep her.'

She shot him a shrewd look, and saw him flush slightly. Then, suddenly switching her mood, she laughed at the two men, and swept up her gloves and cape from the chair where they had lain.

'Well, now you know. Given you something to think about, eh, Vicar? Time for 'ome, Major.'

When Lottie failed to turn up at the vicarage before church next morning it was not difficult for the vicar to work out the reason.

'You were very wrong to run off carrying tales like that!' he told Nanny Ord angrily.

'Maybe I was, and maybe I wasn't. But I've seen the way you look at 'er.'

'Look at whom?'

'Lottie! And at your age, too.'

'What are you talking about?'

'You know well enough what I mean.'

He laughed harshly. 'You can be a devilishly nosey, suspicious old woman, can't you, Nanny?'

'Aye, laugh as much as you like. That girl would be better away from 'ere.'

He sighed, and looked round his study.

'Have you noticed, Nanny, how everything in this room is so old? Nothing fresh, or young, or even new?' He blew the dust off the top of a book.

'Well, you've been 'ere a long time. And no woman to see to things.'

She left him. The church bells were starting up for morning service. To his ears they sounded harsh, tuneless, joyless. He went through the day like one walking through a dark cloud; and learned from Elsie, in the evening, that Lottie had not been home.

Louisa was at Bishopsleigh, waiting for news. Nobody in the village had seen Lottie. Pale and abstracted, Louisa looked through the contents of the walnut box, which Nanny had mysteriously retrieved from wherever she had been hiding it. Old letters, from her to Charlie. A lock of blonde hair—Margaret's—and her faded photograph. And a Valentine card, clumsily painted; the one Lottie had made for Charlie, so long ago. Louisa stared at it, unconscious at first of a movement near the door. When she looked up, Lottie was standing there, watching her silently.

'And where the 'ell 'ave *you* been, young lady?' she

227

demanded, angry with relief.

Lottie's face gave nothing away. 'Upstairs,' she said. 'In the nursery.'

'Well, let me tell you, you gave me the fright of a lifetime.'

Lottie scuffed the ground with her toe. 'Sorry.'

Louisa beckoned her to the desk and put the Valentine into her hand. The girl flushed, and frowned, and put it down, saying nothing.

'Funny, eh?' Louisa said. 'Come 'ere, let's 'ave a proper look at you.'

She turned Lottie's face towards the light and studied it. There was a smudge of nursery dust on one cheek. Louisa approached it with her handkerchief, but Lottie shrank away.

After a moment she said, 'Lord and Lady Haslemere. They was like something in a fairy story when I was a kid. Then, when Lady Haslemere got ill, I remember you comin'. I remember Lady Haslemere dyin', an' all. I thought it were your fault.'

'How could it have been my fault?' Louisa asked sharply, and, getting no answer but a shrug, went on, 'Look, my girl, you and I don't know nothin' about one another. But for all that, we're mother and daughter. It's a fact—flesh and blood. If you want a decent start in life, I'm willing to give it to you. I want you to 'ave a better chance than what I did.'

Lottie stared. 'You managed all right!'

'Yes, I managed. I did well. But it was hard. Too hard, I shouldn't wonder.'

The reality of it all had begun to sink into Lottie's mind. 'But I'm sixteen!' she burst out. 'I've lived 'ere all mi life!' Tears were standing in her eyes. 'When I were little, I thought Lord Haslemere were the nicest man in the world. 'E never told me off, see, even when 'e knew I'd been in there, in 'is old playroom, on t'rockin'-orse . . . Oh, go away! Everything's spoiled. You've spoiled everything!'

Louisa's head was bent over the little walnut box. 'Well,' she said quietly, 'I'll be at the hotel in Harrogate if you want me.'

Somebody besides Louisa had had little sleep on the night Lottie spent in the nursery. The vicar's study table bore a dirty supper-plate and a glass that had held whisky, and across a chair-back his collar was draped. Lottie, perched on the window-sill, surveyed his haggard, unshaven face.

'Didn't you go to bed last night?' she asked.

'No.' He did not look at her.

'I was telling you about this funny dream. It was so real I thought I were awake. I saw 'er, Mrs Trotter, open the door an' come in. She looked so sad, an' 'er face were white as chalk. She come and leaned over me, lookin' at me so queer—an' just 'ere, between 'er eyebrows, sat a big black moth. I reached up to brush it away, but I couldn't seem to touch it. She went on lookin' at me like that for a bit, but she didn't say anything. Then she just got up an' went away.'

'Well, you've certainly given us all the devil of a nightmare. And there's no need to look so disgustingly pleased with yourself.'

'I'm not. I'm miserable. I keep thinkin' of mi Dad—well, I thought he were mi Dad, an' I loved 'im. I wish 'e were 'ere now.'

Alec put his arms round her, stroking the long hair, and looking over her bent head at the bright garden.

'You know your mother will be taken care of, Lottie. Liz will go in every day, and the Major's arranged for her to have enough money.'

Her voice was muffled. 'I don't want to go away.'

'But Lottie, my dear, you've always said "First chance I get, I'm off."'

'I know I 'ave. But I don't want to go now.'

He released her. He was full of anger that things should ever have come to this. He had liked and respected

229

Charlie Haslemere; he liked and respected Louisa. But would it not have been kinder if they had seen that the unwanted baby should be brought up in a fitting home, and given proper education? Such arrangements were common enough among the aristocracy, and Charlie could well have afforded a good boarding-school. Instead, the child had been thrown aside like a weed, to grow wherever it fell, and then to be painfully uprooted. "What man is there of you, whom if his son ask bread, will he give him a stone?" Charlie Haslemere had given his daughter a stone; his only child, who should have been his heir instead of that distant relation in Canada. Hypocrisy, thought Alec, hypocrisy and callousness. And, because he was angry with the dead and the living, his tone was sharp when he answered Lottie.

'Well, you don't have to go. You can stay—your home is here. But how do you see yourself in five years—in ten—in twenty? Lottie, you can always be proud of your real parents—and you always loved your father when you didn't know he was—didn't you?'

She nodded, tearfully, looking up to him for reassurance.

'And what you have here,' he added, 'wouldn't have lasted for ever. It would have changed, you would have changed. You'd soon start to say "Oh, when I was young . . ."' He paused, seeing her face less clouded, and then said cheerfully 'There's one thing I want you to do before you decide.'

'Yes?' She was anxious.

'Make me a cup of fresh, strong coffee.'

She laughed with relief and ran off; he could hear her, in the kitchen, humming a song.

The cab came to the vicarage door at four o'clock. Lottie was ready, a bunch of flowers from Alec's garden lying in her basket, on top of the few shabby belongings she was taking into her new life. The last he saw of her was her face, looking back through the rear window of the cab, at him, the vicarage, the church, the village; a world of which she would no longer be a part.

He turned and went inside, shutting the door on emptiness.

# CHAPTER FIFTEEN

Nobody could have guessed at the state of nervous tension in which Louisa had spent the time since her parting with Lottie at Bishopsleigh from the casual manner of her greeting when the girl was shown up to her hotel room in Harrogate.

'Oh, you're 'ere, are you?' she unconsciously echoed her own mother's brusque mode of greeting. 'Might as well 'ave some tea, then.'

It was, in fact, the most effective way of dealing with Lottie's nervousness. To have gone from the vicarage to a private house would have been an easier transition than to arrive at this huge, awesome building in the elegant town to which she had only been once or twice in her life on day trips. Harrogate was 'grand', full of rich fashionable folk come for spa treatments or to enjoy its exhilarating air. Its steep streets were effortlessly breasted by large, immaculately groomed motor-cars, Daimlers and Royces. Its massive hotels, so much more showy and ornate than Bishopsleigh Hall, appeared to Lottie like palaces. The public gardens and the expansive grassy Stray were brilliant with tulips planted in serried ranks.

So it was calming to sit drinking what tasted only remotely like the strong sweet tea she was used to, and eating little biscuits which were so soft and nice that they slipped easily past the lump in her throat: round biscuits with red or green jelly centres, dainty chocolate fingers, slender crisp pink wafers with something creamy between them. Louisa, out of the corner of her eye, watched them go down with satisfaction. She herself always lost her appetite when she was upset. Getting Lottie to eat, she thought, was half the battle over.

Replete, Lottie looked round the spacious room.

'Am I stayin' 'ere, Mrs Trotter?'

'Till tomorrow. Then we're off, ten o'clock train.'

'Shall I . . . shall I sleep with you?' Apprehensively, she was eyeing the majestic walnut bed, draped in spotless white. It seemed quite a different article of furniture from the ramshackle one she had occupied in Elsie's parlour.

'Not bl . . . Not likely,' Louisa answered hastily. 'You're next door. Nice little room. I'll show you.' It was, indeed, reassuringly small and modest, being designed as a dressing-room or accommodation for a maid travelling with her mistress.

'Is your house in London like this?' Lottie asked, back in Louisa's room.

'It's a 'otel, not a house.' She began to talk of the Bentinck and its people, realising that very little of what she was saying was getting through to the comprehension of her hearer. Talking was difficult. Louisa was not a great word-spinner, or sufficiently imaginative to find the right formula for making Lottie feel comfortable, either with her or in this strange place. Giving it up, she pushed over a pile of illustrated magazines, which she knew from the pictures pinned up over that rickety bed in the cottage were the sort of reading Lottie liked; then, seeing her becoming absorbed in them, she rang to order a tray to be sent up for Miss Richards at dinner time, while she herself went down to the dining-room. Something told her it would be dangerous to expose those frightened eyes to the overpowering splendours of gilt, plush, Corinthian columns, shining silver and napery, and the critical scrutiny of waiters and fellow guests. In any case, the child wasn't fit to be seen in public in that scarecrow outfit of hers.

Lottie slept the sleep of emotional exhaustion that night, after reaction had set in and she had cried herself sodden on the lace-trimmed pillow. Louisa, listening at the communicating door, shrugged. Best thing for her, poor little bitch.

She summoned Major Smith-Barton. Together they knocked off a bottle of champagne. The Major raised his first glass.

'To Lottie,' he said. Louisa looked faintly surprised, but smiled.

'That's right. Lottie. And Gawd 'elp us all.'

She was agreeably struck by the way in which Lottie, refreshed by sleep, began to adjust to circumstances next morning. Excitement put colour into her cheeks, and sent her eyes darting from one new thing to another on their journey to the station. Everything was exotic to her, as if she had walked into an Arabian Night: the luxury of the first-class compartment, the white lace anti-macassars against which she hardly dared rest her head, though Louisa had made her have her first proper bath and wash her hair the night before; the obsequious porters and the attendants who came to summon them to refreshments in the dining-car. And then, the changing panorama of scenery as Yorkshire darkened, tall factory chimneys rising above the smoke of Leeds to the right of them, as the green fields fell behind. Doncaster past, they were in the Midlands, and all the buildings looked different, and strange accents shouted place-names at the stations; and somehow she forgot to be wretched any more because it was all so interesting. Suddenly she fell asleep, heavy with soup and roast chicken, to be awakened at length by Louisa shaking her shoulder.

'Come on, we're almost there. Have yer first look at London.'

A world turned upside down is never an easy place to live in. The Bentinck was certainly not as awesome as the Harrogate hotel, but it was a strange, alien place. To have her own room, for the very first time, and the beautiful new clothes Louisa had bought her the day after their arrival, that was all very nice. The people were kind, though she had a lot of trouble sorting them out, except for Welsh Mary, with whom she felt at home more than with anybody else. And the hall porter's little dog made a great fuss of her, which made him smile friendlily at her.

But it didn't seem real. She didn't even feel real herself, being called Miss Richards still, with Mrs Trotter telling everybody the story they'd agreed on, that she was the daughter of Lord Haslemere's groom. Lottie knew the Major knew the truth, because they'd talked about it with him, and she was pretty sure Mary knew as well. As for the others, Starr, Merriman and Mrs Cochrane, she could sense that they stared and whispered. Who am I? she asked herself, staring into the mirror. In the fairy stories, the goose-girl who was really a princess always turned into one properly, as soon as the spell was lifted; people didn't go around talking as if she was still a goose-girl.

And she was so lonely. That was another thing. Mum, poor old Elsie, had been silly and exasperating in some ways, but she'd given her adopted daughter real affection, plenty of hugs and kisses, even if they had been a bit beery; and Dad, Elsie's husband, she'd really loved and missed. She could accept that Mrs Trotter, not Elsie, was really her mother, but there were no hugs and kisses from her. Once, soon after arriving, when she'd been at her most homesick, Lottie had run to her for comfort, and been pushed away almost roughly, as though Mrs Trotter wasn't used to touching people and didn't like it very much.

She began to long for her father. Not poor Dad, but Lord Haslemere, her real father. From the reluctant Louisa she got a small picture of him to keep under her pillow, and found out which had been his suite in the hotel. Number Three. He was all she had of her true identity; her memories of his kindness, of how one day, seeing her in the wet street with her shoes leaking, he had picked her up and put her before him on his horse, and next day a new pair of shoes had arrived at the Richards' cottage. Only Mary heard anything of how she felt.

'*She* don't want me here,' Lottie told her, not caring what Mary might deduce. 'She don't know what to do with me. *He*'d have known. He wouldn't just have left me.'

The Major was kind. He took her about to art galleries, museums, exhibitions, the waxworks, Wimbledon, helping to make her bit by bit into the woman she had a right to become. But he was not enough to fill the blank in her, or make up for Louisa's coldness. There was a party one night, given in the suite that had been Charlie's. Somehow Lottie got herself invited to it, without Louisa's knowledge, and saw it invaded by strangers; sat taking in the grown-up conversation and the atmosphere of the rooms, so important to her life. It was the next morning before Louisa found her, still there in the sitting-room, among the empty bottles and full ashtrays, a lost and lonely figure. And Louisa was angry.

'What the 'ell do you think you're doing? You can't go wanderin' round all the rooms, takin' vacant possession.'

Lottie stared valiantly back at her. 'Not all the rooms. Just this one. He'd want me to see his room. He wouldn't mind.'

'Look, it ain't his room any more. We've got some guests coming.'

'It'll always be his room, and I don't know how you can let strangers come in.'

Louisa had never known a rival for Charlie, not even poor Margaret, until now. 'Well,' she said, 'I can't wall it up, can I? I've got to earn a livin'. I don't believe in shrines, and he wouldn't, either. What's so special about it, anyway?'

What indeed? The night of the unintentional dinner-party, and of even less intentional love. Lottie was looking her fearlessly in the eye.

'I come from it, didn't I? And he died in it. From his

236

wounds. And if he'd lived he'd have been blind in it. Mary told me. I wish *you* had.'

Louisa was not in the habit of feeling ashamed or apologising for herself. She could only brazen it out.

'Look,' she said, 'I've done my best for you, haven't I? I've brought you here. You didn't want me to start motherin' you, did you?'

But Lottie's eyes told her that she had.

'I can't do that,' Louisa answered them. 'I'm sorry, but it's not in me nature.' She hesitated, then asked, 'Do you want to be a lady?'

'Yes.' The Honourable Miss Charlotte Tyrrell, she thought to herself. She felt it; she knew she could be it. Even her looks were right, now that she had the clothes and the setting.

'You'll have to learn, then,' Louisa said, helplessly for her. 'You'll have to go to school and do it proper. There's one in Switzerland that's highly recommended, where young girls are turned into ladies.' She looked up at Charlie's portrait. 'I think he might approve of that.'

'Be out of your way, then.' Lottie's voice was bitter.

'That's not the reason. I'm trying to think what's best for you. London's no place for you—not yet, anyway.'

'There's no right place for me, is there? And never will be.'

'Oh, now, that's nonsense.'

'No. The Major was tellin' me about society, and how it works. Some funny rules. People like me don't seem to be part of it.'

Louisa got up, gazed round the littered room, and saw, remarkably, an unopened bottle of champagne. With swift expertise she opened it, found a couple of empty glasses and filled them.

As she worked she said, 'I'm goin' to tell you something, Lottie. All my life I've done battle with society. I committed the unpardonable sin of risin' above myself, you see? I've made some good friends in society but I've never really bin accepted where it counts. And long ago I decided that wasn't goin' to bother me. I was goin' my own way, and they couldn't stop me. And you can do the same. You can go to this school, learn the rules, and beat 'em at their own game, if you put your mind to it. And still be true to yourself—like I've bin. Understand what I'm getting at?'

'No.'

'Oh, blimey, you need your father for this.' It was the first time she had spoken of Charlie as anything but 'he' to their daughter. She sighed. 'We're going to have a nice glass of wine, just the two of us, and drink to his memory. That's the best I can do for you. Your first glass of wine—in his presence.'

She looked up at Charlie's portrait, the one Collinghurst had painted of him looking as she liked to remember him, the shadow of coming blindness left out of the frank, smiling eyes. Then she looked back at Lottie. The Major had told her that Mary had not needed his confirmation of the girl's parentage, for it was written in her face, her expression. Now Louisa acknowledged it; perhaps she had seen it all the time, had been reluctant to admit it because it brought her a kind of pain. It was there, all right, and so was his spirit, in the fearless way Lottie tossed back the champagne, then gasped and smiled. It worked quickly, that potent foaming wine, making the girl for the first time at ease in her mother's company.

'Will you talk about him?' she asked.

Louisa drew back. She had never talked about him, to anyone.

'What do you want to know?'

'Just . . . how it was. From the beginning. And how it ended. Got a right to know, haven't I?'

She had never spoken to Louisa like that before, but there came no answering salvo. 'Yes, you have,' Louisa said quietly, 'but you'll have to wait for a bit. You'll hear about it one day, I promise you.'

Lottie nodded. There were things she understood,

instinctively, about her mother. She sipped the champagne, watching how Louisa drank, copying her. She would learn and learn, until she was what her father would have wanted her to be. She raised her glass, so slightly that Louisa didn't notice, towards the portrait, and fancied that the gesture was acknowledged.

Lottie's coming to the Bentinck had been in its way symbolic. The old times were gone, banished by war, the great catalyst, and the old habitués were gone with it, as irreclaimably as the wounded officers who had recuperated in its rooms, their uncashed cheques locked for ever in Louisa's drawer. The Bright Young Things had arrived; some the children of one-time clients, some newcomers who would never, formerly, have passed the Bentinck's portals. They were rich, they were implacably frivolous, they were daring, they lived for pleasure. The girls had bobbed hair and short skirts, and smoked and swore, danced to jazz bands and attended wild parties in strange costumes.

Lottie followed their pattern in everything, and Louisa disliked it and disapproved. There was too much of her in her daughter for them ever to live in harmony together; quarrels, separations and scenes were inevitable. And yet—would she have had Lottie otherwise than she was? Beautiful, of course; as spirited as her mother had always been; educated to the standards of society; and, as Louisa had once suggested to Elsie Richards, ambitious and talented, with a natural flair for music and a voice that was going to take her to the top in the world of musical comedy, the 'thing' of the times.

It was not in Louisa to look back. As the world moved on, the Bentinck moved with it, a natural centre for London's expensive, reckless young people; a pleasure-place, as it had always been, stamped with Louisa's personality even now that the flappers and Piccadilly Johnnies cavorted in it to the tunes of the young Noel Coward, who often came himself and played on the piano that had been Charlie's, once jealously guarded by Louisa from any other touch. Parties, parties, parties; noise and colour and late nights; affected young voices gabbling in modern slang . . .

And in the centre of it, Louisa; carrying her years with beauty and calm dignity, endlessly tolerant because she had seen everything in her time. The Young Things adopted her as a sort of mascot and she revelled in the role, becoming more and more outrageous and eccentric because it delighted them and gave her a position apart from the rest of the older generation, against whose stuffiness they were determinedly rebelling. She, a notable rebel in her time, would always be found on the side representing change and enthusiasm and the Life Force. Twice she had sincerely wanted to die. Now, as she had said, she had experienced enough of death.

The Bentinck had survived the bombs; Louisa had survived battle after battle of other kinds, and great sorrow. Lottie, once resented, had proved to have represented the gate to the new world, that of the 1920s and their hectic gaiety and optimism. Louisa would outlast even them, and far beyond. Alone, admired and already legendary, she would enjoy a kind of immortality as the Duchess of Duke Street.